The Thinker and the Thrush

by

GWYN THOMAS

LAWRENCE & WISHART

LONDON

Lawrence & Wishart Limited
39 Museum Street
London WC1A 1LQ

First published 1988

The text of *The Thinker and the Thrush* has been prepared for publication by Michael Parnell

This book has been published with the financial support of the Welsh Arts Council

Photoset in North Wales by Derek Doyle & Associates, Mold, Clwyd. Printed and bound in Great Britain by Oxford University Press

Introduction

by Michael Parnell

In 1948 Gwyn Thomas was thirty-five years old. After a young adult life of some distress and dissatisfaction he was beginning to settle down. The hated war was over, a Labour government which still promised much was in power, and for some eight years he had enjoyed steady employment as a schoolmaster. He was happily married, his health was better than it had been, and thanks to the efforts of his energetic wife his endless scribblings had begun to find themselves in print. In 1946 no fewer than three separate publishers, plied with typescripts by Lyn Thomas, had accepted stories, each without knowledge of the others' interest. The novella *The Dark Philosophers*, published in an anthology called *Triad One*, was declared a small masterpiece and was soon published separately in its own right in America, where it won generous praise from Howard Fast among others; the stories 'Oscar' and 'Simeon' in *Where Did I Put My Pity: Folk-Tales from the Modern Welsh* excited attention; and the novel *The Alone to the Alone*, when published in 1947, established its author on both sides of the Atlantic as a writer of tremendous individuality and promise.

Given a new confidence by these successes, Gwyn Thomas began to plan a future in which his writing took precedence over everything else. He had been writing almost feverishly for his own pleasure and relief since he was in his mid-twenties, and he had actually entered his first novel for a competition in 1937; although the idea of publication had never been particularly important to him, the compulsion to write coming from deep inside, he was not displeased to find that readers thought well of his work, and now he began to envisage some large-scale books. It was plain that he must build on his relatively recent recognition of his powers as a humorist, for it was this warmer comic tone which made palatable the essential starkness of the vision which drove him to write. Happy in his discovery that people liked to read stories expressed in the sardonic, ironic cadences which made his conversation inimitable, he wrote in the autumn of 1947 a novel about a young man twisting on the horns of a dilemma that fascinated Gwyn Thomas: how, brought up in an ambience that idealised socialism, to live decently after recognising within oneself the ambitions that spring from commercial and conservative values.

The novel he wrote was *The Thinker and the Thrush*, and it was duly accepted by Nicholson and Watson for publication during 1948. Glowing with achievement and relishing the laughter his book called from those who read the typescript, Thomas nevertheless turned immediately to what he conceived as a much larger and more valuable theme, where his more rollicking and farcical approach would be inappropriate. Long obsessed with the tale of Dic Penderyn and the matter of martyrdom for a social cause, he settled down to write his own version of an attempted industrial revolution in a nineteenth-century South Wales valley.

The book took shape painfully, for the project turned out to be immense. Convinced that what he was doing was of a different order from his earlier writings, he sent the typescript to a different publisher, Michael Joseph, and received a most encouraging welcome. Plans were set going to publish *All Things Betray Thee* (though that was not its title at this point) in 1949, and so great were Michael Joseph's hopes for it that Gwyn Thomas began to wonder whether he might be able to give up teaching and become a full-time professional writer.

Meanwhile, however, Nicholson and Watson were proving slower than expected in getting *The Thinker and the Thrush* into print. When it came to Michael Joseph's attention that another and quite different Gwyn Thomas novel was about to appear, he insisted that it must not cut across the publicity he was arranging for the launch of *All Things Betray Thee*; in fact, he said, it must be published in the previous year or in the following, but not during the same year. Despite attempts to accelerate their production, in times much more difficult than today, Nicholson and Watson realised that they could not get *The Thinker and the Thrush* into the shops by Christmas, 1948. Thomas, certain that it was more important to publish *All Things Betray Thee* as planned, withdrew his comic story from Nicholson and Watson and put his MS into a drawer against some future opportunity.

All Things Betray Thee was recognised on publication in 1949 as an extraordinary, beautiful and poetic novel, and though it did not do as well commercially as its publishers had hoped, it was a very considerable success. In the USA, under the title *Leaves in the Wind*, it was equally highly regarded, and Gwyn Thomas's career seemed set fair. In the event, things turned sour. His reputation in the States suffered as the political mood there, whipped into anti-left furies by

Senator McCarthy and his cohorts, caused him to be identified as one of the enemy, so that his subsequent books were looked at with increasingly hostile criticism or, worse, ignored altogether. At home Thomas quarrelled with Michael Joseph when his next book, an ambitious historical novel set in Spain at the end of the period of Moorish domination, was rejected on what may in retrospect seem insubstantial grounds. Finding Victor Gollancz willing to publish him if he would write more in the serio-comic left-wing vein established in *The Alone to th᾿ Alone*, Thomas produced *The World Cannot Hear You*, the first in a series of half a dozen very funny, highly individual novels for Gollancz all set in or near the Rhondda Valley from which their author had sprung.

In all the change and confusion, *The Thinker and the Thrush* was lost and forgotten.

When Lyn found among her husband's papers, a good while after his death in 1981, the manuscript of the novel, she quietly set about typing it up again. She did so more to keep in touch with the spirit of the friend and lover she sorely missed than with any thought that the book might yet be published. When however she showed it to me, as Gwyn Thomas's biographer, the story struck me as so appealing that I felt it would be appreciated by a wider public. Lawrence and Wishart having already published posthumously Gwyn Thomas's lost first novel, *Sorrow for thy Sons*, as well as issuing a reprint of *All Things Betray Thee*, fortunately agreed.

* * *

Stobo Wilkie may seem an unlikely sort of hero for a Gwyn Thomas novel. In a number of ways he is not very attractive. It is not, however, his craftiness and deceitfulness that repel us so much as his social views. Like other shopkeepers in Thomas's fiction (and in his non-fiction!), Stobo represents an acquisitive and conservative selfishness, a suspicion of open-minded thought, a specious identification with the haves and a lack of concern for the have-nots. Stobo wants to 'get on' and doesn't much mind how he does it. His fortune depends on his keeping in with Mr Ellicott, the shopkeeper whose business and savings he hopes to inherit; his business success depends on his keeping in with customers for who he feels little but contempt. When he does at last acquire a measure of social concern, it is essentially to further his career, to go where the power and influence are, rather than from any real notion that he may be able to help people more effectively.

It is not as simple as that, however. Stobo's personality comes off the page much more sympathetically than one might expect. In his way he too is a victim of a confused and directionless social system. His first-person narrative allows us to perceive beneath the corrupt surface an interestingly baffled mind, a rather pathetically frustrated young man to whom his friend Colenso Mortlake's idealistic socialism makes little sense but who recognises in Colenso's attitudes a higher human possibility than in the pragmatic utterances of his other friends, especially the Moggs. He is an intensely comic figure, whose sexual hang-ups provide the opportunity for some hilarious moments and reflections and whose misadventures at the hands of both his friends and his opponents makes the reader like him in spite of himself. At bottom he is, despite everything, optimistic, tough and resourceful, and we care about the dilemmas he is negotiating. Aware of sin but sinning anyway, he appears to represent all that should be most abhorred about weak and materialistic individuals in a grubby society, but his values are put forward fairly and even persuasively at times, and the ironic presence of the author constantly challenges us to weigh our own attitudes.

Gwyn Thomas considered a number of possible titles for his novel. One on which he seems to have settled was *The Thinker and the Thrush*, the name of the pub to which the philosophers and businessmen of the area repair to restore their tissues and make their contacts. At a later stage he replaced this with the simple *Stobo*, which may be thought more appropriate, for Stobo is at the heart of the whole narrative. So intriguing a figure was he to his creator that he recurs in various forms in later work: as Councillor Eryl Pym, for instance, in the 1956 novel, *A Point of Order*, and in the subsequent reworkings of that book as a radio play (*The Alderman*, 1966) and as a theatre play (*Testimonials*, 1978). On reflection, however, *The Thinker and the Thrush* seems the better title and has been retained.

Stobo's story consists of a series of comic reversals for himself set against a background of manoeuvres and encounters in a social war. The South Wales town is here called Bandy Lane; it appears to be closer to the sea than the Meadow Prospect or Mynydd Coch of later novels and stories, outside rather than inside the enclosing wall of the line of hills bounding Rhondda to the south-west; but Birchtown (Pontypridd) is not far off and in most ways Bandy Lane is exactly like the communities of all Thomas's novels. The town itself is industrialised and ugly; the surrounding hills are attractive and on their slopes there are farms and delightful pubs in little hidden valleys. There is a Constitutional Club (Con Club) and a café run by a foreigner, in this case a Greek,

Manolos Kiprianos. Through the town flows a dirty and polluted river called the Moody.

In this zone march and counter-march a cast of characters who will prove not unfamiliar to those who know Thomas's published fiction. There is a host of people like Sir Gwydion Pooley, local magnate, and Banfield Marsh, proprietor of the Cosy Cinema, who make only the most fleeting appearance; then there are the peripheral characters who play a small but significant part in the proceedings here or there, like Shifnal Pugh the horse expert. Then there is a central crowd of interacting protagonists like Wyndham Wilkie, Stobo's father, the apathetic milkman in whose interests the intrigues are set on foot (he is a sort of predecessor to Uncle Edwin in *The Stranger at my Side*), Melancthon Mills and Dunkerly Dodge, philosophers and social workers, ironically called 'progressives' because they believe in 'getting on' at no matter whose expense; Samson Blakemore the villainous farmer and his ally, Lucas Phillimore, who exploit Wyndham; and Stobo's girlfriend Angela and her dotty family.

All beautifully named, they play their part here in what might have been recognised, had it appeared in 1948 as planned, as the first novel of Thomas's true maturity. It does not appear here quite as written, for, as one might expect of a Gwyn Thomas novel, the typescript which Lyn produced was of a longer and rather more self-indulgent novel, full of indefinitely extended metaphors and with some very loosely constructed sentences. Thomas never found a sharply critical editor at Gollancz, which is one reason why his books may not have been quite as successful as his publisher hoped; hailed by reviewers as brilliantly and dazzlingly written, they were some-times perceived by readers hoping for a joyous and easy read as being unexpectedly difficult. Whether Nicholson and Watson intended to publish *The Thinker and the Thrush* as submitted by Thomas cannot now be established, but Lawrence and Wishart felt that the typescript ought to be tidied up and reduced more to the dimensions of a standard novel. This I undertook to do. Nothing was changed or added, but the typescript was gone through with a thick pencil, and as many words and sentences struck out as seemed possible. Some may feel that the resulting book is the poorer for the missing bits, but it seemed to me that in cutting short some of Thomas's wilder flights of rhetoric, in removing some sections (mostly from the mouths of certain characters) which, though comical and interestingly reflective, were nevertheless digressions from the story and central themes, and in leaving out the second halves of sentences that already seemed to have made their impact in the first half, I allowed a much more sinewy and muscular text to emerge, and I hope I may be forgiven for my cheek. (It is worth perhaps considering that if I had not so edited it, the book might have remained unpublished. The original manuscript and typescript may be consulted at the National Library of Wales in Aberystwyth.)

The book seems to me to be a very good one. It has a well organised shape, and the writing is taut and nervous; it is full of witty observation and comic image, but these are under firm control. The theme underlying the occasional farcical interlude and the general play of comic interchange is deeply serious; the picture of South Wales valley life which emerges is a little distorted but essentially true. It is a book which balances humour against a great darkness; Stobo says, early on:

I went around the back to wash the disinfectant smell

off my hands, convinced that there would never be enough carbolic to render wholesome so willingly and helplessly scabrous a globe.

The novel was written at an important stage in Gwyn Thomas's realisation that his searing social anger was more effectively conveyed obliquely than through the direct attack he had tried using in his younger days. Laughter is his significant and disabling weapon against the smug, self-absorbed conservative enemy, and although the comedy of *The Thinker and the Thrush* has its sombre undertones, here Thomas's style is to be found at its most vital and confident. No one is spared; the 'progressives' with their feet of clay, the idealists with their tendency to extremist nonsense, the exploited with their apathetic acceptance of the iniquities from which they suffer, all are invited through cleansing laughter to reassess their position and do better. But the book is no moral tract for the times. As the citizens of Gwyn Thomas's world go about their business we share with them life as a somewhat bizarre amalgam of experiences, where joy is somehow derived from misery and wisdom from ineptitude. Readers will not easily forget such occasions as when Wyndham Wilkie's friends help him deliver the milk with a new spirit of efficiency and generosity that stuns the customers on his round, or when Stobo and his Angela go to supper with Mr Ellicott and Stobo fails to see how the old man dotes with a plainly sexual passion on the person of the young woman. Holding it all together is the gradual revelation of the complex and oddly disturbing character of Stobo Wilkie, teased and exploited by his friends, taunted and humiliated by his enemies, set newly thinking by the cruel philosophical honesty of Dr Poinsette, but learning to trust only his own impulses despite everything.

Many will find this novel a most happy discovery, both those who know of Gwyn Thomas's writing already and those of a younger generation who may not yet have encountered it. Its appearance signals a new stage in the revival of an unjustly forgotten reputation.

* * *

Gwyn Thomas was born in 1913 in Cymmer, Porth, in the Rhondda Valley, the youngest of the twelve children of a largely unemployed miner. He was educated at the Rhondda Intermediate School and St Edmund Hall, Oxford, where he read Spanish and was profoundly unhappy. As part of his degree course he studied for some months at the new University of Madrid and noted with horror the approach of the Spanish Civil War. After some years of ill health, during which he was sporadically employed in government-sponsored education schemes in South Wales and various parts of England, he started work as a schoolteacher, first in Cardigan and then, from 1942, at Barry Grammar School. He established a reputation as a novelist in the decade after 1946, and eventually gave up teaching to become a full-time writer and broadcaster in 1962. He enjoyed success as a contributor to *Punch*, as a playwright for the theatre, and as an occasional columnist in various newspapers, and increasingly as a writer and performer for radio and television. His death at the early age of sixty-seven came as a shock in 1981, and many both inside and outside Wales felt a sense of personal loss. He was survived by his wife, Lyn, who has now left their home in Peterston-super-Ely to return to Barry.

Gwyn Thomas's writings currently in print include the fiction *Sorrow for thy Sons* (1936, but not published until 1986), *All Things Betray Thee* (1949) and *Selected Short Stories* (1984; a new, expanded edition, 1988); the autobiography, *A Few Selected Exits* (1969, republished 1985); and the essay collection, *A Welsh Eye* (1964, republished 1984). His two early short novels, *The Dark Philosophers* and *The Alone to the Alone* were reissued together in one volume in 1988. His novels not currently in print but well worth seeking out include: *The World Cannot Hear You* (1951), *A Frost on my Frolic* (1953), *A Point of Order* (1956) and *The Love Man* (1958). His plays include *The Keep* (1961), *Jackie the Jumper* (1963), *Sap* (1974) and *The Breakers* (1976); his first three plays, *The Keep*, *Jackie the Jumper* and *Loud Organs* are scheduled to be published together in one volume in 1989. A *Writers of Wales* monograph on Gwyn Thomas by Ian Michael appeared in 1977 and a full-scale biography, *Laughter from the Dark: A Life of Gwyn Thomas* by Michael Parnell, was published in 1988.

1

Mr Ellicott looked out from the little tabernacle of his cash desk. He hummed and smiled at me as I sweetened the shelves with warm water and disinfectant. This was the great Monday morning ritual, and while it was being done Mr Ellicott would wave out of his shop any customer who dared make demands on him before eleven o'clock. It was he personally who gauged the amount of disinfectant to be used, for he claimed there was a sourness about the world that could well do with a little chastening from carbolic.

I had worked in Mr Ellicott's shop since leaving school at fourteen and we were firm friends. He had no wife, no children, and I was his only assistant. His business was brisk and dependable, if riddled with seams of bad and worsening debts. For a year past, troublesome veins in the legs and an utterly tired heart had kept him to his desk for the larger part of the day and he encouraged me with his smile to keep up the desperate tempo at which I worked, when customers lined both counters. He could easily have engaged another assistant but I had persuaded him not to. He had promised the business to me when he decided to quit definitely and I wanted no competitor for his favour. I had made myself Mr Ellicott's right hand. He had come to rest on me. I knew it, and I saw the future as golden, for I had detected many ways in which the business could be bettered and enlarged: refrigeration to cut down waste on perishables; an ice-cream corner; an annexe for the sale of pastries. No one could say that buzzing like a white-coated bee from one side of Mr Ellicott's shop to the other had dulled my brain. When the bacon-machine was not whirring, when the customers' prattle had fallen still, I could hear my thoughts thrusting with strong purpose forwards.

Mr Ellicott sniffed. 'Oh, it smells so fresh. You're a good boy, Stobo.'

'It's the way you brought me up, Mr Ellicott.'

I was already regarding the business as my own, mine and Angela's. Angela was my girl. When I reproved Mr Ellicott's debtors, and his easy-going friendliness and the thoughtful melancholy caused by his bad veins had increased their number over the years, it was done with a first-hand enthusiasm that brooked no answer. What I said was: 'How can you have the face to defraud anyone as nice as Mr Ellicott?' but what I meant was: 'How dare you reduce by so much as a penny the value of something for which I have worked so hard, so long, which will one day be mine?' There was nothing immoral about all this at all. I could have gone to the Technical School when I was twelve and done well as a draughtsman or fitter down at the Bandy Lane Trading Estate, but even at that time my delight was to poke around Mr Ellicott's warehouse, making quiet fun of the inefficiency of Nestor Flagg who was then Mr Ellicott's assistant. I think I worried Nestor into the grave with the way I kept raising my eyebrows in surprise at the quaking quality of his every gesture.

The cleaning finished, I replaced the pile of fruit tins on the shining shelves, running my fingers delightedly over their coloured wrappers and over the high-grade green paint with which Mr Ellicott had treated all the woodwork. As I replaced the last tin on the last shelf, I heard the buckets that flanked the entrance jangle. I had always disagreed with Mr Ellicott about the placing of these buckets, thinking they had a vulgar suggestion about them which would be better masked in one of the darker corners of the interior. I thought that too much hardware lowered the tone of a grocery shop. But Mr Ellicott had insisted on their being there, arguing that a bucket had a frank, homely air about it and besides, my predecessor Nestor Flagg having been a little deaf, a clang of metal as an approaching client brushed through the entrance served to put him on his guard.

The second I heard the buckets I knew who was coming: Mrs Chiddle. She lived two doors down from the shop and was a widow. I considered her an impudent and immoral woman because the way she had baited the hook for Mr Ellicott would have disgusted even that Izaak Walton about whom I have heard talks in the Centre. Young as I was then, I think Mr Ellicott owed his freedom from Mrs Chiddle to me. I had heard plenty of stories about her. When Mrs Ellicott died she had been in the shop twenty-four times a day. She had not submitted a single order and had it filled, but come in for every article separately. Mr Ellicott, seeing her so constantly at the counter and the cash-desk, had begun to feel a sense of incompleteness in his bed also and that is the kind of thought that sends a man down the slope. That was just at the time I first went to work for him, and if I had not been so diligent in reminding him that his heart and leg veins were in no state to support the strain of serious passion there is no doubt that he would have married Mrs Chiddle, if only to save the bother of having to talk to her so often in the course of a single day. She was also wearing out the buckets with her ceaseless traipsing.

Mr Ellicott shouted greetings to Mrs Chiddle and called on me to give him some assistance in getting out of the cash-desk which had now come to fit him like a waistcoat since idleness had put fat on him. Mr Ellicott was no Don Juan but he believed that as long as he ran a grocery shop he should personally serve all those who had come anywhere near marrying him. So, leaning heavily on me, he advanced, the gaslight glinting on his thick horn-rimmed glasses and wearying thatch. He showed every one of his retired teeth to give greeting and service to Mrs Chiddle. I watched every move with close attention and unease, for I was an earnest young man, touchy as a boil to any evidence of immorality.

Mrs Chiddle was broad and stout, slowed down in her movements by a thousand arguments against living which all her days had propounded, a friendly woman beating her fists against a rock-face of unfriendly circumstance. She smiled at me, knowing that I, in my small officious way, represented the vigilant, hostile side of Mr Ellicott's conscience. He took his stand behind the butter and cheese counter, ready to do her bidding within the limits imposed by the grocery trade in a Christian place.

I felt sorry for Mrs Chiddle all the same. She was a lonely woman, but then Bandy Lane was as full of loneliness as of air and both had grown stale for lack of motion. There had been something pathetic in the way she had made herself up into a hot, untidy bundle and thrown herself at Mr Ellicott's head. There had been a note of sadness struck off from her zeal which had taken part of the skin from my mind and left the pity of it raw. But she had had her eye on Mr Ellicott's business and that was bad. So, whenever she came into view I would remind him with word or glance of what he had told me about the way in which his heart and veins had him poised at an angle which would shoot him into the Black Meadow at the onset of any sustained bout of lust.

As I stood there that morning I decided that some sharp gesture of discouragement directed at Mrs Chiddle would not be out of place. The smell of disinfectant on my hands made me feel keen, intense, austere, and I felt a master of the grocery trade from both the hygienic and ethical angles of approach.

Mrs Chiddle's technique of intercourse with Mr Ellicott was strange and you would not find it mentioned in any of the handbooks. She stood with both hands on her taut chintz apron, her eyes on his, both sighing, as if what they saw was all the delicious untrodden distances their feet had never reached. From the sound of their sighing and the raptness of their staring at each other one gathered a sense of significant ceremony. Had I not been an interested and automatically hostile party I would have liked that interlude of meaningful dreaming in the small sea of food smells, but I had myself to look out for. True, any thought of serious romance between Mrs Chiddle and Mr Ellicott had been as well gaffed as a salmon and was no longer even twitching at the bottom of the boat. Her body had lost shape as thoroughly as his heart valves had lost strength. But Mrs Chiddle was still an emblem to remind Mr Ellicott of what he had lost and was still without, and who knew whether one morning his valves might not take a whiff of Easter air and sing some anthem of resurrection? And his leg veins might reclaim part of the ghost they had given up and trot like mad after some bit of enchantment. So Mrs Chiddle, as emblem, had to be fought.

She sighed again and asked Mr Ellicott if he remembered the old times. He said yes. Of course he did, because she was there six times a week with the same chintz apron, the same broad, sad face, the same plangent alto voice that seemed to darken the cheese with its richness, to remind him of them, to rub them into his withering senses like a sauce, to prick and disquiet him with impossible longings. 'They were good times,' said Mr Ellicott, and he closed his eyes as if he wanted his mind to walk back without hindrance to some faraway field of fulfilment he had briefly known.

'And those days we went away with the choir,' said Mrs Chiddle.

'Oh God, yes. Those days, those mornings when the sun was always strong. Or is the sun always inside one?'

I frowned. Mr Ellicott did not open his eyes. The past recalled by Mrs Chiddle was as broad as the earth and he was happy to get lost there. He no longer had the dynamic impulse that keeps the senses of a good businessman tethered like tidy goats to the cash till, so he could afford these moments of detachment. And while he stood there bemused, Mrs Chiddle got busy. She stood right by the best creamery butter and the round of fresh Caerphilly cheese. Into these she pitched, gouging out lumps from the dampish cheese and helping down each mouthful with a finger swathed in butter. I had not decided whether she came into the shop hungry and helped herself there to still her stomach or whether there was something in the nostalgic mood she provoked in herself and Mr Ellicott that made it necessary for her to go fingering butter and cheese in this way. This morning she went further. She moved a little along the counter and plunged her hand into a bottle of sweet biscuits, of which she fished out six and put them into her mouth. That, I thought, was the moment to tackle Mrs Chiddle, for they were large biscuits and she would have needed to be a ventriloquist to throw her voice over a heap of stuff as high as that.

'Mr Ellicott,' I said, 'I don't like to break in on your fine thoughts about the old days but I have to tell you that whenever you go off into one of these trances Mrs Chiddle, who by rights should be in the trance with you, practically clears the counter of food. It used to be just the cheese and butter but this morning she has started on the sweet crunchies, one of our best biscuit lines.'

Mr Ellicott winced but still did not open his eyes, for all the world as if he were up to some act of love in the darkness behind his lids. Mrs Chiddle glared but made it even harder for her to reply by slipping three more crunchies into her mouth.

'And besides,' I said, and my voice here became harder, more telling now because I was dealing with a point that had made one of the best passages in a talk I gave to the senior section of the Bandy Lane Youth Centre, 'To Sell and to Serve', 'And besides, I'm not saying Mrs Chiddle isn't clean but it doesn't inspire confidence in other customers to see these products being mauled. I've seen people getting a worse grip on the handlebars of a bike than Mrs Chiddle has been keeping on that round of Caerphilly. Every day I've got to go round after her wiping off finger prints with the muslin. If you ask me, Mr Ellicott, she's exploiting your weakness and kindliness. She's nothing better than a looter.'

I would have said more because I had three big facts about contamination by fingering which I had picked up from a Ministry of Health leaflet, but Mrs Chiddle took two quick steps and caught me a homer on the side of the head and called me, as clearly as she could through all that food, a cheeky young something. She left the shop and in the glass cabinet we kept for loaves of madeira and fruit-cake I saw that my face was very red. I always wore stiff white collars on the tight side for neatness to show how much more serious I was than the average trader in Bandy Lane who tends in physical appearance to be as slapdash as a tramp, with no more than two buttons in three secured and keen not to make their clients feel inferior by wearing collars soft as love, grubby as urchins and four or five inches away from the neck. But hangmen have used looser nooses than the collars I wore, and they were the most assertive bits of whiteness in Bandy Lane, an off-white area if there ever was one. It was the pressure of the collar that made me blush when Mrs Chiddle hit me. It was certainly not for shame for I had seen my duty and it had been done. It was the collar, and the smell of butter and cheese on her hand reminding me of the way in which a bunch of unscrupulous jokers can go about nibbling and tasting a grocer out of house and home, all as friendly as you like. A reference to old times, a closing of the eyes and your stock vanishes as through a trap-door.

I had expected to see Mr Ellicott scandalised by my exposure of Mrs Chiddle and willing to praise me for the iron hand I was now forging in my muslin glove. But when he opened his eyes he just hobbled back to his desk, refusing with a look of distaste the arm I outstretched to help him. Once at rest behind his ledgers he relaxed and began to laugh.

'Dig out your collar-stud, Stobo,' he said, 'and let some air into your emotions. Morally you're a jack-in-the-box and a nuisance. Your heart is choking to death. Of course I knew that Mrs Chiddle was helping herself to butter and cheese. My butter and cheese, not yours yet, you see, Stobo. And why do you think I kept my eyes closed? To make sure that she wouldn't be shy about pitching in until she had satisfied herself. Some mornings the poor girl's been so slow in taking what she wanted I've almost fallen asleep, so long have I kept my eyes shut. Butter and cheese are dear for the average widow. Cows have not heard of widows or they would deliver the stuff direct to them. You'll learn, Stobo. I hope you'll learn, or you'll be a corn on the foot of living more tender and sore than these damned varicose articles of mine. We help each other over the hills and into the grave. Carry as many people as you can, Stobo, and reduce the bumps. You're too wound up. Let the springs rest easy.'

And he laughed again and went back to his reading of the wills in the county paper. I knew I could have floored him in a trice because Melancthon Mills, my friend and Warden of the Social Centre, had talked to me more than once about the abuse of charity. Melancthon's father had been in business and had kept floating in and out of the County Court on a tide of indiscriminate credit. He knew.

I went around the back to wash the disinfectant smell off my hands, convinced that there would never really be enough carbolic to render wholesome so willingly and helplessly scabrous a globe.

When I got back Angela was there with the huge basket she always brought for shopping. At the sight of her I slipped back into the kitchen to give my tie a final tug, my hair a last subtle pat. The best was not too good for Angela. When I returned to the shop I did not go straightway behind the counter. I went into the middle of the shop where she was standing, took one of her hands and kissed it. Now, this manoeuvre was not common in Bandy Lane. If the average inhabitant came on to you doing that, either you would hide your hand or keep your eye on his teeth, for social urges in this zone are so raw the bone shows. But Angela accepted the tribute as to the manner born. All ladies who have laced and satinned their way to loveliness of form and utterance since man's beginning spoke through her. But this hand-kissing was not primarily her idea. We were both in a play being put on by Dunkerly Dodge, one of the Assistant Wardens at the Centre. Angela was an adventuress and I a count. My part was very small, just walking on, seeing Angela and kissing her hand to show that I am a count and smitten. I had easily persuaded Dunkerly to give me the part, for he knew how keen I was on developing suavity for the social side of my career.

I wish there were a pamphlet with numbered headings which could explain all I felt about Angela, for my feelings still remain, in sum, a mystery to those about me. Odo Mayhew, a real thinker, a clerk in the Finance Department of the Council and stage manager of the drama group at the Centre, has often told me in that penetrating melancholy way of his – for Odo, in spite of the quietness of his job, has known a lot of grief – that there are some wounds that draw their own appointed daggers. I, Stobo Wilkie, must be one such wound.

Angela was dressed in a white blouse, snowy as my collar and almost as neat; a brown cardigan, a fawn skirt and shapely, well-polished shoes. Her hair, dark but full of lights as a handsome night, was piled thick upon her neck, blue-black like grapes. At any time of day you would always see Angela turned out like this, a picture, a credit, not like most of the other girls in Bandy Lane who, before six in the evening, were not ashamed to slop around the streets looking as if they were modelling for an unparticular ragman. I first saw her at the age of five and even at that age the elements of some abiding and nourishing secret had fallen into place. The way her back tilted away from her thighs, her head from her back, represented for me the two supreme angles of this earth, and while obsessed by the thought of Technical School at the age of twelve I had been very keen on geometry and daft on Angela. To me, then as now, she was the junction, the point of passionate union between light and dark, peace and pain, the very last creature on all this globe ever to have entered the being of a man in the grocery trade.

I looked across at Mr Ellicott. His head had disappeared again behind his paper, absorbed in the flux of inheritance in the Bandy Lane zone. I winked at Angela and she handed me the neat slip of note paper on which her half-weekly order had been written in her mother's copperplate hand, the hand of one who, in a more vigorous context, might have forged banknotes and told the Band of Hope and the Social Insurance what to do with their precepts.

I moved swiftly about the shop, seeking the articles that Angela desired. The mission was difficult for two reasons. The first gave me great pain for I was a lover of honesty, and if grocers had some such exemplar as Hippocrates to whom one could swear an inviolable loyalty of intention and practice I would have been tapping out anthems of purity to him on the till every day of my life. But for Angela I took to double-dealing as a duck to water, although I can imagine the drier sort of duck having doubts where I had none. For Angela I would have deceived God, let alone Mr Ellicott. So on all possible articles I gave her liberal overweight, operating the scales with whistling speed and ease that would have foxed a lynx. When I was banging the stuff down and creating ten types of diversionary rumpus with the weights to assure Mr Ellicott that I was in full command and in no need of supervision or help, I also had Angela sing in that fine flexible alto of hers on which Mr Ellicott doted, so that even if he did look up it would only be to smile at her, to nod his head in rhythm with the music and encourage her to carry on, which Angela would do because she also doted on her voice. At the moment of the offence and while she was in the shop I had no scruple. Had Mr Ellicott been an odd leg and I a shark in hungry waters I could not have gone at him with busier jaws. But once alone again the pang in my moral sense was like a nest of boils. Odo Mayhew has told me that he has never met anyone who is such a tremor of reservations as I, and that this is a good thing because if you quake once in a while there is still hope.

The second reason was the quality of articles Angela had on her list. Her mother was the fussiest eater in Bandy Lane, and some of the titbits she asked for would not normally have been found in the food shops of this area: tinned crab, Viennese sausages that laughed right through the tin at the uncouth bread-stuffed items you would have got from the butchers of Bandy Lane. Mrs Lang's stomach was just about Bandy Lane's last link with the aristocracy. Her palate refused to compromise. Either the best or starve, that was her slogan. When I saw the price of some of the dainties I slipped into Angela's basket or sweated blood trying to make her credit right with Mr Ellicott, I sometimes wondered how long it would take her mother to starve if I could persuade her without coarseness that even the stuff she was getting from me was not the best that could be had.

'How's your mother, Angela?' called out Mr Ellicott.

'She's not been out much lately, Mr Ellicott. You know how she gets sometimes. Afraid to meet people.'

'I know. She's high-strung. There's better blood in your mother than in most. Blue, if you follow me. High-class.'

'You're right, Mr Ellicott,' I said, emphatically slipping a small free packet of cream-crackers into Angela's basket. 'Whenever I'm with Mrs Lang I feel small, humble. It's the blood, as you say. So blue. There's a lot of blood in Bandy Lane that's got no colour at all.'

'Plain grey,' said Mr Ellicott. 'Twenty years ago I said about your mother: That girl should never have been in service; there isn't a lady in all the land that couldn't have learned from her. Oh God, the grace. It's a thousand pities she's not had more luck with your poor father, Lyndhurst Lang. How is he now? Is he back at work?'

'Started last week but says he's taking it at a cautious tempo.'

'Good. Lyndhurst has had a lot of bad luck with his health. Even blind germs find him. Never mind. You and Stobo will make a good pair. He'll have a good business. He'll be able to give you the sort of life your poor mother should have had. You and Stobo come to supper with me tonight.'

'We've got a practice at the Centre at seven. Can we come after?'

'Any time you like. It does me good to have you in my kitchen. Two young strong people.'

I blushed to hear him speak so kindly of us as I glanced into Angela's packed basket, full of so much stuff virtually stripped off Mr Ellicott's pelt. I smiled my gratitude at him and my adoration at Angela. As she left the shop I was making a mental list of those mothers of large families who would be in during the day with long shapeless orders which would allow me a dozen chances of underweighing and overcharging to redress the balance tipped in hell's direction by my weakness for Angela. Sometimes, tormented by the talks I had with Odo Mayhew and Dunkerly Dodge on the need for a passionate selfless integrity which would burn away like a blowlamp the drab paint of dead false ages, I resolved to have done with this chicane and pay like a man out of my own wages for what Angela got in excess of her stated demands. But I was due in two years' time to make my first big down payment on the sum mentioned by Mr Ellicott as the price he would ask me for the shop's goodwill. Not a penny could be spared from my account at the Post Office. Often Angela charged me with being too much like a monk in the interests of the savings book. But her smile was as broad as mine when I showed her each tiny step upwards of the total. Odo Mayhew, to whom I confided all my ambitions, told me that money was dross and this dedication to hoarding and self-interest would burn my fibres black. But I did not listen too attentively to him; in the matter of money he has been practically driven off the hinge by the foolish financial antics for which he has to account as clerk to the Borough Treasurer.

2

I got home from the shop at seven. I hurried over the last of my tasks because I was worried about my father. He was in most ways a quiet, likeable man, but only the dead could have showed less initiative. I was quite frank about this in my own mind. I wanted to show him all the patience and affection I could, for he was a lonely man, but I often wished that nature had given me a father with a surer grip on life or at least the means of giving me a helpful push up the business ladder on which I had set my feet. You never saw anyone look as baffled as my father when I came out with these metaphors about ladders and feet. He had never come across existence as an upward progression. If ever I got a push from my father I hesitate to think where I might land.

He had worked for years as assistant herdsman and milk roundsman to Samson Blakemore, who kept a small farm on the hillside above Bandy Lane, and there was no doubt that this work for Blakemore, slaving hard at enfeebled cows in draughty barns at the crack of dawn, accounted for much of the depression and self-defeat into which my father had now sunk up to the neck. His sad, small head still remained in sight, but precariously, and if you saw him give a jerky movement it was certain he was kicking away what little he still had left to stand on.

Our house was empty when I got there. There was

no sign of food having been prepared. For a second as I stood by the door I was ill with awareness of what my mother's going had meant to us both. With her there had been no luxury but there had been light, food and a unifying rivet of care. But I realised that this type of brooding could be a dangerous ailment and put it out of my mind. I assumed that my father had gone off on one of his solitary rambles round the town and that he would buy himself a packet of chips at the shop of Manuel Valera, a Spaniard, to whom my father delivered milk and for whom he sometimes did such odd jobs as potato-cleaning when Manuel was short-handed.

I made a slight meal, then hurried over to the Centre. In those days it was my real home. On my way there I thought, a little furtively, of the mechanics of deprivation on this earth and of the raw holes left in some of us by its infallible hooks, and I felt, but in an essentially quiet, gradualist sort of way, of course, that something should be done about it.

Someone stopped me and said that he had seen my father walking about with Colenso Mortlake. That made me feel no happier. Colenso was an old friend of mine. We had been at Elementary School together but he had gone on to do five years at the Secondary school and was now an electrical engineer with a firm of contractors whose work took Colenso all over the land. I had not been sorry to see Colenso start on his travels, for his was a sour and rebellious view of life. If ever there was any reverence in Colenso he kept it boxed away from me. When he was a member of the Youth Section at the Centre he made repeated efforts to interfere with the fine teaching done in the Religious Instruction and Civics groups, saying that the doctrine put forward by the teacher encouraged a comatose servility in the student. I as a committee member seconded Dunkerly Dodge when, after Colenso had made a bitter verbal attack on Sir Gwydion Pooley, the steel magnate, a wonderful citizen and a patron and president of the Centre, he moved that Colenso be expelled. Colenso was called in, heard what we had to say, smiled in his ironical yet pleasant way, wished us many feudal returns of the day, took some electrical tool from his pocket, waggled it at us in a suggestive way and said he looked forward to the day when he would have our minds at the end of a really hot wire. A typical jest by Colenso, that, very involved, very disturbing.

So now he was back with my father. I considered that bad, because for years Colenso had been in and out of our kitchen, thickening my father's grey mood by telling him that he was no more than a serf to Samson Blakemore and that if he continued to get up before the chickens and cart milk round the town for such a sullen and retrogressive element, he would vanish one day in a cloud of lunatic despair. And with every word that Colenso let drop into my father's mind I could see the cloud forming.

At the Centre I caught the last part of a committee meeting on the charges to be set for the summer camp which we ran in the West Breconshire mountains. It had run at a loss the year before and Melancthon Mills, our Warden, smooth as marble, wise as an owl and a true friend, had sought the advice of our patron, Sir Gwydion Pooley. Sir Gwydion had sent back by return, covering the immediate loss with a cheque, and we all clapped at the lovely apposite click of his benevolence. But in his letter Sir Gwydion warned us to be on our guard against letting the members have too much for nothing, since this would warp their sense of values, create thoughtless egomaniacs and not selfless citizens, and advised us to increase our charges next summer. This we decided to do, substantially, for that was our whole aim as a Social Centre, to cut down the number of thoughtless egomaniacs.

'Sir Gwydion is a thousand times right,' said Dunkerly Dodge. Dunkerly had the most winning manner in all Bandy Lane. He had a strong voice which he used as objectively as a snake-charmer's pipe, and a fine accent developed in two years he had spent with a repertory company in North Wales. Now he was establishing records as the agent of an insurance company and of a firm that supplied club-checks for which the clients paid him a shilling a week. 'I've seen some very warped-looking young elements around here. Let them have a just appreciation of what they are being given.'

After the meeting I went with Dunkerly and Melancthon Mills into the canteen. I bought them tea and cakes, for I wished to discuss with them the problem of my father's inertia and decline. 'I'm worried,' I told them. 'Most nights he sits in the house in his old flannel shirt staring into the fire with such a look you can see the coals turn from red to grey just to keep in step. He doesn't say much most times except that he would like to join my mother in the Black Meadow if the burial rates were lower and the Christian doctrine of an afterlife a bit truer. Slow, alarming stuff like that, enough to bring the milpuff up out of the chairs.'

Melancthon's eyes clouded and he laid his hand on my shoulder to show that I had his sympathy in having to listen to material of that sort, for his father had a total collapse after thirty years as Treasurer to the Bandy Lane Rationalist Group, a band of voters who had given up most of their time and pocket money to the eviction of God, a long job in Bandy Lane.

'He recites the names of his favourites among those cows he has to milk up there at Blakemore's,' I said. 'Maisy, Daisy, Lily and Milly, Dulcie and Dolly. He says they're all so weak he's found them trying to get a sit-down on the milking stool, and that the milk he gets from them is about as nourishing as pop.'

'This is serious,' said Dunkerly.

'It is,' I said. 'He neglects his clothes. Half the time he wears no trousers. That comes I suppose from being so much about animals and is a sort of reaction too against Blakemore who is austere and wears a pair of trousers, my father says, of serge as thick as Blakemore and strung almost up to the neck.'

'I've seen Blakemore in that rig,' said Dunkerly. 'He looks a bit on the trussed side. He almost breaks his arms trying to get things out of the pocket. It belonged to his son, that very big boy, who died of the appendix. Blakemore was very proud of him and he's always having to explain about his size when you ask him why his trousers look so abnormal. It's quite likely, as you say, that your father has a hankering after bare legs at home after seeing so much cloth on Blakemore.'

'He's like that these days. And he gets these desperate fits on him, whatever he's doing, and he crawls back home. I've seen him lift a cup to his lips, then ask "What's the use of tea?" And down goes the cup.'

'A shame, that,' said Melancthon. 'This sick, rebellious questioning of the ends for which we live is bad. Every question asked in despair is a rat chewing at the rigging of the vessel of social confidence. Your father, Stobo, sounds as if he has finished with the rigging and is now getting his teeth ready for the deck itself.'

'Yes. All he does is curl up in his armchair, loosen

the ribbons of his underwear and say that if life has shattered him then he has the right to go about looking shattered. He says it would *really* shock people if he went about looking as degraded as he feels. He said if I would find him a beach, he would comb it. That's the stuff he says. Frightening and anarchistic. What's the cure?'

Melancthon said nothing. He had clearly caught some whiff of the authentic fundamental disgust that lay behind my father's attitude and it must have chimed with some mood of failure arising from the great difficulties he often stumbled over in running the Centre. He leaned on his fists, stared down into his tea and said nothing. But Dunkerly seemed to have run right round the problem and spotted all the doors that led to its heart.

'The root of the problem lies in Samson Blakemore, the dirty undignified way in which he keeps that farm of his. He's never encouraged your father to take a pride in his work. Of course Blakemore is rather more than half off the hinge. I don't blame those sons of his for going off and leaving him there all alone. All he's got left is that cousin of his, Lucas Phillimore, and he's an even rarer element than Samson. But between you and me, Stobo, I think your father could have done a lot more to help himself. He's never taken any pride in that horse and cart of his. The cart rattles like the fear of death and it's a wonder he doesn't land up at the bottom of that stony old farm road covered with cheese. And whoever got the ideas of calling such a sad-looking animal as that horse Jolly? And what kind of costume is that your father wears when he's on the job?'

'Costume?'

'That bowler. That dark suit.'

'Oh, his old funeral outfit. It's the only suit he's got left and he'll never need it for a funeral again because he says that with the sable outlook his mind now wears every day of the week it would be just an impertinence to celebrate any individual death. And in any case he says Blakemore and Phillimore like to see him going about his tasks with a suggestion of misery because life strikes those two also as being a bit of a hearse.'

'If there were some mental equivalent of a bottle-brush those two could well be scoured from ear to ear. We've got to get a brighter equipment altogether for your father. Has he been losing business lately?'

'A lot. The Conjoint Milkeries and the Co-op have taken a lot of his custom.'

'No wonder. He stands there with that bowler hat getting lower and lower over his ears every day. When he raises his arm to get the horse started he looks as if he's laying a curse on the milk. And it's terrible to hear him utter the name of that horse: "Jolly, Jolly," he goes, in a voice that sounds as if he's lowering the whole outfit into the tomb, churns and all. A man has got to believe in what he sells. Does your father believe in milk, Stobo?'

'God knows what his beliefs are exactly. But he feels affection for those cows, so I suppose he believes in their milk.'

'Good. Well, leave it to me, Stobo. I'm going to get to work on this. Bandy Lane's too full of people like your father. Life gives them a soft tap and they crumple up as if a leopard has just landed on them from the tree-tops, and when they crumple they hate to see anyone standing upright. Your father would like to drag you down with him.'

'Oh, I don't know, boy.'

'I do, Stobo. I've been about. I've been an actor. I've got an eye for tragedy, like other people have for whippets. It's amazing how people hug their knife to their own bowels. As conscious self-disembowellers the Japanese are as tyros compared with most of the elements in Bandy Lane. Whenever any voter lifts the cup of tears to his lips for the longest and noisiest sip of all, I hear the curtain going up and life is flooded with a light that yields all secrets to me. And what I didn't learn on the stage I've picked up in the insurance and club-check business where you see the voters on their most exposed and pitiable flank.'

'Thank you, Dunk. I knew you'd help me.'

'And Melancthon will, too. He's in a bit of a daze at the moment. But he's been like that ever since he read that pamphlet on Plato and the Youth. A real sage and a saint is Melancthon,' Dunkerly lowered his voice, 'but he could do with a spell in my business to bring him to grips with life. Frankly I don't think Plato could even get nominated for the Council in this zone. The entrails get more twisted as the rhythm of our wants grows brisker.'

Dunkerly and I left the table, leaving Melancthon to his thoughts. 'Life's a bit of a woman,' said Dunkerly, and he slipped his arm around my shoulder. 'The more you get to grips with it, the more it glows, the more it wants to give. Of course, that's very adult talk, Stobo, not often to be heard in the Youth Section of a Social Centre. But I know you'll bear it in mind.'

I nodded. I was impressed but puzzled, for at that time I was nimble-witted only in the matter of groceries.

3

I was happier as I made my way back from the Centre, but my happiness did not last long. When I opened the door I saw two suitcases and I knew that some kind of sinister novelty was brewing. There was also a sound of singing in the house, melancholy singing of the sort which we have turned our back on in the Centre as keeping the fibre of Bandy Lane soaked and dark.

Around the fire were my father, still dressed in the suit and hat he wore on his round, Colenso Mortlake and Leo Watham, a dustman with the Bandy Lane council, a gentle and poetic sort of man who had long been friendly with my father. Leo's nerves had suffered when he had been transferred from an ash-cart drawn by a huge, slow horse to a motor lorry which lurched around Bandy Lane at amazing speeds disposing of rubbish with blinding zeal, driven by one of the most ambitious young elements in the town, Hadrian Mogg, who was out to create an impression on the Council officials and in doing so was sending his colleagues who had survived from a quieter age into the County Mental.

My father and his companions were eating chips and humming an old Celtic air that was as round and black with age and grief as my father's bowler.

Colenso looked at me expectantly, assuming a warm welcome, but I wanted to make it quite plain to him that his road and mine were no longer the same. I respected him for having done so well with the electricity, but I wanted to show him that I had plumped for quiet progress and a settled and honourable future and wanted no part of his challenging and upsetting ironies.

'Colenso is coming to stay with us,' said my father, the listlessness of his face lifting briefly. 'Isn't that good?'

'No,' I said. 'There's no room for you here, Colenso.'

'Of course there is,' said my father. 'He's brought his bags and all.'

'I'll go if I'm not wanted,' said Colenso, but he stuck fast to his chair, knowing that he had my father hypnotised like a rabbit. 'I got home from that big hydro-electric job in Scotland this afternoon. I sat down to tea with my mother and stepfather. We were having fish and chips. My stepfather is a very religious voter but I didn't know that while I was away he was promoted to a leading position in his sect and he's blazing with zeal. There I was talking away in a smooth godless flow. My mother is a bit deaf or she would have warned me that my stepfather has his torch out for the nearest infidel. I was saying that the job we'd been doing up in Scotland would give power and light to an area which has had only fanatical bigotry and meanness to keep it warm since the beginning of time. This, I said, was a fine example of man's power to confront rationally all the old dilemmas that have made him such a terrified frog, jumping and croaking from one totem-pole to another. Then my stepfather's fork came down about a hundredth of an inch from my fingers. At first I thought that the little tailor-shop where he works had weakened his eyes and that he had mistaken my fingers for the chips and was spearing hard out of hunger. But then he did it again and I could see there was no mistake. Chips were the least of his concerns. He told me that while I had been speaking he had seen the fish on his plate discolour and shrink and he told me to take my bags and go or, instead of using just one fork on the target, he would be coming at me with the whole drawerful of cutlery. So here I am, on your mercy.'

'You can stay for the night, Colenso,' I said. 'I don't blame your stepfather. He's been in an exalted state ever since he got the headship of those fundamentalists in Nyasa Road, white-hot with conviction, handing out an extra crutch to the pious and putting a sharp end to disbelief. Why can't you be agreeable, for God's sake, and keep the peace? Pat a neighbour's phobias and throw them a biscuit. You'd do as much for a dog.'

'I really do try to,' he said, his broad face as genial as could be and his thick, jetblack eyebrows up to show innocence. 'What's the matter with you, Stobo? What have you got against me, boy? You could swear I'm a stranger, a leper.'

'Oh no you're not, Colenso,' said my father. 'You're welcome, boy. Don't mind Stobo. He's in with a lot of queer ones since he started going to the Social Centre and courting that Angela Lang.'

'That's right,' I said. 'Turn on me for trying to get on. Melancthon Mills once said, Colenso, that there are some who see life as a conspiracy; others see it as a glorious opportunity. You, I'm afraid, are muffled up and collecting funds for the first group. Look at my father. Once he was the happiest milkman in Bandy Lane, a model employee, singing as he got out of bed. Then you go denouncing Samson Blakemore as a kulak or something, you tell my father he is the worst sort of peasant and the only reason he should keep his cart-wheels oiled and clean is to serve a as tumbril when he is taking Blakemore to the knife...'

'Don't be daft, Stobo,' said my father. 'I thought those things out for myself.'

'I was helping your father,' said Colenso. 'I'm trying to lift him out of his coffin and you stand ready with the hammer to fit him in again. I found him walking in the streets of Bandy Lane so serenely sad that if Bandy had a better flavoured river he'd have been in it with pleasure. We were joined by Leo Watham here, who has lost whatever happiness he knew as an ashman since the passing of the horse and the coming of that Napoleon of the refuse tip, Hadrian Mogg. So I took them to that pub where they have a discussion group and a male voice choir, The Thinker and The Thrush. We were welcomed by the discussion group and I gave a short talk on Samson Blakemore, defining him as a half-evolved kind of domestic animal, and Leo gave a fine rendering of that poem, "The Man with the Hoe". He pointed at your father the whole while, hinting that he is the finest example of rural oppression since the French Revolution. The chairman, Waldron Mead, formally denounced milk and urged your father to find a smoother trade. We almost had your father in a mood to march up the mountain and bury Blakemore in his own midden and crown him with the day's curds. But he's always too nice, too genial. If ever death were to grope and stumble in the dark your father is the boy to lift it up and set it right.'

'That's you all over,' I said. 'Full of negation, packed with mischief. My father has a tidy little job, one he was lucky and privileged to have right through the years of shortage, and you turn him against it, against Mr Blakemore who is a landowner, a man of substance even though he does seem a bit slow to wash. But you won't succeed. I've discussed the matter with Dunkerly Dodge and he's going to take Dad in hand and give him a new outlook.'

My father threw his chip-paper into the fire and looked at me gently, curiously.

'God help you, Wyndham,' said Leo to my father. 'I know that Dodge. A fussy, thrusting voter, like Hadrian Mogg. Between them they'll have us right in the Jordan before we can approach the National Health for water-wings.'

'And I don't like the idea of you taking my father into pubs, either, Colenso,' I said. 'Don't forget that I've got a bit of a reputation to keep up here now. And that particular pub you took him to is a terrible place, a nest of dissenters, plotters, no-goods. Your stepfather stood on a porch there one night, reeling as he caught the reek of ale and calling for Lot.'

'Salaam, Rechab,' said Colenso, and he laughed in his adroit, delighted way. My father and Leo, to show that their wits had been sharpened by the session of drink and poetry in The Thinker and The Thrush, laughed too. I turned away, shorn of argument. Laughter always disables me, for I am at a loss to know how much to allow inside the igloo at any given time. My father, thinking I had been hurt in my brush with Colenso, came up and laid his hand on my arm.

'You carry on, Stobo,' he said. 'I'll do as you say. I'm sorry to have been so down, such a mope. I don't want to shame you, honest. My mind and heart are in ribbons, and if you and Mr Dodge can stitch them back into a flag that will brave the breeze, good luck.'

'That's the spirit, Dad. And if Colenso comes sidling up to you with his bilious doctrines about the gaping wounds in the flank of the species, just dip his shirt-tail in paraffin and supply his stepfather with a match. The warmth would do everyone good. And you, Colenso, go back home tomorrow and make it up. There's another side to your stepfather, you know.'

'Another side?' asked Colenso suspiciously. 'What's he got in reserve? What more can such a voter do for me?'

'I got this information from Dunkerly Dodge who collects for the insurance and the club-checks in that Nyasa Road district where your stepfather holds most of his meetings. In that area all you see of the average voter is a tuft of top-hair on a lake of debt. But lately people have been clearing off debts as fast as they can, even getting Dunkerly out of bed to get their cards up to date. That's only been since your stepfather has been bringing such a piercing and immediate sense of hell into their thinking. He makes a special point of lambasting debtors because there are so many people who owe him for suits he says he wouldn't have made less if he had been carrying on his tailoring business in one of those warm islands where the voters make do with a small leaf in front and the broad blue sky behind. Any man who is good for trade cannot be wholly vile.'

I could hear Colenso's mind assembling most happily the material of his reply and among the materials I could see a dialectical nail long enough to pin my head to the floor for those bold statements I had made about trade and God. So I nipped in with: 'It's late. Come on, Dad. You've got to be up early.'

'With the milk,' said my father and we all laughed. Since the dusk had first fallen across his joy in life that was his only regular joke, and it behoved us to encourage him.

4

The very next day Dunkerly set with a vengeance about the reclamation of my father from the wilderness. It was my half-day from the shop, and he arranged an important meeting with Samson Blakemore. 'We should put that element in an iron lung of suggestion,' he said. He got my father to start subscribing to a clothing club at ninepence a week and he promised that the goods would be made instantly available. 'I want your father to have a whole uniform of snow-white raiment for his milk deliveries. For two reasons: to shame and cheer Blakemore into a blither outlook; to give the voters more confidence in Blakemore's milk and stop the drift of custom towards the big bottlers. Besides, it'll give your father a sense of the poetry of his occupation and that's something nine-tenths of the working class could do with having injected into them in pill or enema form. Clad in white, coming down the hillside behind his gleaming churns, if he can ever make such dull-looking articles gleam again, he will sing his way around the beat.'

We had a short meeting at the Centre before setting out for Blakemore's. Dunkerly was dynamic, with his long fawn overcoat trailing behind him, collecting the people he wished to come with us. I thought he was making the delegation too large and I could see it was going to embarrass my father to be one of such a procession, but Dunkerly said he wanted our reproach to make a real dent on Blakemore. Colenso was one of the party. I had tried to explain to him that on such a mild and uplifting mission, designed to pull Samson Blakemore out of the Middle Ages as far, let us say, as Bosworth, he had no place. But Colenso said he would keep well in the background and the quiet, amenable way in which he said that persuaded me that the good progress he was now making in the electrical industry was filing down the more jagged of his edges. Dunkerly was quite upset to see him and he kept muttering to me that if the electrical company knew what a viper it was nourishing at its pylons it would concentrate a shower of free watts on Colenso personally. All the same I could see Dunkerly look enviously at Colenso's large brown slouch, his new blue nap overcoat and the very confident look that Colenso had put on since he became associated with schemes of light and power which, he said, were going to transform the face of Britain. Dunkerly said that it took a lynx like Colenso to have found anything about the face of the little old country that needed transforming, and I agreed.

The most interesting members of our group were two Austrian visitors and the brothers Mogg. The Austrians were a fresh-complexioned, keen-looking pair of elements who were out to study our youth organisations which were apparently much less formal and brutal than the samples they had known. They took a great interest in everything, but their English was poor and this was a great comfort to boys like Dunkerly who never really wanted to stop talking. Helmuth and Max wore green suits with a kind of Norfolk jacket and their fair heads were always bare. Dunkerly pointed out that the tall, clean, blonde look of the boys, in such contrast with the jet, dwarfed look of many voters in Bandy Lane, marked them out as the natural leaders of Europe. Dunkerly's head tended to be on the light side and he was often overtly Aryan in remarks of this kind, and he did not like it when Colenso, speaking up for the aboriginals of our hills, said he would believe that when he found that the fair curls on Helmuth's head were worth more on the open market than the black straight material he carried about.

The brothers Hadrian and Offa Mogg were about the most ambitious duo in Bandy Lane. Their father Peter Mogg had developed a whole series of defensive complexes after keeping his finger tightly plugged in a staunchless wound of apprehension. About the time his children came along Bandy Lane was having trouble with its river, the Moody, and Mogg saw life as a succession of mounting floods. He had named his two boys after barricades and dykes. Hadrian was the youngest man ever to reach foreman's rank in the Borough Engineer's department, and he was now in charge of the garbage lorries in which Leo Watham was being driven to nervous ruin. It was Hadrian's aim to become a Sanitary Inspector. His schooling was stopped when his father overdid his zeal in the Bandy Lane floods of 1931 and got himself washed out to sea. He studied in his spare time and had a notebook in beautiful copperplate to which he gave the title, 'Filth in Theory and Practice', in which he proved that Bandy Lane in some details of its private hygiene was several blushes below the level of certain primitive peoples who, until Hadrian had taken his torch around the division, had held the medal for free, easy and loathsome ways.

In his research Hadrian had been helped by his brother Offa who was the senior reporter on the *Bandy Lane Bulletin*. He ran a special column of intimate revelations which he signed 'Oculus Voster', and he had a very large, finely drawn eye at the head of the column to help voters who had no Latin. Between them there was not a thing that Hadrian and Offa missed. They were like an infra-red device fitted to the head of Bandy Lane and once you saw their disgustedly observant look you knew that nothing would go unremarked.

I was not surprised to see Hadrian there, for he had often told me that he considered Samson Blakemore's torpid approach to neatness and my father's offhand treatment of the churns as sources of danger on which he was doing a monograph for his work on filth. 'Frankly,' he told me as soon as we got to the Centre where we were to meet Dunkerly, 'I'm glad Dodge is making these moves to get Blakemore and your father to strike a more jubilant note. I know Blakemore lost his sons, I know that your father lost his wife and then his place on the Bandy Lane bowls team when grief robbed his hand of its old steadiness and skill, but grief is a germ-spreading pest, Stobo, and in an efficient system of mental sewage there would be a broad pipe for its disposal. I have been listing those two as blood-brothers to the bubonic-bearing rat for some time. I have seen his cows back away from Blakemore on grounds of gloom and grime, and I don't like your father's method of dishing the milk out into open jugs. Some people leave the jugs out all night to save being called out of bed. The thought of what happens to those jugs has often made me cry out in my sleep. Think of the dogs alone, especially the nosey and incontinent sort that seems to swarm in Bandy Lane. Tell me, Stobo, have you ever seen a dog that was able to resist the sight of an uncovered jug?'

Dunkerly was looking at us critically. 'I've been thinking,' he said. 'Our appearance needs to be more jaunty and life-loving. We've got to show Blakemore that the day of sullen endurance is done and the hour of smiling assertions is at hand.' He turned to Max and Helmuth. 'I know that your blonde heads have a fine cleansing suggestion about them but what I would fancy for you are those hats with feathers that are worn by voters around the Tyrol. Have you boys hats?'

The Austrians said they had hats in their boarding-house but they were featherless.

'Go get them. We'll see about the feathers.'

Helmuth and Max slipped out to the house two doors away where they were staying. We followed Dunkerly to the office that was used by the two sub-wardens. It was full of boxes and models. We had just been holding a hobbies competition for the under-fourteen section of the Centre and it was astonishing what these young elements had got their hands on. The two prize-winners had been the twin sons of Offa Mogg, Baldwin and Maginot. Offa had encouraged the boys to develop a vigilance and care for detail equal to his own and they became collectors, Baldwin of birds' feathers of every type and Maginot of birds' eggs. The range of their work had taken everybody by surprise and the collections had been carried in in boxes the size of an adult's coffin. My father said that if there was still a bird among our hills not bald or childless it was not the fault of the Mogg twins who seemed to have plucked or looted everything on wing or in nest. The boys had got into some trouble during the weeks just before the exhibition when they were trying to fill in the gaps noticed by Offa, himself a bird-watcher, in their collections. They had been accused of actually going beneath courting couples in dingles and hedges for feathers and eggs and this had led to a lot of confusion and anger, for in those circumstances not even so glib a little element as Baldwin Mogg could make his purpose clear. More than once some hasty lover had branded them as pimps and assaulted them, only to find his name and deed spotlit in the next Thursday's column of Oculus Voster in the *Bulletin*. If the assaulter happened to be a married man, the brighter the light, the keener the stare of Oculus, for Offa was never the man to put up with such manoeuvres as adultery in any context. This brought fresh waves of violence down on the boys from voters whose joy had been gutted by Offa's exposure, and by the time the exhibition opened it was wondered exactly what would be in those long, sinister boxes – the eggs, the feathers, or the twins.

Dunkerly asked Offa's permission to use some of the feathers. Offa said that Baldwin would be glad to serve the public in any way. When the two Austrians came back they were given two of the longest feathers Dunkerly could find to fit into their hats, far too long in view of the low-lying, crushed-tweedy nature of those articles.

Dunkerly looked at my father's bowler as if in difficulty about the kind of ornament that would best lift it and him out of the doldrums. He picked a feather that looked as if it had been plucked from a very short blackbird and told my father to fit it in, not too obtrusively because he did not want to strike a note of burlesque, but in such a way as to show that my father, though still on a low key, shared the genial life-view of the rest of the party. 'You'd better have one, Colenso,' he said. 'And make it prominent, so that Blakemore will see from the start that our intention is to have his spirit as sweet and light as a meringue.'

We started out towards the steep path that led to Blakemore's farm. We were accosted by several voters who thought, from the nodding plumes in our hats and the artificially cheerful looks on our faces, that we had found some new, open-air way of going off the hinge.

Hadrian Mogg walked by my side. After complimenting me on the good progress I was making with Mr Ellicott he switched back to the topic of himself, which in the case of Hadrian was as broad and deep as anything you could think of. 'Thank God things are beginning to move a bit in my life too, Stobo. Honestly, I've known so much frustration in my time it's only been the shallowness and draughtiness of the bins that's prevented me from curling up inside one of them and throwing in my lot with the other refuse. When I started with the Sanitary Department they were still using the old horses and carts. You can imagine how it hurt me to be going round trying to keep the streets clear sitting behind such a socially undisciplined thing as a horse. A calm, bucolic air hung over the whole business of ash and waste. I was working with Leo Watham and that prospective father-in-law of yours, that knowing but essentially inert voter, Lyndhurst Lang. We were on a cart with a horse called Drowsy. No horse ever had a better name and my guess is that Leo and Lyndhurst took turns at giving this animal drinks of ether to wash its oats down, it dawdled so. When a strange sickness struck at the horses it was my plea that persuaded the Borough Surveyor, Rutland Swayne, to switch over to motor lorries, and the vigour I brought to the job put half this town's flies on the Social Insurance and almost drove Watham and Lang into the County Mental.'

'You certainly played the bear with Leo,' I said admiringly. 'He told me you were like a lighted firework lodged in his fork and for a whole stretch he could not see a bin without breaking into a trot and throwing it into an imaginary cart. And he accuses you of having poisoned Drowsy and the other mounts as part of your plan to finish off what little beauty there was left in the ash trade.'

'Anybody trying to get on is slandered like that. It'll happen to you, Stobo, don't worry. You'll find that Mortlake there spreading the tale that you are dosing Ellicott with hemlock to clear the road of succession. No, in a quiet way I loved Drowsy, but issuing a death certificate in any shape or form to that animal was just being subtle.'

'Do you think we'll help my father at all with this trip, Hade?'

'Probably. It might help draw Blakemore out of his seclusion and back into the social life of Bandy Lane, and there's nothing like leading a healthy social life to put personal sloppiness into the right perspective. Do you know that Blakemore would have been in trouble with the government for the tumbledown way he keeps his farm if he hadn't been so spick and span in the days before his decline. When his wife was alive, a big, active woman, a saint of cleanliness and harmony, the place was a gleam of whitewash. When she sang even the cows hummed, and Samson was so quick with his bucket and shovel to deal with such material as excrement you could see the cows glancing around as if worried to know they were making so little impression on this globe. Then Mrs Blakemore died. The sons drifted away and Samson's cousin, Lucas Phillimore, a strange element, came to live there and the light went out.'

We approached the farm. Dunkerly gave orders that Max and Helmuth should look delightedly round and laugh as if thrilled to be back in touch with farming at a thousand feet above sea level.

'A farm of character,' said Offa Mogg in a loud voice. 'The yeoman tradition, our spine and stay.'

Hadrian was looking at the puddles and piles of the farmyard with anxiety and took in with bitter disgust the drab stained walls, the unadorned windows of the farmhouse.

The front door of the farm opened and out came Lucas Phillimore. About forty-five, he was much taller than his cousin, with grey hair and features of a pale moth-eaten handsomeness. There was a curious tightness in the skin around his eyes and a world of defensive craftiness in his stare. His clothes, scagged in many places and unclean, were of good quality and stylish in a manner strange to Bandy Lane, more often to be met with on the bodies of thriving cattle-dealers in the parlour-snugs of compact, pursy market-towns. What Lucas had done in his years away from Bandy Lane not even Offa knew.

Lucas glanced at us with dislike. He examined our feathers and then glanced at the few chickens which were pecking about in the yard as if to say we had probably been up to some bit of rape before he came out. 'The place for carnivals,' he said in what I thought was a very fine, superior accent, 'is down there on the main road. Go down there.'

'Good day, Mr Phillimore,' said Dunkerly. 'We have brought two Austrian friends along. They come from a land of mountain farmers and are interested to know how their opposite numbers manage here.'

'Their opposite numbers are two noughts,' said Lucas acidly, 'and they are just managing to keep out of the workhouse.'

'Could we have a word with your cousin?' asked Dunkerly.

'Won't I do? Am I an idiot? Can't I answer questions?'

'We'd rather have a word with Mr Samson Blakemore.'

'Look at him,' whispered Colenso to me. 'A decayed gentleman, and decay only grew up when it came to gentlemen. A moral cretin of the most sinister type, his life a narrow causeway between the black lakes of regret and waste.'

'Samson!' shouted Lucas towards a small structure that looked like a closet. Its walls were uncertain and precarious. 'Yes,' said Lucas, 'that's the closet. There's no flush because one tug on the chain and you'd come out with the roof on your head and the tank on your watch-chain. There's a measure of subsidence around here that makes every sneeze a hazard.'

There was a muffled sound of recognition from within the little structure.

'My cousin is in private session,' said Lucas. 'He thinks hard. He sits there most afternoons working out programmes for the next hundred years and wondering what he'll do about the three field system when he's only got two fields left. Between ourselves I think the blight that got into our potatoes last year also landed between Samson's ears and put a shroud on his brain. He talks to his sons who are no longer here and now he's working up a whole case that Wyndham Wilkie there, our milkman, has alienated the affection of our cows, turning them against him.'

I glanced at my father. He was looking quite sympathetically at Lucas's pale, twitching face. His own expression had not changed, as if these prophecies of doom and woe were familiar to him.

'As a matter of fact,' said Dunkerly, 'that touches on our business, Mr Phillimore. We've been worried by Mr Wilkie's condition down at the Social Centre, and as we are rather interested in industrial relations we thought we might come up and help you all work out a friendlier and healthier basis for your joint activities.'

'Look,' said Lucas. 'If my cousin weren't so busy chatting with his past and linking arms with the dead he'd have given Wilkie the poke years ago. You can hear the milk curdle when that element approaches it. He dresses for the round in a way that makes people wonder whether his cart is loaded with churns or urns.' He lifted his voice. 'Samson, there's a very peculiar turn-out here, and bringing up the rear is your milkman, Wyndham Wilkie, who has brought all the loons in Bandy Way up here to demand greater justice for him.'

The closet door opened. Out came Blakemore. He was wearing the remarkably tall trousers that had belonged to his huge son, Martin, now dead, of whom he had been very proud. The trousers were black and, coming so far up the chest, gave him a strong monolithic look. He approached us slowly. He stopped and looked at us carefully. My father was the only one on whom his eyes did not linger. My father was embarrassed and upset and wished to go, but a gesture from Dunkerly kept him in place. Samson looked long at Max, Helmuth, Colenso, Hadrian, Offa and myself. His face became tender and his eyes filled with tears. Then he turned and went into the house. Lucas followed him and closed the door.

'I think we've done the trick,' said Dunkerly. 'Did you see how soft and forgiving his face became then? He's probably been regretting his anti-social ways for some time and this little visit has given him the decisive shove. What in God's name causes lives to crumble like his? But I think we've applied the poultice in time. He'll come out of there laughing, sweeping and laying on the whitewash with both hands. This is going to be a red-letter day for your father, Stobo. In a few minutes he'll be inside there drinking tea with Mr Blakemore and receiving apologies for the unfriendly way they've treated him over the last few years.'

A front window of the farmhouse opened with a

loud harsh squeak. Samson, his face now utterly purged of the tenderness that had appeared in it so briefly, came into view. In his hands was a small rifle. Behind him we could see Lucas grinning in an evil and masterful way, pointing out this and that member of our group as if recommending them to Samson as targets that demanded priority.

'So you want to alter my way of living, do you?' asked Samson in a voice that sounded as if he were still opening the ungreased window. 'So you have the little journalist making notes which will prove my fitness for the County Mental. You have those two well-scrubbed foreign boys to poke their fingers in my filth and shame me.' He lifted his gun. 'Get out. Get down that path or I'll shoot those damned feathers out of your hats and then with the next round I'll remove all support from beneath the hat.'

We turned. With a spurt Dunkerly regained his natural position at the head of the party. We went down faster by far than we had come up.

Hadrian Mogg was more thoughtful than ever. 'That mood of tenderness was just a snare,' he said.

'There's something about farming which brings out the foxy side of mankind,' said Colenso.

'He probably gets some little impulse of love just after he's been to the toilet,' said Hadrian. 'It's a lonely, pensive function and inspires many baffling moods. That's what we had today. Then the iron jaws start closing again and love hangs on to the last of its limbs wondering what the hell has happened. This is another fact for my handbook and it's going down in red ink. Frankly I think it would be a good thing if some voters were kept in the closet all the time.'

'The trouble,' said Offa, 'is with that Lucas. He's the mischief-maker. He poisoned the mind of Samson against us as soon as he got him in the kitchen. I'm going to find out something about Lucas. He's a menace. What about Wyndham now, Dunkerly? Don't you think the best thing would be to find him a job away from Blakemore?'

'Oh no,' said Dunkerly. 'Let's keep at what we have set our hands to. Our function as artists in adjustment is to heal frayed tissue, not tear it apart.'

Colenso quietly observed to me that Dunkerly had probably taken out a comprehensive death-policy on all of us, then bought Samson the rifle out of the commission.

5

That evening I called in at Angela's. I took along with me a bundle of illustrated papers which depicted social highlife from every angle, showing groups of people at fox-hunts and banquets. After getting a headful of this material it was difficult to even think of Bandy Lane for several hours. Mrs Lang, Angela's mother, who had spent her early years in service with some aristocratic family in the north of England, would go into a trance of admiration for a whole week at the sight of one of these papers, and, since she would never have been able to afford them on the very small wage earned by her husband Lyndhurst Lang, she was grateful to me for obtaining these copies from my friend, Gethin Pugsley, the caretaker of the Bandy Lane Reading Room, who gathered them up and passed them on to me in return for a small helping of cream biscuits about which he was daft.

In Angela's kitchen I found Mrs Lang, a tall,

long-faced, sad woman, standing in front of the mirror making a face as she dissolved beneath her tongue one of the aspirins she was taking for her everlasting headaches. She said that once her brain-cells properly understood what a degraded and depressing voter she had married in Lyndhurst they had gone on to full-time aching. Lyndhurst was lying full-stretch on a deep armchair in a corner. His neurasthenia had been out in a strong sun and had come to full bloom since he had become a second charge-hand at the furnaces in which the town's refuse was burned to be used later in the making of tarmac. Lyndhurst had always taken a cautious, unsmiling view of life but now that he was seeing existence as an endless parade of doomed offal he had touched rock-bottom; there was an unforgettable pallor on his face when he told me of the way in which some of the town's sterner religious doctrinaires, like Colenso's stepfather, would come to the doors of the burning chamber and call out to the furnace attendants, a quartet of quiet rationalists of Lyndhurst's kind who had tried at odd times to lay cooling fingers on the hotter heads among the pious: 'And so it shall be with you all!'

Mrs Lang fingered through the first of the magazines. It was full of pictures of such finely bred people it made the self-confidence of the average prolie shrink to the size of a pea. Mrs Lang drew me by the arm to share her reading and asked if I did not see a resemblance between some of the ladies pictured and herself. There was a resemblance, for Mrs Lang had the authentic stamp of one whose face had been stretched three or four statuesque inches beyond the normal length by centuries of looking serene and contemptuous. Privately she was convinced that the blood of those northern aristocratic families flowed in her veins. She had whispered to me more than once that her mother had conceived her while serving at some baronial hall and that the oaf whom she had come home to marry, a lumbering voter called Cynddylan Jakes, was not the father at all. I never made any complaint to Mrs Lang about this because I knew how she warmed her stiffening fingers at the fire of these beliefs, but I did not think the way in which she spoke of her own father was altogether wholesome. I appreciated the value of blue blood, none more so, and I was glad that Mrs Lang in her days as a servant had been exposed to contact with the elect, but all the same I did not see the point of allowing one's thirst for blue blood to draw one into claiming to be what Colenso Mortlake in his outright way would call a bastard. I remembered seeing that Cynddylan Jakes, and while clumsy and no duke in costume or speech he seemed a tidy old voter and a tolerable father.

Then Mrs Lang broke into an excited cry and showed me a large photograph of a tall colonel on the gang plank of a ship off to some colonial war. 'Why, of all things, Stobo,' she said. 'This is the young master. When I was in service with his mother he was a lad no bigger than our Oswald and Edgar. And here he is, off to the gorgeous East to keep a firm hand on the flagstaff.'

'Oh, Christ,' said Lyndhurst, groaning and opening one eye. 'Tell the young master to come down here and lend us a hand with that tarmac. Those clinkers from the furnace are playing hell with us.'

Mrs Lang turned white and stamped her foot on the floor in a fierce gesture of the sort I had often seen on the screens of our two cinemas, the Comfy and the Cosy, but never before in a kitchen. 'Don't dare talk about Master Philip like that,' she shouted.

'Why not?' asked Lyndhurst bitterly, and I could see that he was now prepared to break the surface of the stupor in which he spent most of his evenings and make an issue out of this Master Philip. I tried to make peace.

'You ought to see him in the picture, Mr Lang. Medals and ribbons all over, and spurs. A model. A bit like that genteel voter you see in the fag adverts, with the white moustache, but Master Philip's is still black.'

'You are not fit to wipe his boots, any of you,' said Mrs Lang. 'And don't you dare, Lyndhurst Lang, to use that sort of language before my boys.'

It was only then I noticed Oswald and Edgar sitting in a sort of well created by the end of the sofa and the armchair in which Lyndhurst was sprawled. They were twins and often appeared in tableaux that puzzled the public in company with the twin sons of Offa Mogg. The two boys, as always, were sitting quietly as mice reading together a Christmas annual of informational bent from which they had already picked up enough facts and figures to floor the Cabinet. But in all other respects they were sub-vital. Their eyes were distended by a vigilant timidity, fed on too many suspected terrors which were always ready to come before them, fleshed and actual, at their nod. Their skin appeared shrunken by rain, faded by the mists. This limp transparence dated from the period six years before when Lyndhurst's wage had been chipped by recurrent bouts of nervous sickness and Mrs Lang had fretted herself into a five months' stay in the County Hospital for the mentally ill, causing Angela to leave the County School where she was in her third year and take charge at home. There had been little to nourish the boys. Their hair had achieved a climactic mousiness, as if each hair had crept up separately from the wainscoting, as if the roots had taken one look at their begetter, Lyndhurst Lang, and decided that a quiet, pain-evading inertia was the correct line.

Mrs Lang had made up her mind that her sons were to go into the County School. She badgered Lyndhurst and, after I began courting Angela, me too, into bringing them every book that tested one's general knowledge, and by now the boys were bent double under a load of unconnected data. But their arithmetic was as poor as anything in the zone. Prothero Wilce, the teacher in the scholarship class, who had lost hair, teeth and hope in the task of grafting a minimal culture on to his candidates, said that Oswald and Edgar were the first boys he had met to succeed in shoving arithmetic to a point lower than zero. I had interceded with my friend Odo Mayhew and he now gave the boys a little coaching at the Social Centre, but I saw that my request had been a mistake. Mathematically Odo's mind raced along on a supersonic plane and by taking one look at a town he could tell you how far behind its total rates yield it happened to be. He regarded calculation as a natural function like digestion, and not even in his nightmares had he been able to conceive of boys so gravely in need of magnesia as Oswald and Edgar.

There was no doubt that the boys had been ill starred in their allocation of teachers. Prothero Wilce, ten years before, had seen his entire scholarship class scuttled by an arithmetic paper that contained several tap sums, problems that inquired how soon a cistern with a leak or with the plug out would fill or empty at a given rate. This defeat had caught Prothero in the middle of knitting a second foot to an ulcer and it had saddled him with an anxiety neurosis about running water until his whole curriculum in arithmetic seemed to feature only taps and tanks. It was terrible to watch Prothero over a table, sallow, sunken and haunted, suddenly become oblivious of the moment's business and grip the table as yet another problem in cubic capacity dropped into place. Odo on the other hand, while comparatively sane about taps, was definitely obsessed with the finances of local government. Upon every successfully levied rate he laid his lips hotly and the sums he set Oswald and Edgar reflected this cult in the clearest of mirrors. I could not blame them for being backward in reckoning. They had not had a proper chance. The universe of calculation built around them by Odo and Prothero was as bleak and grey as the great ice-barrier which so hampers voters off to the pole. Between them they had conveyed to Oswald and Edgar that all the characters in arithmetic are either drowning or chained by debt to the local authority or both.

'How are the boys getting on with their arithmetic?' Mrs Lang asked. 'Is Mr Mayhew pleased?'

I did not know what to say. Only the day before Prothero had told me that the boys' sense of number was definitely pre-Cro-Magnon and that it would go hard with the waterworks of the future if the citizens turned out to be as indifferent to the issue of running taps as Oswald and Edgar. Odo too had been sad on the subject. He said that if a generation were coming along as insensitive to rates as the twins then he and the Treasurer, Selwyn Phelps, could go on the streets singing duets from Selwyn's last speech to his union, 'A balanced audit is a lovesome thing, God wot,' laying just the right double stress on the fiduciary and religious notes. But I could not tell Mrs Lang these things. In the abstract I am for truth. One of the best papers I ever read to the Careers Group at the Centre was 'Truth as an Ally of Business'. But I often find that, as a steed to ride on, the truth is too tall an article for the very low-roofed premises in which most voters crouch, perfidious and bandy. So sometimes I get the steed to kneel and I find my head is rapped less often against the ceiling.

'They're getting a better grasp of the stuff all the time, Mrs Lang. Quiet, but very lucid, that's how Mr Wilce described them. Mathematical moles. Often they seem to be working in the dark and then you see the tump.'

'Good, good. Of course the County School will be good for a few years, but they will need the mathematics later for Sandhurst.'

'For what?' I asked, puzzled, for the only Sandhurst I knew at that period was a brand of sausage-meat that sold well among the voters with large families.

'Sandhurst, the military academy. The school of the elect. The only real gentlemen's club. It surprises me, Stobo, that you haven't heard of it. You grocers keep yourselves too much to yourselves.' Mrs Lang's eyes powdered me and swept me up. I could see that I had bruised myself in her opinion by not knowing about Sandhurst and my vest was quite wet with the thought of what she would have said if I had come out with anything about the sausage-meat of the same name.

'Where did you say they were going?' asked Lyndhurst.

'Sandhurst,' said Mrs Lang, leaning forward and bristling. I could see from Lyndhurst's face that he had no more information about Sandhurst than I had had. I smiled at him moderatingly, not wishing him to say anything that would upset his wife.

'And what do they intend doing there?' he asked.

'They'll become soldiers. Officers of the King, if such words mean anything to you, Lang.'

'Officers of the King, my God!' Lyndhurst blew out a hoot of disgust. The mention of armies always had this effect on him. Dunkerly Dodge had told me that he had been upset more than once while collecting dues from the Lang home to hear Mr Lang make such a mockery of national discipline. Dunkerly was all for it. He was a leading sponsor of the Boys' Brigade and he would have been in the Territorials if his wife were not already complaining that he spent less time at home than a tom.

This touchiness about the military ran in Lyndhurst's family. His brothers Joby and Jethro had been prominent objectors in some past war and, even after being warned by several shrewd voters in Bandy Lane that it would be playing into the enemy's hands to recruit two such fractious and Tolstoyan elements, the army put uniforms on them. They deserted a few times and were back in Bandy so soon after being put on the train to join some platoon that the boys in the discussion group at the Thinker and the Thrush, which was full of non-violence men, claimed that the brothers were being thrown against the outer wall of some rubber barracks by way of punishment and being bounced back to their starting point. The Mayor of Bandy Lane said that the prompt reappearance of the Lang boys was giving the war as frivolous and futile an air as those wars in the Middle Ages. As he had prepared a speech on the fallen, and no one from Bandy had yet got killed, he urged the government to get those boys pinned down and at least wounded to give glory in the division a little shove. The boys were treated to persuasion. Their wits were weakened under the strain and they ended up marching around Bandy Lane Square stark naked and holding a banner which they used just for announcement and not for concealment, for there was nothing coy about the Lang family: 'The only uniform we will wear, that of humanity.' They were sent to the County Keep, partly for ridiculing the ethics of militarism, partly for walking about nude in a square that is really too draughty and morose for anything but decorum and thick serge.

'Look, Lydia,' said Lyndhurst. 'If those kids are lucky they'll get jobs with me in the macadam plant, and to get even there they'll have to keep their heads soaked in cod-liver oil for strength. If there's no place for them there, and if Hadrian Mogg hasn't by then settled the rubbish problem of the planet once and for all, I'll get them onto one of the ash lorries.'

I watched Mrs Lang. All the words moving inside her were toothed and snarling and snapped their refusal to join in anything so simple as a sentence. I placed my arm on hers and persuaded her to sit down. 'Oh, Mr Lang's a bit crotchety. Don't mind him and don't worry about the boys either. If Sandhurst values general knowledge, they'll end up as field marshals.'

'My God,' said Mrs Lang. 'Why did I marry such a man?'

'If you can hold the past still long enough,' said Lyndhurst, 'we can both question it.'

Angela came in at that moment. She poured herself a cup of tea, gave both her parents a peculiar, impatient look, and accepted my arm as we walked to the Centre. She was carrying her head wonderfully erect and this made her slightly taller than me; but I, such was the quality of my love for her, was not in the least humbled by this. Some laughed at me, some envied me, and I had spent enough time in business to know that envy can be pre-eminently a fertiliser.

6

In the main corridor of the Centre Angela and I parted company. She went to the cookery class and I went into the lecture room. There I found a muted earnestness. Dunkerly Dodge had just unwrapped a parcel of goods which had been purchased by my father through one of Dunkerly's clubs. Dunkerly had allowed my father's account to mature and become operative much sooner than was usual because of my standing as guarantor. Normally a voter signing on to make weekly payments was required to pay in for eight weeks before being allowed to buy the suit, gramophone, headstone or encyclopaedia which he wanted. This was because in the days when Dunkerly was establishing his practice he had allowed many of his clients to obtain the goods after the first payment, and so many of them vanished as from that point it was thought that Dunkerly's clubs were functioning as a sort of bomb on which these voters sat as a means of being blown right out of sight.

There was quite a number of people in the lecture room with my father. Dunkerly of course was right in the centre of the group, showing off the quality of the two white coats and two white aprons which had been obtained for my father. Dunkerly was fondling these garments as if they were vestal robes and my father some element who was now swearing off the libido for as long as life would plague him with such issues. My father stood quite still and passive as he was fitted up. To me it was a big and refreshing improvement, and the crown of it was when Max and Helmuth presented my father with a new hat of Austrian velour to replace his bowler. Dunkerly told us that the two boys had studied my father's hat ever since arriving in Bandy Lane and had reached the conclusion that it was the most depressing thing in Britain.

After the presentation of the hat we all retired to the music room where Angela sang to Dunkerly's accompaniment songs like 'Mine, Mine, Vienna Mine' and 'The Blue Danube', and put a lot of loose-hipped abandon into the rendering of some gypsy ballads that brought Max and Helmuth simmering out of their Central European reserve. 'Oh, the blue Danube – I would like to live there and die there,' she kept saying between songs and I could see that her fine artistic imagination had cut its way clear of the black, black Moody which was our river. She grasped the hands of Max and Helmuth, her eyes full of romantic tears as if she were expecting them to get her on the boat there and then. I was glad to get her away on the excuse that Mr Ellicott was expecting us. Going just then saved us the trouble of listening to Dunkerly trying to instruct my father in the first steps of yodelling, which Dunkerly thought should be a part of the new image my father was to project on his morning milk round.

The night was clear, quiet and frosty as we made our way to Mr Ellicott's. Whenever we came to a circle of light made by a street lamp, she would whirl round the lamppost while humming some snatch of the Austrian music Dunkerly had been playing. Her movements were graceful but I was glad no one was about because I was gaining a reputation in Bandy for being steady and reliable which I did not want to lose. I was glad of course that Angela was a devoted daughter and a pure girl – I had never been allowed to make any sort of uncertain advances towards her – but I wished she could have been as soberly restrained in all phases of her conduct as she was in keeping my desires blinkered and decent.

Inwardly but with discretion I blamed Dunkerly for this phobia that sometimes beset Angela to rub life up into a lather of high artificial spirits. Three weeks before she had played the lead in a drama at the Centre. She wore a gown of black satin which Dunkerly had managed to borrow from Lady Prunella Pooley herself. Angela played a countess coming back to Paris suffering from some fatal disease she has contracted in the Far East. On the same ship is Dunkerly as smooth in his ways as Angela's satin, also going back to Paris. His health is fine but when he lands back in France he is going to be guillotined for a murder many years old. The detective in charge of him was myself, a sober, ruthless type of man but with enough tenderness to be melted by this tragic love into an act of clemency, slipping the cuffs off Dunkerly so that the doomed pair can go waltzing and dreaming about the boat. It was very beautiful but Angela should have known better than to let her mood overflow from fantasy into the rate-paying existence of Bandy Lane. For days she looked at me with loathing because I was the one who caught Dunkerly out there in Peking. When the play ended the only people not crying were a few dozen voters in the corner of the Centre where no sound can enter and where no one can follow the plots of the plays we put on. Angela was going down the gang-plank of the ship, throwing a last little bouquet at Dunkerly and clutching her heart to show that disease feeds on the bitterness of our self-created situations and that hers is now closing in for the kill. I slipped the handcuffs back onto Dunkerly and with a fine smile he gave the flowers such a sniff he left the stage with a petal at each nostril.

With the thought of that play in my head and my ears full of singing from the Grange Street Mission on our right my emotional load was almost unbearable and I was glad that life packs such sanity-bringing aspirin as food and debt. The people in the Mission, a sad lot who had combed the hymnals of all denominations for songs that put hope and gaiety down for the count, were singing a hymn that held man's plight on earth up for attention as clear and bitter as a pickle on a fork. I shouted to Angela to hurry up and bury her dreams. Colenso told me once that it would do some terrible damage to Angela one day to have her existence torn constantly between these two planes, a woman of wealth, poise and distinction in the plays and a prosaic, amenable drudge in her own home. Colenso also urged Dunkerly to put on plays about the common folk, in which whole families on strike would be seen trying to shout their lines over the racket of their own belly-rumbles and marching with torches to prevent their leaders being hung. Such plays would give Angela a saving sense of drabness. But Dunkerly answered that since citizenship in an area like Bandy Lane gave the average voter such a gutful of reality, he regarded the stage as a kind of stomach pump to siphon the stuff out in readiness for an infusion of dreams.

Coming out into the centre of Bandy Lane we paused to stare at the advertising stills in front of the Comfy and the Cosy, discussing details of expression, costume and coiffure. We had seen both shows earlier in the week, with complimentary tickets for the shilling seats given to Mr Ellicott for plastering the door of his warehouse with bills. Angela would have preferred to sit in the one-and-threepennies but, as I told her, when a man is saving to buy his own business and has a girl who likes to go to the cinema two or three times a week, free admission is a gift from God.

We went into Mr Ellicott's around the side. He was delighted to see us for he was very lonely. We went into his kitchen which served also as his parlour, a place of solid wood and red plush. In different parts of the room, inescapable, were pictures of the late Mrs Ellicott, whom he had met during a stay in the Paddington district. She had been a contralto singer of some repute and most of the pictures showed her in gypsy costume, carrying a lot of gauze and spangles, in such operas as *The Bohemian Girl*. She was a woman of breadth and vitality, with something of the quality of the red plush that sang from every corner of the room, urging one's senses to lie down and rest.

Mr Ellicott had himself laid the table for us. Each time I had had supper with him had raised a memorable lump on my palate because the food I had with my father at home, although supplemented by some free gifts from Mr Ellicott's stock, was as flat and tasteless as the oilcloth we ate it on.

Mr Ellicott led Angela into the room, for he was a courtly old voter. We almost shouted for joy at the sight of the table. He had brought a record load of cooked meats and tinned fruits, pears, Angela's favourite. Often, with one of the larger type of tinned pears between her teeth, tears would come to her eyes, partly through ecstasy, partly because the chilling sweetness gave her gums a shock. There was also a bottle of red tonic wine of which, I often suspected, Mr Ellicott drank quite a lot. Not that he did not need it, having such trouble with his legs and heart and being consumed with sorrow about widowerhood. I was glad to see him drink anything that would bring him cheer, although this particular tonic wine had what seemed to me a forlorn taste that would have depressed a horse. Normally he never offered us any but that night there were glasses for Angela and myself; of course, I would refuse the glass he would pour out for me.

We sat down and began to eat. Angela, always hungry in Mr Ellicott's and made hungrier by her session of song and excitement with Dunkerly and the two Austrians, was through two slices of tongue before I had put the mustard on mine. Mr Ellicott leaned over and spooned practically a jarful of his hot piccalilli onto my plate, saying 'This is the stuff to put a balance on your bank book,' and I made as if I was going to put the stuff down with delight although I knew that within minutes I would be envying that Alpine element who slipped into a crevasse and came into view again fifty years later, very cool and serene, still grasping his ice-pick but dead and in the middle of a glacier.

Mr Ellicott did not want pears. He watched Angela pitch into them, sighing with pleasure at the sight of such beauty and relish on one face. He sipped his wine and let his eyes wonder from one of his wife's photographs to another. 'This is good,' he said. 'A big fire, young and dear friends; it makes me miss Teresa less.'

'It must have been a terrible blow, Mr Ellicott, losing her like that.'

'My mind is in an immovable socket, Stobo. It points always towards her.'

'That's how my mind would be if I lost Angela. Always in that socket, staring at the place, all the places where she had been.' I wanted Angela to hear that but her head was full of the sound of her teeth sinking into her pear and I was on the point of repeating the whole statement when Mr Ellicott broke in.

'That's a wonderful business, to sit quietly night after night and keep the wound of a great loss open and fresh with salt tears. That can be as exciting as love, to watch for any hardening of the skin into callous forgetfulness, to press the fingernail of remembrance into it to keep it soft and full of pain.'

'That's the way, Mr Ellicott,' I said. 'Keep it fresh, keep it soft. Don't you think so, Angela?'

'Oh, yes,' she said, but she looked so blank I could have been referring to the Caerphilly cheese for all she had followed of our talk. I wondered to myself whether Mr Ellicott did not sometimes overdo this cult of desolation. Offa Mogg told me that Bandy Lane had never seen such devotion as Mr and Mrs Ellicott had given each other. She had been a passionate, bountiful woman, just the thing for Mr Ellicott who as a young man had been on the shy and covert side. All the years of their married life he had been curled up compact and warm as a done crumpet on the hearth of her kindliness. He insisted on her wearing clothes as like as possible those she wore in her gypsy roles and there were some who said she would end up dragging a supplementary barrow behind her for her bangles. She had died suddenly. She had always prided herself on being immaculately ready at the table to pour out Mr Ellicott's first cup of tea as soon as he had washed his hands after leaving the shop. She had been as good as her word to the last. He had come into the living room one evening and found her sitting at the table, her hair flawlessly piled up in its waves of black profusion, the skin of her face firm, unwrinkled and nourished by years of care, her neck and arms adorned with the heavy amber beads that were her great fancy. Her hand was stretched out towards the teapot and she was dead. She had died with uncommon neatness. For a whole year Mr Ellicott had taken no tea. When he resumed the custom it was only with his eyes on her pictures and his cup raised towards her in staring salutation.

After our meal, Angela sat down at the piano. This was part of a fixed ceremonial. Mr Ellicott got out copies of all the gypsy songs his wife had sung and as Angela gave them out in tones every bit as potent and ringing as Mrs Ellicott's he kept time with a large tambourine. His fingers travelled over the smooth wooden frame and the silver bells of the instrument and the heat in his eyes dried his tears as he stared at Angela with an admiration which I would have found peculiar had I not been sure that in her he was seeing the ghost of his own Teresa. He came to sit by her side. He asked me to go into the shop for another bottle of the tonic. It took me some minutes to find it and when I returned I could have sworn that he had his head near to Angela's and that he had his hand on her right ham, but the light in that part of the room was tricky and too much good food always gave me a touch of delirium. In any case, Mr Ellicott was like a father to us both, a more tender and solicitous friend than ever my own father had been to me or Angela's to her.

The bells of the tambourine made a sad rustle as he laid it down. I hurried to uncork the tonic wine, upset by the confusion on Mr Ellicott's face, eager not to have him think that I had thought what I had when I came into the room. As I decanted the wine my head was less full of Angela and Mr Ellicott than of what Colenso had once said about the cult of sorrow generally hurrying Mr Ellicott on to the Black Meadow. The sight of the bells on his tambourine made me think of those buckets around the door of his shop, noisy vulgar articles in any context. When he went, they would certainly go with him.

Mr Ellicott looked up at the flimsy safe in which he always kept considerable sums of ready cash. He used the banks but he liked to keep part of his affairs private in order to keep the government's tax collector on edge. 'If you had been a daughter of mine, Angela,' he said, 'your life would have been very different.' Angela looked at him enquiringly. I filled his glass again because I could see his old forehead bulging with rich promise. 'You'd have your desire, to be a fine actress, an actress for good, for money, I mean, in London. You wouldn't have to go cap in hand to the people who run the Sir Tegla Pooley award, only to have them turn you down. But how was I to help you properly in a place like this where people talk so?' He put his hand on her body again but this time lightly and away from the thigh. 'But if you had been my daughter, by God the story would have been different. Never mind though. The money will come to you through what I'm planning to do for Stobo in the business. From beyond the grave Teresa and I will look at you reliving our own wonderful happiness in this room.'

'Thank you, Mr Ellicott,' I said, seeing that Angela was too slow in making a proper reply. 'We shall listen for any stirring that will tell us that you and Mrs Ellicott are watching and wishing us well. On each anniversary of your departing we shall sit here together and and drink your health in the tonic wine, or tea, if you prefer.'

'You've got a fine spirit of loyalty, Stobo. As for the toast, stick to tonic wine. Tea is black to me since the wind blew down my strongest wall and left me to be fingered by every frost.'

At the mention of the Sir Tegla Pooley award Angela's face had hardened and I fidgeted uneasily in my seat. I asked her to sing one of Mrs Ellicott's most powerful items, 'Conchita's Curse' from a musical play written by Waldo Lucroft to words by Odo Mayhew who had heard about those gypsies living in caves near Seville and was worried about the rates position of such dwellings. But she did not hear my request. Thinking bitterly of the Sir Tegla Pooley award, she raised her glass and I could hear the vindictive rasp of her breathing in its hollows.

The award had been established by the father of Sir Gwydion Pooley to honour the memory of a sister of his who had died of meningitis when she was starting her acting career in London. The grant was to further the talent of any young actress selected from candidates drawn from the whole area covered by the Pooley steel enterprises. Angela had been trying for five years and although she was always singled out as the star at every drama festival staged at the Centre she had never been selected. I had played some little part in that fact and that was why I fidgeted. Naturally I wanted Angela to stay by my side. If she had listened to her father, an anarchist with no conception of the moral mechanics that shape life, she would have gone off to London leaving her mother to sink into her terrible morass of despair and debility. I knew that Angela's ambition, fed by the flattery of Dunkerly Dodge who is himself sometimes lacking in a sense of proportion in these matters, would have driven her to this act of desertion.

The first time that she had put in for the award I

was frightened out of my skin when Melancthon and Dunkerly both told me that she was the firm favourite. In my anxiety I went to Offa Mogg and told him about my fears about the step Angela was taking. What Offa said led to my first act of willing skulduggery, conscious cunning. It was a hard experience for me because I am not naturally and spontaneously evil. I have to let the thing rain upon me, soak into me, before I am ready to perform an act which my first judgment would denounce as loathly. Offa told me that there was a clause in the award's act of establishment which specified that the chosen applicant had to be a person of absolute moral fitness. By a few hints, said Offa, we might debar Angela on this score. I told Offa I had struck men for saying less than that. I hadn't, of course, but Offa is no bigger than I am and a man does not know what he may do under stress. Offa told me that to safeguard our position on this earth and often to protect our loved ones from their own folly we sometimes have to develop the darting malice of a sewer rat, and as he said that you could almost see his eyes gleaming in the furtive shadows of the main municipal pipe. So, assured by his grasp of the cloak-and-dagger side of life, I gave in. To get into the conspiratorial role I put my head so close to Offa's mouth he could barely get his lips open to outline the programme.

I told him that as Angela's patient and only lover I, of all people, knew that morally she was as unblemished as a Sunday School log-book and that it was only out of love for her and knowing how fond of her Mr Ellicott was that I was consenting to what I felt was the thrust of a poisoned knife into Angela's back, and that was no kind of intercourse to be favoured by a boy brought up among the Congregationalists. Offa said that only the merest hint of irregularity in this

— 76 —

matter of sexual conduct needed to be mentioned to the chairman of the board and that would be that. We then discussed the nature and extent of a hint and after a fair amount of quibbling, natural in the context, we arrived at a workable definition.

'Let's have "How Can I Live Without You?",' said Mr Ellicott to Angela. He made the request in a shaking whisper as if he had been repeating the title of the song as part of some inward rite of frightening intimacy. He grinned in twitches as if he had been caught at something.

'Oh, yes,' I said, glad of a diversion. Angela began playing and singing. She did not lean over the keys but sat bolt upright. There was no light and shade in her singing. Her every note was a sunstroke and things throbbed in every part of the room, with Mr Ellicott and I at the head of the queue, shaking like a pair of clappers. Angela's posture was no accident. During the years of effort she had planned her campaign. She had noticed that whenever Sir Gwydion and Lady Prunella appeared together in public they always looked at each other with what appeared like a gay devotedness. Not knowing that life can be very duplex in these matters, she assumed that Sir Gwydion must regard his wife as the very model of what a woman should be. So Angela patterned her expression, a play of the eyes and mouth in a suggestion of healthy delight, her clothes, with a difference of thirty or forty pounds in the cost of materials, her walk, firm yet feminine, on Lady Prunella's. In the dark they could have passed for sisters.

But she did not get the award. She was furious and bitter and I pretended to be as much enraged by Sir Gwydion's decision as she was. I tried to get out of Offa what evidence of unfitness he had laid before Sir

Gwydion, but all he did was look inscrutable and say that he had merely acted as a surgeon in the affair, slipping in the scalpel of a little lie to shave off a tissue of diseased possibilities.

Then came the joke. Offa discovered and told me that Sir Gwydion and Lady Prunella were not at all in love. They put on that look of radiant affection just to set a good example to the prolies of Bandy Lane who are often careless about marriage, jocosely indifferent to the rules laid down for it by Church and State and, in some parts of the town, exist in a permanent sexual mêlée that had wearied even visiting anthropologists into taking up something easier. The Pooley marriage had first been an affair of love, a fine fusion of blood, steel and finance. Lady Prunella had introduced her brother into the firm. He was a poet and a Fabian who believed that the proletarian body could be drained of its impurities with a hot poultice of compassion and collectivism. This angered Sir Gwydion who had never heard of poetry and did not understand that the Fabians are a quite constructive lot, firmly loyal to the old ways, coolly appreciative of hierarchy in reasonable dress and in no way Bolshevik. So out of the firm went Lady Prunella's brother, and Sir Gwydion and his wife had been at variance ever since, so Offa had learned from a maid in the hilltop mansion. Lady Prunella called him such names as 'materialist clown' and 'unpoetical oaf' and many another phrase picked up from the poet, which made Sir Gwydion's ingots shrink with injury and ire, for he had always found the bulk of Bandy Lane a handy lump of cap-touching servility and this barracking in the boudoir was likely to shake his hair out.

So, if you wanted Sir Gwydion to have an instant down on someone, woman or girl, let her resemble

Lady Prunella. There had been, therefore, no need to make that point about Angela's having been in any way loose, and for nights after the discovery my cheeks burned with such shame at having told so hideous a lie and all without need you could have read the whole story of man's shabbiness by the light of them. Time and again I broke out into feverish trembles at the thought of what would happen if Angela ever found out.

It took a bit of doing to keep her on an even keel after those four annual disappointments. We arranged huge and exacting parts for her in plays translated from the Spanish by Melancthon Mills. Melancthon had for some years been a clerk in an oil firm at Caracas and he had translated several plays which he claimed had been written by Venezuelans. Some of us felt that the pulse of Spanish drama had never beaten more slowly than in these plays. One particular one in which Angela had a great success and which helped her over the worst patch of her resentment about the Pooley award showed her as the daughter of a sick and tyrannical mother who keeps herself alive by feeding off her children as if they were so much cheese. She has used up four daughters who are now in the Black Meadow, flattened by the old woman's tantrums, and the last is Angela over whom she is lingering as if she were a rarebit. The mother lives to be a hundred and ten, Angela to eighty, and the effect of great age was well arranged by Odo Mayhew who fixed them up in a kind of sackcloth that struck a grisly note and made them look as if they had been dead as long as the play claimed they had been alive.

Everyone expects Angela to poison her mother or to be poisoned by her, but they must have a very simple approach in Caracas because all that happens is that the old woman dies at last just a few moments after Angela's ancient lover has had a stroke after his fiftieth refusal, and by her bedside Angela kneels down and asks God in a bitter prayer to explain the laws of outrageous waste which have permitted her life to be lived on so crass and pointless a pattern. Then a halo forms around her head to show that the old woman was right all along and that to serve yourself up like a hot crumpet to a parent who fancies a bite is the path of wisdom. In the halo's light the wrinkles vanish, the stoop goes from the shoulders. We had never seen this happen in the flesh in Bandy Lane where maimed lives have a way of remaining stolidly maimed, but it might come off in communities less involved in the neuroses of protest than ours.

The halo, done by Odo as a crown of electric filaments, was very good. The first night it misfired and almost burned Angela's ear off, but after that it answered to the switch and we had all the work in the world to convince Odo that if he rigged up the whole cast with these hats of neon it would spoil the effect. The sight of this miracle drove a lot of people back to church and chapel, and this pleased Odo who said that there is a link between local government and revealed religion: once people spurn the Ark of the Covenant you also find the temperature of hope and confidence falling in the Rating Office.

Angela finished playing the ballad. Mr Ellicott had his head down upon his pale clenched fists. Angela turned to me with interest but without love. 'Do you know what Colenso Mortlake says about such songs?' she asked.

It was a shock to have the name of Colenso dropped like a stone into the pool of our tenderness. I shooed at her with my eyes, urging her to have self-interested common sense enough not to go irking Mr Ellicott with any of Colenso's barbs. Mr Ellicott did not look up. His nerves were drinking at a well of carefully decanted tears, his senses sound-locked and far distant.

'He says that such songs thin the blood to water. He says there's a whole industry setting up these spurious targets of pity to waste the total force that might make our loves grow up and get on with the job of making life clean and tidy.'

'Oh, he's a wise one,' I said, but I had to keep my voice down and that robbed my tone of its irony. Angela nodded as if to say that she had always known Colenso was a sage.

'He also says that any man who goes around sniffing at the ashcans of old loves, old memories, should be fitted up with a large, snug ashcan of his own, with him inside.'

I rattled a cup to deaden the impact of this statement. 'That's what Colenso would say.' I made my voice buzz with malice.

'Have another pear, Angela dear,' said Mr Ellicott, who was upright again. He passed the large cut-glass bowl over to her. She helped herself but, even as she cut through the soft fruit with her sharp teeth, enclosing it behind her full lips and squeezing the sugared juice from it with a moan of joy, her face did not grow sweeter, less reflectively hard. She emptied the dish. At last the flavour of the fruit, the warmth of the fire and the tonic wine helped her to overcome her mood of fractiousness and she managed to smile back into Mr Ellicott's small worn eyes.

'Oh yes,' he said in a voice that had suddenly become feeble, 'in the long run, through me, through Stobo, you'll be better off, Angela, my dear.'

We had one short round of singing, this time of a

quiet, pious trend, and then we said goodnight to Mr Ellicott.

7

The following week the effort to renew joy and pride in the life of my father began in real earnest. My father was slow to respond because his spirit had put on leaden trousers with a fresh combination to be mastered for the opening of each new day. The main reason for that was the effort of Colenso and Leo Watham during their sessions of evening talk to denounce this whole attempt at regeneration as a dangerous reactionary bit of clowning. I had no luck with Colenso. On the very day I had expected to see him pack his bag for Scotland to resume his work on the dams up there he told me he had accepted a job with a company that was building a ring of small power stations around Bandy Lane and that by the time he had finished he would have us all ill with light. 'Also,' he said, 'I am curious to know what happens to your old man.'

While my father allowed the darkened underside of his mind to admit that Colenso was right, and that the kind of co-operative gaiety for which Dunkerly and I took up the tongs would probably involve him in some even more compulsive brand of woe, he put himself in my hands, glancing at my fingers with tolerance but without much conviction.

He did not at once put on for duty his uniform of felt hat, white coat and apron. He would sit in the kitchen in the evenings with this finery on, looking clean and trussed as a new mummy. He did not make a dent in his hat because he said he could not bring himself to lay his hand roughly on material as good and rich as that Austrian felt. The hat's crown was high and gave my father, as he sat there under the critical eyes of Leo and Colenso, the look of a worried gnome.

We heard that Samson Blakemore and Lucas Phillimore did not take kindly to the attempt on our part to dip my father in radiance and run the dish-cloth down his spine. Samson said he liked my father the way he was and he would suffer no alteration. 'We are for the grave,' he said. 'No jigs along the way.'

'Blakemore told me this morning,' said my father, 'that he'd come down with his pitchfork and prod like a frying sausage any voter who criticises his quality as a farmer, and he regards this effort to spruce me up as a criticism of himself. I wore my new hat today. Just the hat. It seemed to set him off.'

'What we are doing is supposed to be a criticism, Mr Wilkie. It's a subtle indictment of Blakemore's whole squalid refusal to keep up with the present,' said Dunkerly.

'I just wanted to warn you, Mr Dodge, when I mentioned the matter of the pitchfork. So that if you see Mr Blakemore with a tool of that description, do not hang about, or I'll know where to look for the prongs. He was roaring at me like a madman. He came into the byre where I was milking Molly. He shouted at me in such an angry way that Molly, who takes my side always, ceased to yield, and he said it was the height of my hat and those silly feathers tickling Molly's flank and giving her idle thoughts that had this effect. He hit the hat off my head. Mr Blakemore can be very unreasonable. And all the time Mr Phillimore stood by the cowshed door chuckling to himself. He kicked the hat back to me. You see the faint stain there on the left side. It landed on a spot where Molly had expressed herself. But I gave the hat a rinse as soon as I got home.'

'He won't intimidate us,' said Dunkerly. 'We'll have that man back in the bloodstream of Bandy Lane again, a red, healthy little corpuscle.'

'You'll only find him in that role if he's spotted some length of vein he particularly wants to spoil,' said Colenso.

Hadrian Mogg had bought a few tins of paint for my father's cart but Samson Blakemore would not allow it to be applied. 'He will decide in his own time when the cart needs painting,' said my father.

'That will be when you need a national SOS to track down the wheels.'

'He says the smell of paint annoys milk and throws it off balance.'

'Any milk that can stand up to Blakemore without going giddy or stiff could lodge in a paintworks without ill effect. If I didn't think it might do him a world of good, I'd mix a pint of this paint into his stew. The worms have set up their own government in the woodwork of that voter's soul.'

'It's that Phillimore who's the really Mephisto-phelian element in that team,' said Offa. 'Watch him.'

'He's a distinguished man,' said my father gently, 'and unhappy for that reason. He's come down in the world.'

'Anybody who comes down in the world and lands on Blakemore's farm has had a long drop,' said Colenso. 'Phillimore must have broken both legs.'

'Once he was a steward on a big estate in the north Midlands. A toff. But he got into some sort of trouble.'

On a Sunday morning we gave the cart a diligent

washing down and a few small initial instalments of paint. The cart was very dirty. 'Wyndham,' said Hadrian Mogg to my father, 'did Blakemore intend to cultivate these floorboards? I bet he was hoping he would have a fresh field here. He could have raised a crop of mangles in that depth of dressing. No wonder your horse Jolly looks dead-beat lugging as heavy a tumbril as that about, with a ton of top soil thrown in to give it extra dressing.'

'I never know anything about Mr Blakemore's plans,' said my father, smiling at the pools of muddy water that stood around the cart in proof of our hours of cleaning. 'He wants things to be the same one day as they were the day before. It seems as if he does not want to annoy life with too much attention, as if he is afraid he will sting it into another round of such calamities as he knew in the past. He doesn't tell me much. I stick to selling the milk and he sticks to shouting at me. It may do him some good to shout at me, so I never tell him to lower his voice although it sometimes makes my head ache.'

'What kind of function is that for you to fulfil in the life of another, Wyndham,' asked Colenso, 'that of a spittoon?'

'We all have our uses, I suppose,' said my father, and I was pleased to see Colenso turn away in helpless disgust from the firm armour of my father's resignation.

'Evil will continue to grow in our vines,' said Colenso, 'as long as there are those whose mouldering patience and wantlessness manure the roots of their branches, as long as dumb humiliated lives are the layers of the wine-press, the black vats in which the wine is stored, the sullen throat down which the stuff is poured to promote the spinning torment of our kind. Your old man, Stobo, is so natural a victim he must inspire a mood of malice even among the dead. Among the living he brings such an itch to be laying a bruise on him that as soon as we can persuade these doctors to look beyond the crude and operable disorders which are the pride and mainstay of their cult we shall get your father classified officially in the next edition of their encyclopaedia as a disease.'

The next day we went to see the old horse-dealer, Shifnal Pugh, who had been persuaded by Hadrian Mogg to fix up some tonic mixture which would dust the glands of my father's horse, Jolly. Colenso warned us against the visit. 'In his days as a dealer Shifnal was very mean. At the last market he attended in Carmarthen he made so low a bid for one of the horses and in so contemptuously clear a voice the horse decided to make an issue of it. Shifnal spent twenty minutes running around the statue of General Picton on Carmarthen Square with an earful of hoof and the horse just behind him neighing about exploitation and the rate for the job. He's been against horses ever since. Don't forget, it was Shifnal that Hadrian called in to treat the ashcart horses. Within a fortnight the ashcart service was completely motorised. Not a horse left. Remind me to get my black serge out for Jolly.'

We found Shifnal to be a torpid little element. He wore, indoors and out, a large flat cap and a coat of the same check material, the once bold squares now dim and myopic. Around his legs he wore a pair of jodhpurs that had been cast off and presented to him by Sir Gwydion Pooley. Sir Gwydion was a tall man and Shifnal had had to lop off part of the bottoms of the trouser legs, giving these articles a puffy, baggy look that made him, from certain angles, seem to be walking about on his knee-caps. Considering how servile Shifnal's attitude was in some respects, that would not have been surprising.

When he had come back into the western counties he had lived as a horse-dealer in various county towns, negotiating the sale and purchase of steeds that became older and less upright each year until he reached the bottom of his professional sump and finished up as the overt agent of a group of continental knackers. As soon as Shifnal entered a field with a horse in it you could see it dusting off its policies. When Sir Gwydion found out about that he tried to get his jodhpurs back but they were the only covering Shifnal had and he told Sir Gwydion that although he knew he was stabbing man's best friend in the back prior to seeing him canned he had to keep the draught off his legs.

In his earlier days he had worked as a stable-hand at Newmarket in the stables of various peers, and this had given Shifnal a strong sense of hierarchy. He attributed a large part of our social decay, and most of it according to Shifnal was located in and around Bandy Lane, to the drying up of those families who had the money and kindliness to keep endless strings of horses. Dunkerly and the Moggs could never have enough of these Newmarket anecdotes and they sat enthralled as Shifnal told them of the titled elements who had dropped into his stable and congratulated him on his work with the animals which, so Shifnal claimed, was never less than magic. They had never failed, he said, to ask about his rheumatism, to smile and pat him on the back and say: 'Well done, Pugh, my man' or 'Keep smiling, Shifnal'. 'And these,' Shifnal would say, 'were real peers of the realm, supreme toffs. The men who made history.'

'Who made history squirm,' said Colenso, who was also interested in these stories of Shifnal's but in a revolted way and he was frank in his belief that Shifnal had suffered in youth not so much from rheumatism as stiffness of the mental hinges.

It was on a Thursday evening that we went to see Shifnal to find out what he could do for Jolly. Colenso came with us. Supplies from the headquarters of his firm for the power station job had broken down and he would be on slack time for a fortnight. That being so, he told us with a smile, he would now be able to give us unlimited time as a partner in the scheme to renew the social upholstery of my father and Blakemore.

Shifnal was stooped over the fire. He said nothing as we filed into the kitchen. Dunkerly, always in character, gave out a few calls and cries associated with horses, as 'Tally-Ho!', which we had never heard in Bandy Lane. Shifnal had grown rather conceited since Melancthon Mills had invited him to the Centre to give a series of talks on 'The Newmarket I Loved', stressing just the love of horses and the social solidarity of peer and stable-boy but playing down the betting because Melancthon wanted these talks to give a more wholesome tone to a group of boys who came to the Centre to rest in between talks with the Probation Officer.

'Have you thought of a little tonic for Wyndham Wilkie's horse, Shifnal?' asked Dunkerly.

'I'll have to see the horse again. I'm used to handling bloodstock and the last time I saw that Jolly pulling the milk cart there was probably more blood in the churns.' Shifnal wore a heavy white moustache and spoke with one of the deepest voices you ever heard. Colenso put this down to his habit of sitting with his head stuck about a foot up the chimney and swallowing soot which darkened his larynx, but Dunkerly said he spoke this way in tribute to the owner of the first stable in which he had worked, a man who had lost the original rich timbre of his voice being brotherly with stallions and telling such elements as Afghans in a high shout to give up all thoughts of home rule.

We arranged for Shifnal to see Jolly again on the following day and he promised to deliver a pill which would put a foot on Jolly's mane and have its urges jumping about to a definite rhumba beat. 'Don't overdo the monkey gland,' said Colenso.

We sat down and Shifnal described to us a scheme he had been pondering of taming and training about half a dozen of the ponies that roamed the hills around Bandy Lane, fierce animals that would as soon give you a hoof as a neigh, and use them to start a mounted detachment of the local Boys' Brigade. 'That would take the minds of these kids off such things as rifling gas meters and looting orchards,' said Shifnal.

'It would take their minds off everything else, too,' muttered Colenso to me. 'Here are these kids already confused by having to dodge the hoofbeats of a hostile and stupid society run in the interests of the more senile of our tribesmen and now this Shifnal wants to make it more literal by having them kicked to death by ponies.'

'What was your remark about the monkey gland, Mortlake?' Shifnal asked Colenso in a haughty confident tone, as if he had just fished up a retort that was going to give Colenso a clip from which he would never recover.

'Don't overdo it. The milk trade on these hills needs a stable rhythm and Wyndham would not thank you for being pranced about like a circus performer.'

'We'll leave any talk of monkey glands to you, young man,' said Shifnal. 'It's you who are the one who pours out black Darwinian bile at The Thinker and the Thrush and such places that specialise in libels on God. Morally, Mortlake, you are a bit of a monkey yourself, up and down those pylons and denying man's divine origin.'

'Oh, don't mind me, Mr Pugh. I'm young, I'll get over it. My old man had the migraine and there was an ache in every doctrine he handed on to me. I'm glad to see you trying to help the Boys' Brigade and Wyndham Wilkie, especially Wyndham because he stands in need of a strong lifeline.'

'Don't you worry about a lifeline to Wyndham,' said Dunkerly. 'We'll take care of it.'

'I don't worry,' said Colenso, and in a lower voice he added to me: 'When these voters connect with that lifeline, you watch your old man's feet.'

'What have his feet got to do with it?'

'They'll be some distance from the ground and his body will be twitching slightly.'

'You never looked better, Shifnal,' said Dunkerly. 'A body full of healthy air and robust smells, a head full of healthy thoughts.' We looked at Shifnal. He was old and shrunken. Colenso as usual had his mouth to my ear for a comment: 'Life doesn't need all the ointment Dunkerly lays on it. He just makes it slippery without benefiting the wounds. Just look at Shifnal. So small he could curl up inside the leg of his jodhpurs and rent the other unfurnished. It would take two gorillas to carry the monkey gland that would do him any good. And his age! The waxing moon of human stupidity, deathly daft. If Hengist and Horsa had cavalry, Shifnal was the boy to supply the mounts.'

'What I will give Jolly,' said Shifnal, 'will be bland, wholesome and well-designed, like the old gentry, God bless 'em.'

'To you, too, Shifnal,' said Dunkerly, 'we are going to restore lustre. It's all part of the fight we are making at the Centre to combat the blind, impersonal mass doctrines of the past, levelling down, the cult of spite and sullen uniformity. We seek all those whose inner glory, whose human outlines have been smudged by indifference or penury. You, Wyndham Wilkie and all who are crouched too recessively in the shadow, for you all there will be a pointing up of our inherent but dimmed individual colouring.'

'You'll need an endless spring for all that cleaning,' said Colenso.

'To seek the freedom of this species through acts of individual liberation is to try to disperse the darkness of midnight with separate candles.'

'What the human heart desires with indomitable love, Colenso, that it will have.'

'As the agent of all the human hearts that have been worn by indomitable love to the basic pathetic stump with nothing to show for their pain but a card from the dealer in old stumps telling him that the price is down on last year, I wish you well.'

'It's a good job that Shifnal wears such a big cap and keeps his head more or less up the flues,' said Offa. 'If he got a headful of that sort of talk he'd jump right out of his jodhpurs.'

8

We were up with the dawn the next day to launch my father on the new plane of good cheer. Dunkerly, Offa and I were wearing bright yellow scarves, the product of a weaving group which had been started at the Centre. We waited for my father at the foot of the path which led down from the farm.

He was wearing his new hat and his white coat and apron, and his churns, which for the past year or two had been about the most lustreless things in Western Europe, had quite a shine on them. True, he looked, at first glance, no less bleak and recessive than he had done before, but we put that down to mere habit for it is axiomatic that if, for years, a man has been in the way of scowling disgruntled at the unfavourable hour that fidgets between night and day, he will not break himself easily of the custom.

Angela, who was fond of my father and wished to help him in every way possible, was with us and gave a fine quality of yearning to the yodelling that Dunkerly and Offa set up. My father kept his mouth shut except for an occasional cry of 'Milk!' which sounded to me most sad and unmusical, as if he were coming around calling for a dead man of that name. I went up to the side of the cart and told him to try and join in the next yodel because I agreed with Dunkerly that the cheerfulness of the sound, its suggestion of a freer, cleaner, gayer world would double the milk order in the district. My father let out a sound but it was about ten Alps short of the effect we have heard off and on from the genuine Swiss.

Dunkerly told my father that for the time being he could stay in the cart while he and Offa ran to one side of the street and the other filling the jugs which had been left on the doorsteps and window-sills. My father tried to explain to Dunkerly that this was one of the older parts of the town, very dour in its outlook and firm in its belief that people should not create too much of a racket on the streets because of the men on shift work trying to sleep at the wrong time of the day and because, on principle, they believed in facing up to life with a muted air of grievance. But these arguments made no sense to Dunkerly and Offa to whom any veil of silence was something sinister, to be ripped to pieces and thrown aside. They rapped on doors when pushing the jugs back into place and shouted such greetings as 'Chin-chin!', 'Cheery-bye!' and 'Wakey, wakey!' which were not native to the territory. I could see several voters with sleep in their eyes and scratching themselves with pagan openness, pushing back curtains, looking at us and jumping back when they did not see my father, thinking that a wing of the milk trade had been taken over by a group from the County Mental. The only creature in our turn-out who struck a normal note was the horse, Jolly, between his shafts looking sick of the earth and bored with mankind.

At one house Dunkerly did a kind of gay double-handed tattoo on the door, lifted up his head in a laughing yodel, and shouted: 'No more sleepy-bye, milky-milky!' Then he bent down to get the jug. The door opened and one of the most miserable looking voters, unshaven and savage, leaned out and caught Dunkerly a blow on the back of the head that laid him flat on the doorstep, his face the colour of the scoured step from shock and unconsciousness. 'That,' said the man, 'will teach you noisy bastards to go defiling the peace of this street and waking me up.' He slammed the door shut.

Dunkerly was out cold for a whole minute and not likely to get warmer quickly at that time of day. The handle of the jug could be seen just behind his head and Colenso said how nice it was to see so explosive and restless a voter looking so quiet and so like a Toby jug, a harmless article. I was surprised to see Dunkerly so overwhelmed for he had remarkably strong muscles in his neck, specially trained during a course in salesmanship to give his voice a merry resonant ring and his head a jaunty undefeatable air.

I thought that what might have affected him most was the sudden sight of that sad man, Granville Josephs, so obviously drenched in hellish unanswerable misery and resolved to shake off the largest possible number of drops of it onto Dunkerly whose gaiety must have made him strike Josephs as being very much on the dry side.

We got Dunkerly active. Blindly he charged Josephs' jug with milk. 'Who in God's name was that?' he asked, forgetting his usual suavity.

'That was Granville Josephs,' said my father, a little complacently I thought in view of the pill Dunkerly had just had, as if he were proud to have shown that he had customers so much out of the ordinary.

'What has he got against milk and milkmen?'

'Nothing. Normally with my own quiet approach to the churn and the jug I never see Granville from one year's end to the other. Granville's house is small and his wife is mean. He had a lot of daughters and his wife took in a lot of lodgers, some roistering and lecherous voters who navvied on the foundations of the steel plant. Granville was afraid his daughters would be molested and he got insomnia keeping awake to detect any vibrations that suggested evil. The place was full of vibrations because of the subsidence in this part of Bandy Lane that keeps the whole place more or less on the move and Granville's nerves were jumpy as frogs and just as hoarse from giving the alarm. When the daughters really wanted to be molested they had to give Granville a herbal drug to keep him on his back and off the landing, a mixture that would have put a dervish to sleep. So Granville still suffers from the insomnia and he often wishes his daughters were back with that anaesthetising herb. He doesn't get to sleep till six and he sleeps till ten. Mr Dodge must have woken him just after he got off. Think nothing of it, boy.'

Dunkerly laughed and shook his head as if making light of the experience but still looking as if his nerves were braked and cautious. His eyes, usually so brilliant and aware, were like misted marbles. Angela made a move to loosen his yellow scarf to put his head in closer touch with his feet because his movements were no longer straight, logical or continuous.

He had given us an order not to be meagre in our measure. Some of the orders were for a quarter pint, for pensioners or very poor families, but Dunkerly was appalled at seeing so little milk in a jug, could not believe that my father had heard the order right in the first place, charged him with being a poor salesman or his clients some brand of freak, and then went on to fill the jug.

'There are some very poor elements about here, Mr Dodge. They've been accustomed to getting such tiny rations they've got no idea the cow is such a lavish animal. There are some families who put up with dark unmilked tea except when they get hold of some condensed in a tin or sit beneath falling plaster from the kitchen ceiling. Don't give them too much milk all of a sudden, Mr Dodge, it'll be too rich for them.'

'Let me be the judge of that, Mr Wilkie. No wonder your milk round has been getting bloodless at the edges. You've been keeping the needs and expectations of these people at too low an ebb. As long as we have half-pint milkmen we'll have a half-pint civilisation. No reference to your physique of course, Mr Wilkie. Custard must be rarer than radium in this corner of the division. Give these people a taste of luxuriance, of abundant living, and you'll see a new flush of vitality creep into their faces. Fill that jug right up, Offa.'

Colenso was delighted with all this talk. On a

cleverly tempered elegiac plane he spoke quietly to Dunkerly and Offa about kids in that very street who in the years of utter shortage had got themselves into the *Picture Post* and into footnotes of Medical Officers' reports for the ghostly variations they played on the theme of sub-nutrition, having graduated to a kind of classically pure rickets, from bent bones to just a bend, no hint of bone.

'My God,' said Dunkerly. 'Mind you, Colenso, if you were decking out these facts with any of your usual doctrinaire bias I wouldn't listen to you for an instant. I don't like the misery of my fellow man to be made the pawn of party passions. We've got to be objective even about rickets. There may be a general tendency to warp in the bone of man, regardless of calories. But the tone of pity in your voice, harmonising with that glorious red now rising over the rooftops inclines me to take you in earnest and the thought of those poor kids who were not even thick enough to stay in their own trousers makes me weep.'

'Don't weep in the milk,' said my father. 'These inspectors are sods for purity, as far as cream content is concerned anyway.'

Then my father became the hub of a universal miracle, with Dunkerly and the rest of us dipping our scoops into the churns regardless of individual orders and of Blakemore's need to make an economic go of his herd. When my father complained that there was going to be a lot of confusion among his clients as a result of this new policy Dunkerly brushed him aside as having been too much of a peon in the service of Blakemore, and told him to read Adam Smith with the wick full up next time.

As household after household along the hillside became aware of this new dispensation which was filling their jugs to the brim instead of just damping the bottom as in former days, they came out of their houses enthusiastically and crowded around the cart, thinking my father had now killed Blakemore and was setting up the New Jerusalem on his own account. They congratulated him on his transformed appearance and praised his hat as the most colourful article they had seen since the carnivals of many summers before. They raised their brimming jugs and said they were sorry now that they had not read and believed all the prophetic pamphlets which the militant parties had been shoving through their letterboxes for a century past and which they had often put to unintended and bathetic uses.

This phase of our journey was golden, and Colenso said that as he looked at the transfigured faces of these elements who were now getting somewhere near the amount of milk which the life-force had envisaged as a norm before scarcity became an ethic, he was sorry that he had forsaken the path of direct political evangelism and taken to anything as neutral as light or heat mechanically contrived. 'When all is said and done,' he said, emptying his scoop into jug after jug, 'the wildest and darkest thing on earth is the heart of each man, each woman. To glimpse, even on a cold and shabby road like this, the unity of human experience, that is the ultimate wisdom, the only happiness that my sort, the penniless lovers of mankind, can ever know.'

When Dunkerly got to the point of knocking on doors and asking for an extra jug in which to house the bonus, I suggested to him that he might be overdoing the charity of our helpings. Some of the people just took one look at us and bolted out the back way. Dunkerly did not share my doubts. 'Nonsense, my boy, nonsense,' he said. 'All we are doing is opening out a new horizon for these people. The habit of deprivation has grown like a veil over their eyes and we are the boys to tear it away. Today they are receiving twice, thrice their normal portion. Their palates will sing thanksgiving. Their hungers will come up from the cellar into a great lighted hall and they won't go back. If you can divorce your revolution from theories and ground it on individual experience there can be no retrogression. Tomorrow they'll come out and ask Wyndham for the same amount as they had today and they'll pay for it. That done, Blakemore will dare not offer him the same miserable wage and conditions as he had before.'

I nodded enthusiastically but could not help feeling that Dunkerly was wrong about Blakemore and about my father's clients. Knowing the difficulties he often had now getting paid for the small orders he received, I could see him needing Blakemore's shotgun to guarantee extra payments. Then we heard Offa's scoop banging on the bottom of the can.

'All the milk's gone,' he said proudly as if he had done something special in touching bottom before anybody else. 'Now we can go and have some breakfast at Kiprianos' café. This milk delivery is a quicker trade than I thought.'

'But we haven't half done the round,' said my father. 'Those bonuses you've been handing out, Mr Dodge, should have gone into the jugs of voters who are still waiting for their milk.'

Dunkerly took out his big curved pipe and sat on the tail of my father's cart to think this out. He smiled suddenly to show there was no longer any problem. 'Don't worry about that, Mr Wilkie.'

'I'm not exactly worrying, Mr Dodge. I don't worry much about anything any more because this hat and white coat give me such confidence. But when the confidence starts wearing off I'm afraid that Mr Blakemore and Mr Phillimore are going to play hell with me when they find that my receipts for this morning's deliveries are down by half.'

'That's all right. We'll have a little whip round to bring your total for the week to the correct level. And as for the customers who are still without, I'll ring up a friend of mine who is in that combine, the South West Dairies, and he can make an emergency delivery to all the addresses on your list that have not yet been supplied.'

'Thankyou, Mr Dodge.'

'Not at all, Mr Wilkie. And tomorrow, mark my words, a doubling, a trebling of orders all along the line except perhaps in the case of that mad insomniac who is beyond the healing range of men or anything else. You will be received with new respect.'

Then we went to Kiprianos' place for a sandwich. When we left we were approached by Shifnal Pugh who looked at Jolly and my father with such analytical contempt I did not know whether he meant his progressive pellet for him or the horse.

9

We were never to know how right or wrong Dunkerly was about what would happen the next morning. Thanks to Shifnal Pugh, the delivery was far from normal.

We met my father and his cart once again at the foot of the hillside path. Only Dunkerly was present, because he wanted to be on hand to explain and persuade if any voters became nasty at having had more milk than they wanted or wished to pay for. Our first call was at the house of Shifnal Pugh who for some reason wanted the pill to be administered at first light, as if he were modelling himself on those old-fashioned executions. He was standing on his doorstep when we arrived, looking tense and important. He sniffed the air. 'A sweet morning for a canter,' and he looked critically at Jolly, who looked as if any gait over half a mile an hour would cause him to drop down dead.

'Over the springy turf, with the wind stinging your face,' said Dunkerly, sniffing in time with Shifnal. 'It would be wonderful, being bandy as a cowboy and having that thrill every day of your life. Have you got the capsule, Shif?'

'Here it is.' Shifnal slipped the capsule into Jolly's mouth and gave the horse such a sharp slap on the top of the head that it must have come within an ace of driving the pill right through to the other end of Jolly's central pipe. We went our way with Shifnal's deep, rather sinister voice telling us that within a brief time Jolly would be neighing with renewed strength and *joie de vivre*.

As we came into Plantagenet Terrace we saw Granville Josephs standing in his small front garden studying the tiny collection of flowers which, in that part of Bandy Lane, always looked confused as if they had taken one smell of the sulphurous odours that came up from the steel works and were looking for the seed from which they had originally come in order to crawl back into it again. Dunkerly dived behind the cart. 'There's that zany, Josephs,' he said. 'He's probably out to finish the job he started yesterday. If you don't mind I'll nip off up Tudor Avenue here.'

'No, no,' said my father. 'Stay with us, Mr Dodge.

Granville is a nice element for all his sadness and fits of temper. Look at the loving way he's bending over those blooms now.'

'Probably getting fresh strength from the pollen to work off on me.'

We all started greeting Granville well in advance to test his feelings and indeed he waved at us in the most friendly way. He brought out his jug, carrying some kind of nosegay of dead-looking chrysanthemums of which he seemed very proud, although for myself I thought that the voters in the Black Meadow would have sent them back to Granville with a ghostly growl.

'They are very lovely,' he said, holding the flowers up gently with his fingers. 'Like some of us, they've had a hard time of it. By the way, Mr Dodge, I'm sorry I was so short with you yesterday.'

'Oh, that's all right, Mr Josephs. At an hour when even the birds are only half awake we can't expect much from humans.'

'Was it a real whanger I gave you?'

'A beauty. I'm still winkling bits of doorstep out of my skull bones.'

'I'm glad of it. It shows my anaemia is getting better. I got weak as a cat with that. Now you reassure me, Mr Dodge.'

'Any time you want to test yourself, give me a shout.'

'Thank you. But my insomnia and my daughters, they are still a nuisance to me. Have you heard of my daughters, Mr Dodge?'

'In detail, boy. I've often likened you in the Literary Group at the Centre to King Lear.'

'Lear? That element should have operated with twice the number of daughters and a Social Insurance card where his crown used to be. Then he'd have something to grow a white beard about. Dividing a kingdom between three daughters is one thing. Dividing two bedrooms between five is another, and the wife and myself trying to fit in our little twilight of desire in the existing gaps.'

'Don't start Granville talking about his daughters,' said my father. 'He's got a lot of material there and it'll turn the milk sour as sin if he gives you the tale with all the trimmings.'

'True enough,' said Granville. 'When your heart's an ashbin not even that Hadrian Mogg with his lorry can give you easement.' Then he started praising Jolly and the smart look of my father. We explained to him about Blakemore and our campaign but he did little listening. He said he'd like to lead a life as daft and slow as Jolly's. 'That's what I've always admired about the combination of Jolly and Wyndham Wilkie,' he said. 'Two fine interlocking types of coma. Don't let them change your mind's wallpaper, boy.' And he gave the horse an affectionate, powerful slap on the flank.

The blow must have landed on the pill itself and scattered its passionate ingredients to every corner of the horse. Jolly gave one neigh and started off down the road at what for Jolly was a blinding speed, with my father, reins in hand whether he wanted them there or not, leaning back like a charioteer.

They did the complete circuit of Bandy Lane without any slackening of stride. My father was frightened out of his wits, especially when churn after churn, can after can went flying from the cart on the sharper slopes, banging and denting the metal and spilling the milk into the gutters. A lot of people, who had been told of Dunkerly's plans for my father, thought that this was a publicity venture to bring attention to his fine qualities as a horseman and to the excellence of Blakemore's milk which was now nourishing the gutters as well as the voters. They stood at corners cheering as the cart passed and calling out their friends to see my father and Jolly on their next trip around.

Jolly stopped at just the same spot he had started. We helped my father down and for several minutes, although the horse had now returned to his normal stupor and he was on the firm road, his hands were still outstretched as if he was clutching the reins and his body was still backtilted at the same charioteering angle we had seen in the race round the town. We could not get a word out of him.

'You know, Stobo,' said Dunkerly, 'it's no wonder that your old man is so ravelled. That Josephs would undo chain-mail with his brands of woe. His demands for pity would thin the blood of an ape. We'll have to make your father deaf to such people because it's clear his round is festooned with them and they've been using his compassion as the most reliable nag in the local stables and as a result he's got a worse case of glanders than Jolly. If I can find some pellets that make for a pitiless cynicism, I'll send them round post haste. Emotionally the poor feed on each other's hearts. That's why they are able to live so cheaply. Fish and chips made an effort to break them of the habit, but with fish at the price it is now they're back at the old antic.'

We scoured Bandy Lane for the missing milk cans. We found them all but were short two lids at the end of the search. We loaded them back onto the cart and my father drove them sadly back up the mountain. We asked him if he would like us to come with him to explain things to Mr Blakemore.

'No, don't come with me. Don't try to explain. Just leave me alone. I don't think you boys with your fancy ideas fit into my life at all. And tell Shifnal Pugh that if he's got another of those pills he'll know what to do with it.'

Dunkerly, who hated any vague directions, was going to ask my father to expand on this, but for once I was able to lay a wise hand on his arm and urge him to silence.

When my father came home at dusk his face looked bruised, as if he had been beaten. His hair was disarranged and there was no trace of his hat. Colenso was furious as he watched my father dabbing away at his face with a flannel. 'If those two jokers up the mountain laid a finger on you on account of those spilled cans, I'm going up there and ram them head first into their central dung-heap.'

'I fell,' said my father. 'On my way down. I was so tired I slipped and fell.'

'What did they say?' I asked.

'Nothing much. Mr Blakemore just shouted as his way is. But Mr Phillimore kept on about me being the one who had gone around Bandy Lane making slanders against them and calling the farm neglected. He had heard too that most of the people I failed to serve yesterday and who got their milk from the South Western have now gone over to the South Western for good.'

'He's a genius, that Dunkerly,' said Colenso. 'He's a good stage manager but I'd like to know who wrote the play.'

'I've got to pay for the milk and the two lids out of my wages, and I've got to help with the potato crop. I've got to go around the houses of those whose trade I lost today. I'm sorry I have to do that, because I hate talking to people, trying to persuade them.'

'I'll come with you,' said Colenso. 'I'm not as busy as Stobo.'

'And don't go trying to make a big drama out of

this,' I said to him. I saw that he was making the veins of his forehead bulge, a thing he always did when he was projecting himself into the role of revolutionary leader. For my father I was glad that no worse settlement had been arrived at. 'I suppose you'll take Dad over to The Thinker and the Thrush and have him standing on the table singing "The Marseillaise". Don't forget that Mr Blakemore has his viewpoint too.'

'So have all the creatures on this earth, but that doesn't entitle them to be employers of human labour. Blakemore is an ignorant bigot, less cultured than his dullest cow, and the same goes for Phillimore with the notion of his being sinister thrown in for extra weight.'

I let Colenso run on, a little guilty that it was he and not I who was patting iodine into my father's cheek, but I was on my guard against Colenso's habit of exploiting my father's every little grievance to promote the cause of fanning our militant courage.

I adjusted my collar and hat. My hat was a trim little pork-pie item, fashionable among the youth of the town at that time. Angela had poked fun at it the night before, accusing it of being banal and unoriginal. As I stood before the mirror some of her phrases took on significant overtones of contempt that cut into my flesh. I disliked uncharity of mood, especially in Angela. It was enough that her mother was so funny. I turned to my father. 'Could I have a lend of your new velour, Dad, for tonight?'

'Mr Phillimore took it, Stobo. Took it for keeps as part payment on their losses.'

I ignored Colenso's grunt and left the house, studying Mr Phillimore's viewpoint.

10

A week later Offa Mogg and I sat together in the debating room of The Thinker and the Thrush. It was early in the evening and we were alone. A big fire burned at both ends of the room. There were three solid oak tables and chairs to match. Around the walls were photographs of some very wise-looking voters who had been chairmen of the debating group. Above the main fireplace was the largest photograph of all, one of Tridwr Vaughan who had been the landlord of The Thinker until his death five years before and an active debater. It was while debating the abolition of any kind of state church that he had dropped down dead in full view of the audience, and his views that night had been so frankly godless that there was some talk of his having been got at by an avenging bolt. It was Tridwr who bought the fine tables and chairs, much against the will of Mrs Vaughan who was on the pious and grasping side and regarded the debaters as a clutch of garrulous louts who would have been better off supping their ale while sitting on the wooden floor, devoting less time to arguing about free love and more to winkling out splinters. Mrs Vaughan had now retired from the business and lived in a tiny flat at the top of the building, reading a lot for the first time in her life and becoming bitterly controversial as the sun of this new interest struck harder at her nape. Now she apologised off and on to Tridwr's ghost for having taken so little interest in the topics of the day while he was alive.

Offa and I were silent and abstracted. He had come along only because Granville Josephs was opening in a debate on the motion 'Have children always been a curse, or is it only just lately?' Offa had come to regard Granville with his griping approach to the housing shortage and his denunciations of family life as one of the most morally decadent voters in Bandy, and he had promised to report the debate in the *Bulletin* in terms so scathing to Granville that my father would in future write him off both as companion and customer.

My own silence was deeply personal. The night before my feathers had been badly ruffled. I still had Angela's toothmarks in both my ears and there were a dozen places on the rear side of my dignity that needed embrocation. I had known that her impatience with her mother had been reaching the point of climax but I had been shocked by the type of little thing that had eventually made her explode. Of course she got no sort of wage at home because the money earned by Lyndhurst Lang at the macadam plant barely kept the family in food. So on the Tuesday Angela told me that since Wednesday was her birthday she would be obliged to me if I would buy her a very smart jacket of brown suede which was on show in the window of Madame de Vere, who was a local girl called Daisy Rees but given over in her mind to French ways and tastes.

I had to take a firm line with Angela. I told her something of the fantastic profit margin allowed herself by Madame de Vere and also that she should be more concerned in helping me reach the minimum sum mentioned by Mr Ellicott as the price of his business. She came out with language which, in the mouth of Angela, our finest elocutionist, I can only call uncouth, such as 'A hell of a lot I care about sharing that spider's web, that potato grove at Ellicott's with you!' The next day she got Dunkerly to go with her to Lovett's, the big store in Hanover Road, to help her get a job in the skirt and blouse department fitting on models for women in doubt behind a very flimsy screen. She did one day there. The very first evening she came home from work her mother was prostrate and groaning, with Oswald and Edgar sprinkling sal volatile on each temple and Lyndhurst threatening to go off and join the same sect as Colenso's stepfather which does for thought and anxiety what America did for the bison. I hurried over and explained to Angela that this collapse was due to Mrs Lang's feeling that she had been hurt and rejected by her dearest child, her only daughter. She weakened and I phoned Dunkerly to tell Mr Lovett that Angela would not be coming back. We helped Mrs Lang to bed where she ate a supper of chips that would have slowed an elephant.

The next night Angela had been like a fiend, without pity or reason. She had lashed at me for having exposed my father to contempt and ridicule in our campaign to make him a more admirable and life-worthy milkman. I rushed her in mid-gall off to the Cosy for which I had two complimentary tickets to the ninepennies. Sixpence more and we had the best seats upstairs. She demanded that we stay to see the big picture twice because she said she found it interesting and relevant to her own situation. It was about a beautiful, talented girl, wasted and cheated by her parents, her lovers, and her employers, who gets her own back on society by stealing, gambling, dancing all through the night and being wanton and fleshly throughout in a way that caused every jaw in the sixpennies to drop almost out of sight. Angela told me that she had now had such a skinful of the Judases who were out to trip her up at every step that she was going to plan such a programme for herself. I was horrified. I asked her if she knew what was meant by being wanton and fleshly. Out came the definition like a bullet from a gun and I could see that as far as theoretical knowledge went Angela had come out of Eden at the trot. She wanted me to take her to see the same show the following night; she wanted to study the details of this woman's expression of delight when she was outraging her old friends and especially when she was breaking her old mother's heart.

When I told her that I would not pay Banfield Marsh, the manager of the Cosy, full price for a show I had already seen, she savagely called me Diamond Jim and flounced off, leaving me to bear in mind a scene from the film in which the heroine, with more ironical laughter than has been heard since the earth tore off from the sun, defended prostitution in the presence of a priest, a friend of the mother, and rounded things off by trying to edge him into the queue.

So there I was, without Angela and feeling uneasily deprived, in the debating room of The Thinker and the Thrush with Offa Mogg. It was a place I attended with a lot of doubt and I had consulted Melancthon Mills about the propriety of it. But Melancthon said that as a man in trade I would have to know all conditions of men and that an example of sober restraint would do no harm to the voters I would meet in the debating room. My maximum order was a short shandy taken in even shorter sips.

I did not disturb Offa in his thoughts. That afternoon he had been discussing with Melancthon

Mills a book which they had been reading on those reformatory Boys' Towns set up in different parts of the world to provide a social outlet for boys who were either vagrant or maturing towards delinquency. The book accorded well with their mood for both suffered from a panic fear that the generation to which their children belonged had given up honesty as a bad job. Melancthon's trouble was that he did not have nerves strong enough to assimilate any conduct the least out of plumb. He had been nourished so long by himself and his parents on the legend of his own blamelessness that at the slightest whiff of brutal or lascivious behaviour you could see his neuroses tying themselves into another knot and his hair looking for a new place to fall.

He was not helped by our new Probation Officer, Ventris Lee. Ventris was one of the most serious voters you could ever imagine. A long-time friend of Hadrian Mogg, he had qualified late for his post and took the same view of juvenile offenders as Hadrian did of insanitary practices. It sometimes struck me that the young, to Ventris, were a kind of festering offal that must be kept from plaguing the entire world by a disinfectant rain of admonition and punishment. Every time a member of the Centre was taken off to the Juvenile Court, and there were boys like Wally Fletcher and Royston Angove for whom the magistrates kept a teapot simmering on the hob, Melancthon, Hadrian and Ventris would stand together and tut-tut so clearly and so long you could see and hear doom putting its shoes on for its sharpest canter.

But Melancthon was most of the time without Ventris' deep-seated woe and clung to the belief that with a slight change of emotional or physical emphasis the rogue, however cemented in evil, would

— 110 —

at last take the road of angelic normality. Whenever Ventris brought him word of a new case he would hurry along to the court full of zeal to give the boy a good character, even though it might be a lad like Wally Fletcher who had once, merely to add an ornament of horn to an ashtray which he had made in the craft-class at the Centre, stolen the rims from Melancthon's spectacles in the middle of one of the longest lectures ever given even by Melancthon to a young offender. Ventris on the other hand would on these trips to court stalk along at Melancthon's side as if all he wanted Melancthon to do was to certify that the boy should be buried in the right quality of lime.

'I think Melancthon is on the right lines now,' said Offa to me. 'In an old industrial town like this the vice forms in seams and layers like coal or iron ore. You've got to break the urban spell.'

'Right over Wally Fletcher's head if possible,' I said. I was still smarting from my last personal encounter with Wally. He lived next door down to us, the son of a sweet but sub-vital little voter called Galway Fletcher who had come from Ireland and looked as if he could not bear to tell the Famine that it was over. I had been assigned to Wally as a kind of moral guardian, but if he had not been devoted in his young and innocent way to Angela, and if she had not been sympathetic towards him, I would have gone out one night to find some stretch of our river, the Moody, deep enough to house and cover a delinquent, and I would have invited the fish to take over with Wally where Ventris had left off.

Two months earlier he had committed a series of small thefts from the butter side of Mr Ellicott's shop: a rasher or two of bacon, a lump of cheese. When caught he had explained to the magistrate, a very old, gullible humanitarian named Creigiau Tothill, that he had meant these articles not for himself but for a sick and widowed pensioner, Mrs Deborah Enoch, who lived in a battered cottage on the marshes that stretched eastward to the sea from Bandy Lane. Mrs Enoch turned up in court looking as if we could have turned the whole butter side over to her and still not filled the great gap of her desires and needs. She walked about with a huge tea-cosy on her head, an ironically strong, black curl of hair dangling from the hole where the spout normally appeared. It seemed that this element, who was still pretty glib in a toothless way, had persuaded Wally Fletcher to bring her any titbits on which he chanced to lay his hand, and it was common for us to have whole rows of cheeses torn and plastered with fingerprints by Wally's efforts to please Mrs Enoch.

Creigiau Tothill's words of praise for Wally's essay in social service sent whole fleets of lads of like bent into the shop and Mr Ellicott and I would have to threaten to skewer these elements if they did not at once make a purchase or clear off. Largely through my protest in the *Bandy Lane Bulletin* and a fine column by Offa called 'Are We Going Too Fast Too Far?', demanding a harsher and clearer-eyed approach to the young criminal, we had put the town on the alert about this problem. 'For elements like Wally Fletcher,' I told Offa, 'I would suggest an iron grille fitted into the ground with Wally underneath, caged and helpless.'

I felt bitter and sounded bitter, for Angela was mixed up in these thoughts I was having about Wally. For myself I shied away from the abnormal and unorthodox. I wanted, as a plain man, to succeed among plain men. Not even to please my old friend Melancthon Mills would I have undertaken that wardenship over Wally, but Angela said 'You think about yourself too much, Stobo, and you are not as rich as all that as a theme. Think of others. Bind up someone else's wounds for a change. A poor persecuted outcast like Wally Fletcher for a start.' And she gave me a look which said that if I refused this act of charity she would never think of me the same again, so I told her that if I could persuade Galway Fletcher to move up I would share with him the confusing job of being a father to Wally.

'I used to think offenders should just be quietly put down, too,' said Offa, 'but I'm wiser now. You must not be vindictive, Stobo. You can flog and flay and gaol until you run out of whip and stone, but sooner or later you are driven back to the simple truth.' I nodded at Offa, envying him the creamy smoothness of his theories. I could see no sternness in his face and I sensed that he had indeed experienced a change of heart about young delinquents. I thought of the phrase 'the simple truth'. Ever since I had first started trying to find a platform of concepts on which I could walk with assurance as citizen and grocer, the truth has appeared to me to have as many faces as the average voter has bones and it kept spinning around as if on a top, staring at me in turn with each one of its strained, bloodshot eyes. The truth was the least simple thing in Bandy Lane.

'The simple truth, Offa,' I said. 'That's it, boy. We are driven back to it fast.'

'Of course we are. And this is it. It is no use prodding sin with a fork as if it were a pickle. We have planted every variety of prong from every variety of angle into the world's thieves and mobsmen since time began and the only effect it's had on these elements is to make them more interested in the pattern of holes made in their hide by our prodding. No, Stobo. In the face of whatever hurt, whatever molestation, if we as a species are still fools enough to offer anything but sympathetic love then we should find a cliff from which to jump. Once you perceive the essential single identity of mankind you understand the deadly danger and lunatic inadequacy of wanton punishment. Do you see that?'

'No,' I said.

'Socially one boy in ten is drinking poison from the start. How to wean him from this diet, that is the problem. And the answer is a thriving co-operative farming centre where these boys will find a sense of dedication, of continuous pride strong enough to absorb all the vapours of self-defensive spites that have caused their moral braces to dangle and their civic pride to discolour. So we are going to kill two birds with one stone.' Offa looked so masterfully subtle I had to turn my eyes away, disquieted by such a total grasp on living. 'We are going to have a preliminary series of talks at the Centre on farming and the healthy effects of open air given by Lucas Phillimore.'

'Who?'

'Phillimore, up the mountain.'

I suddenly found the name and thought of the man odious to me but before the reaction could even knit my brows I was smiling agreeably at Offa. For years I had been like a laboratory dog at the sound of Offa's bells and his tinkle was still compulsive. 'Oh yes, Phillimore. Just the man.'

'Definitely, boy. I draw the line at Blakemore, a demented savage whose head should have been planted years ago in the same furrow as his turnips. But Phillimore has undertones of real gentility. He went to a good boarding school and he has those easy ways of speech and movement that set him off from the average run of morlock in Bandy Lane. True, he's a bit run down at the moment, infected no doubt by contact with Blakemore, but we must not tar him with the same brush.'

'Phillimore seems very anti-social to me. What if he tells you to stuff the Social Centre? What if he's a believer in juvenile delinquency? He looks a bit of a crook to me; I've seen many a villain on the screen of the Cosy who looked like Phillimore's twin.'

'There's nothing wrong with the man that the oxygen of a little flattery won't cure. I'm going to praise him in my column, pay tribute to his suavity and sophistication and make out that he combines the best qualities of farmer and man of the world. If we can get him into close contact with boys like Wally Fletcher and Royston Angove who go off the rails now and then, he will give them an assurance, an unembarrassed ease that will bring out their latent moral brightness like a shower of Brasso.

'Do you realise, Stobo, that most of the world's crime is brought on by a sense of pure embarrassment, a fumbling awkwardness of the ego? A man blinks naïvely at the perfectly natural division of the species into rich and poor and the next thing you know he is assaulting a banker or looting a mansion. How much crime do you find among the well bred? Hardly any. Why? Because they are trained to hold life steady, never to be shocked into some gratuitously offensive caper by its quaking absurdities, which is what happens too often to the poor who are at bottom an innocent and over-ardent lot.'

The room had now begun to fill up. Colenso, wearing a blue suit and a white collar to show that he was one of the officials of the debating club, had come to sit by Offa and me and he was looking at Offa most interestedly. I could see by the play of his eyes that he would like him to go over some of his points again so that he could get his teeth into them. But Offa cut him off. 'Now don't let's have any of your idealistic views of the poor, Colenso, there's a good boy. That stuff's out of date and unscientific. They are an unreliable, unpredictable and fundamentally inferior lot. The lesson of history, and I'm raising my voice here in case you've been stuck on those pylons too high and too long to hear the voice of the past, is that the rich by and large have blandly and wisely been the agents of the only real progress and melioration that the dowdy, undistinguished lump of people have ever known.'

'Would you like me to stiffen your shandy with something?' said Colenso ominously.

'No indeed. You know me. A simple faith, a clear head and never more than a gill.'

'Clear and simple you are, boy. So now you are going to launder Phillimore and slip him like a healing pill into the juvenile section at the Centre. By God, those young delinquents are confused enough already, and with Phillimore added to the mixture they'll go one better than Jesse James and try to hold up the whole process of death and decay.'

'Just cut out those mechanical tropes, Mortlake. You're against anybody who's been to a better school than you. All these convulsions of conduct that land kids in front of the bench spring from the sense of inferiority which is bred by margarine, day schools and mothers who send them out to get groceries on tick. Give a person a natural sense of superiority and he's so busy being superior he hasn't got the time to be delinquent.'

'All right, all right. Just add these notions to the compost heap, Offa, and we'll see what comes up. But you, Stobo, you ought to be ashamed.'

'What for?' I asked, feeling like a corncob between these two millstones.

'Making no opposition to this Phillimore, who has abused your old man to the doors of the County Mental. He doesn't go in only because he's too shy to ring the bell, but one day Blakemore and Phillimore will ring it for him. Bandy Lane will be a milkman short and you'll be an orphan. What kind of evil play are you performing in that skull of yours, Stobo?'

'I try to see both sides.'

'The only thing you ever see both sides of are the buttocks of the mighty which you've been stroking with love and staring at with idiot respect from birth.'

'Don't listen to him, Stobo,' said Offa. 'We see the light ahead. We know what our lads can learn from a man like Mr Phillimore. Good English, a settled assumption of one's own significance, manners like satin. Can you imagine a voter like that going in for petty theft?'

'Two-handed,' said Colenso. 'Subject classes are made in the rascally image of their rulers. The latter rifle continents and enrich themselves by astute bankruptcies, and the former come sharply to a salute of imitation by rifling gas meters and falling behind with the rent.'

We all hushed Colenso to silence as the chairman of the debaters, Holman Bayliss, came in. Offa took out a thick notebook and looked around, sombrely tense, as if he could not consider the evening a success unless Colenso were to follow the example of Tridwr Vaughan, another Lollard who had come sliding down from the peak of his peroration, full of beer, spring onions and thundering apoplexy.

11

During the next two weeks Offa ran several paragraphs in the *Bulletin* praising Lucas Phillimore to the skies, saying how lucky Bandy Lane was to have such an urbane, well educated element, fresh from high administrative and practical experience in many counties, back in his native town. Offa developed the theme that Lucas would be just the man to plant a new, regenerative, non-urban impulse in boys like Wally Fletcher.

Lucas responded well and came down to the Centre to put himself at the disposal of Melancthon Mills. He was a striking figure in his fawn tweed suit and yellow cardigan. He was wearing the hat the Austrian boys had given my father. This angered me but I had to concede that my father owed the cousins something for the milk he had lost during that canter with Jolly.

Lucas agreed to give a weekly talk to a group of youths selected by Melancthon as being likeliest to vanish for long periods into corrective schools, and it was an experience to see in how blank a way these young elements looked at him. He had taken his cue from Offa and had multiplied by three the refined English accent with which he spoke, and there must have been times when his vowel combinations baffled even himself. The boys just counted the number of times Lucas coughed when an over-flattened *a* went down the wrong pipe and wondered.

Melancthon had just come under a new cloud of worry. Dunkerly Dodge had suggested that Wally and his companions were probably sent awry by their lack of continuous communion with beauty. There was a search around Bandy Lane for beauty but none was found in sufficient quantity to keep Wally and Royston out of trouble. Then Dunkerly thought of Thorold Wigley's flower shop, and small detachments of the boys were taken into Thorold's place to get a fill of the blooms. This bored Wally, not because he was against flowers but because Thorold had a way, every time he introduced the lads to some new bouquet, of quoting some shallower types of poetry to drive his point home, and they wished they had some means of driving it right back at him. Wally hopped over the wall dividing his garden from mine and with a sour face gave me some examples of Thorold's lyrics:

> And this is a rose,
> A gift from God, God knows

and, as his *pièce de résistance*,

> All men's woes look somewhat silly
> When you contemplate the lily.

Wally told me that if anyone could be driven mad by pollen then Thorold Wigley had been, and the bees could come and sting him to death for abusing their craft. 'And the way he talks, Stobo! So high, so sweet, so funny. Between him and Phillimore me and the other boys pick up about one word in twenty.'

A further feature was Royston's hay fever; every time he entered Thorold's shop and had a drift of seed into his sinuses he became inflamed and evil as he looked from red eyes at Thorold. The venture ended when Thorold opened a sweet shop next door to his flower establishment. He called it 'The Toffee-Pole' and he said he would stock only the classier, dearer type of sweetmeat. He claimed his shop was really a protest against the vulgar obvious sorts of sweet like Liquorice Laces and Lingering Lumps which gave you hours of hard chewing for a penny and had been popular for years in Bandy Lane, doing a lot to keep the voters sugared and jocose through periods of sinister acridity on the social front. What Thorold wanted was a new deal for the mutilated palates of the area. It was a godsend to Wally and the boys. While they would ask Thorold to show them some bloom in the furthest, darkest corner of the shop, Royston would nip into the Toffee-Pole and just about dig it up for taking away. Wally said they only let Royston loose on the toffee because of his hay fever: 'There are times when we want to listen to Mr Wigley. When we do, Royston's sneezing is a nuisance.'

So they were offered up to Lucas, who spoke to them in his impressive drawl, showing off an expensive brown shoe which he always put up on a chair when he spoke and thrusting a finger into the pocket of his cardigan. His general title was: 'The Land – A Man's Life *or* How Not To Be A Gutter Rat', and he sometimes made languid gestures at the boys as if easing them out of the gutter. There was little in his talks about the practical side of farming and he shut Wally up sharply when he asked why, if he knew so much, there was such a scruffy, barren look about Blakemore's farm. Muttering something about the rough-hewn, homespun pioneer who tried to keep the flag flying on marginal land, Lucas returned to his favourite topic, which was the story of the hunts and parties he had attended in glittering country houses when he served as a steward to a lord in the north Midlands. Wally and Royston and their friends, who had never seen a hunt in their lives and were not likely to see one in that very sombre area around the Bandy Lane Gas Works where they lived, sat quietly listening to him, getting their mental wires so crossed I felt it would need Colenso Mortlake with his whole bagful of tools to allow them to get a plain intelligible thought again.

If it had not been for Angela I think I could have put up with Lucas. There was an air about him; he brought a breeze from the great world. But on the night of Lucas' second visit he met Angela, and something was alive between them. She admired his great height, his soft, controlled voice. 'He's a real leader,' she told me. 'Has he shown you the picture of himself when he was thirty-one and the oldest officer in his regiment?'

'The boys in the ranks were probably keeping him till last,' said Colenso, who had joined us in Kiprianos' for this conversation.

'His clothes are old but good,' she went on, 'as a gentleman's ought to be. Quiet in tone, of course, but with that significant blaze of colour on the chest. I've been meaning to tell you for years, Stobo, that those tidy little blue and brown suits you wear give you a very stale, middle-aged look.'

'In business a sober hue breeds confidence, Angela.'

'And he has that wonderful, manly, tweedy smell about him. I've read about it often in magazines but this is the first time my nose has really had the pleasure.'

'That smell you speak of,' said Colenso, 'is to be found all over Blakemore's farm whether you're sniffing at tweed or not.'

'You can be as uncouth about it as you like, Colenso. What I'm telling you is that when Lucas bends over

— 121 —

me and just whispers in that fine throbbing voice I could nearly faint. Did you know that Dunkerly has offered him a part in the new play?' She stood up and looked at me searchingly. 'Have you noticed that your voice splinters and squeaks when you get excited, Stobo? But Lucas, always low and vibrant.'

Angela left us. In between sips of Kiprianos' coffee Colenso said she was applying this torture deliberately and was only using Lucas as a tool in her campaign to make me a bit more responsive.

'What do you mean, responsive?' I asked.

'Are you a passionate lover? Do you scorch Angela with the kind of heat a full-blooded girl like her is bound to crave?' Colenso leaned over the table looking very technical, as if, in the event of my turning out to be, as a lover, on the cool side, he would arrange with the electricity company to have me fitted up with new warmth.

I pushed my own chair back to remind him that I had long ceased to be the dupe of his notions. 'Just keep your voice down, Colenso,' I said. 'Even in places like this there's no need to be indiscreet. No, you wouldn't call me a passionate lover. A dawdling approach is wise in most matters, but in love invaluable. I've never said or done anything to Angela that I would not have said or done to my own mother.' I was speaking very slowly, for my own sake more than Colenso's. 'I sometimes think I've tamed the animal side of me in this field. Odo Mayhew, who has read a whole series of books on the transmutation of desires, says that it's possible that the separate teeth of my intimate urges might by now have fused into a single beak of commercial acquisitiveness.'

'Quite likely. But I can see Angela fingering this beak and wondering where the hell it's likely to get her.'

'Her strength will be behind me in the business, telling me to peck away. At the moment our affection is as formal as a funeral card. Most days I'm in the warehouse at seven in the morning and it's twelve hours later when I finish. That leaves a man's instincts satisfied and still. Frankly I sometimes feel that I get more excited by the different kinds of dairy produce on Mr Ellicott's counter than by Angela, viewed from the angle of fleshiness.

'I've put her on a high pedestal. Whenever I feel any enthusiasm that can't be worked off stacking cheeses, I kiss the pedestal. The taste of the stone is flat but it's safe and a good discipline in preparation for the years when carnal love will have fallen far back in the queue of interests. My main virtue is a cool diligence and I've taught Angela to respect and even love it. In some ways I may have defects but, by God, as a citizen I'm all there. When I hear of some voters who take advantage of a long engagement to claim the rights of intimacy, I'd like to shoot them down as mad dogs.'

'Just as well you haven't got a gun, Stobo, or the place would be full of dead dogs with eroded engagement rings. What you've just mentioned is a leading tactic with many of the boys.'

'You've probably picked up some very loose notions about women while you've been wandering about fitting people up with power points but you won't find any of my screws working loose. There are some of us who see that lust can be a wanton waste and that the more you repress life the richer will be its eventual juices. I hope you're getting a good headful of these doctrines, Colenso, because I sometimes see a very licentious look on your face that worries me.'

'It worries me, too. There are times when my flame rises fit to burst. But I'm telling you, Stobo, Angela's serving notice that a little flame wouldn't come amiss from you. You may be getting sublimation from the sale of greasy bacon and mop-heads or God knows what, but she's beginning to find too long an icicle in her stall. Repressions may induce rich juices, but Angela looks to me as if she could do with part of her pint here and now. Even to the extent of trying to inflame you by pretending infatuation for a broken down old mountain ram like Lucas Phillimore.'

'You're always trying to read a conspiracy into living. Try to believe that people and things can often be plain and wholesome and reasonable, like our produce at Ellicott's. Angela admires Mr Phillimore. We all do. And there's a touch of loneliness about him that would make an active appeal to Angela. She's been struck too by the fine work he's done as an inspiration to those kids who are in and out of trouble, Fletcher and Angove and that tribe. They've been in no trouble at all lately, not since Royston marched away with almost all Thorold Wigley's stock of toffee.'

'They're taking a rest, that's all. Partly that and partly trying to sort Lucas out. He baffles them. Once they've assimilated him into their bloodstream they will be back to form and Lucas will be walking along the corridor at the Centre, still very dignified but missing his trousers.'

'There are times when I think you are in with those boys, a kind of moral Fagin, spurring them on to these antics by laughing at the very things that should fill them with awe and discipline.' I spoke sharply, for I wanted to take Colenso's mind off Angela and my own off the disturbing thoughts about her that he had set going in me.

'I'm not for or against,' he said. 'I just see that they are surrounded by a very contradictory set of monkeys who see goodness and salvation from such varying and astonishing angles it would confuse a rock, let alone a bunch of boys born practically inside the Bandy Lane gas container with imaginations a million times bigger than their incomes. If ever a circus had as weird a clutch of clowns as Melancthon, Dunkerly, you and Phillimore, the animals would go and sit in the audience.

'But let's get back to Angela. Wally and his friends will get wisdom in the same way as the common folk get their bread, slowly and by working like hell for every crumb. But if you are not careful you are going to find that smugness of yours in fragments and Lucas Phillimore above you with Angela in one hand and a mallet in the other. I see a new light in her eyes ever since that voter came down from the hills.'

Colenso took out from his pocket a pair of shining pliers and began to tap me on the arm with them. He often had a way of producing this tool in the middle of a discussion to create an impression of power on a non-mechanical voter. 'Are you sure you're not subnormal?' he said.

'What do you mean, subnormal?' I said, staring at the pliers.

'What if you haven't got it in you to be an adequate, acceptable lover? You think that your manhood just now is too wrapped up in the problem of trade to be bothered with love. What if some vital part of your passion is gone forever into the way you work the bacon-slicer, into the ardour with which you operate the till? What if Angela has sensed in you some deeper lack than you realise and is making a quick grab at others before life passes her by altogether? She might have noticed too that you are quite happy in the company of boys like Odo Mayhew who is also not active in any orthodox way on the sexual front.

What if you turn out to have entered already on a marriage with groceries that admits of no divorce?'

'Stop waving that instrument at me and talk sense.' I tried to keep my voice firm but I could see Colenso was getting into his stride and I was losing momentum.

'Every woman,' he said, 'needs, in some context or other, a rush of life, a storm of feeling. That's true of the saddest, quietest woman, let alone a big, warm-hearted girl like Angela whose senses, potentially, must be a grenade.'

'What is all this talk about? A rush? A storm? What terms are these for anybody to be using in connection with my girl?'

'A woman needs passionate assurance. Either it can come from love of the desert-sheik type or through gifts. You are no sheik. If you ever had a turban it was used up years ago washing down Mr Ellicott's shelves. If you saw any sand it would probably end up eking out somebody's brown sugar. As for gifts, you're one of the meanest elements I know. Look at that business of the suede jacket Angela wanted for her birthday.'

I would have made a damaging reply but my mind was too full of the mysterious reference he had made to my liking the company of Odo Mayhew. I could answer the charge of meanness, though. 'Mean? Me? Do you realise what I've supplied to that family in the way of food? You know her mother. Her heart is in the country house. She fancies this, she fancies that. I must have been sending her at least ten shillings' worth a week. How can you call me mean?'

'Look, Stobo, you are not courting Mrs Lang's stomach, although I suppose to keep that item sweet would have its part in any bit of all-out wooing.'

With this Colenso stood up and left me, the words of protest piled up in a high clamant drift within me.

Colenso was always like that in his comings and goings. He never said 'hullo' or 'goodbye' because he said these words of greeting and farewell garnished life with sprigs of a too laboured awareness. He appeared and vanished in the quick strange manner of the electricity he helped to spread.

I gulped down what was left of my coffee, taking care to stir the last grains of sugar into the liquid. Kiprianos was standing quite still behind the counter. His hair was grey, his face worn, his body small. The legend was that, despite his unpromising frame, he was a dynamo in the matter of love. He had worn out three wives and was now, they said, debating whether he would be so cruel to himself or to another as to choose a fourth. I watched his dark, knowing face and wondered whether it might be a good idea to question Kiprianos on the sources and methods of desire on the most urgent plane. But, for all Colenso's talk, I really had no intense wish to know and I did not want to be indebted to Kiprianos for facts which, coming from such an unflagging and direct practitioner, would probably have sent me reeling.

12

During the next few days I thought hard about Lucas Phillimore. On one side of my mind was the bland assurance that Colenso had been talking through his mischievous hat, that Angela's interest in the man was the natural interest she would take in a man who spoke without prompting in the accent which was prescribed for us by Dunkerly Dodge in the Dramatic Group. On my mind's other side, the tissue of my thought trembled in the little self-critical wind that Colenso's words had set blowing. I recalled the black impatience, ripening into rage, that had overcome Angela's expression when I gave her the reasons, a long, fair list, for not buying that suede coat.

I thought a lot about what Angela had said about the rapture she felt on hearing Lucas's low, modulated voice. I decided that my own delivery could do with some fixative to prevent breaking in moments of stress and lapses into the more wanton provincialisms of Bandy Lane. I practised in the shop. When I spoke to the customers it was not in the high, enthusiastic, almost piercing tone which I normally used and which carried into every corner of the shop an impression of a friendly eagerness. I now tried to speak in a low, baritone mutter which made it necessary to keep my head down and my pipes steady. This gave customers the idea that I was in some way afraid or ashamed to look at them. I heard several of them go to Mr Ellicott and say 'What's Wilkie up to? Is he talking to someone under the counter?' and 'Stobo is muttering like a bloody spy there, Mr Ellicott. Look at him now, whispering into the cheese like a mite. Almost ruptured myself leaning over the counter to get my ear close enough to make sure he wasn't saying something nasty about me.' And Mr Ellicott came over and told me to put an end to these new methods of talking to the public. 'One thing you must never try to be in this trade, Stobo, is subtle. Look up and speak up, my boy.'

I noticed that Angela was not coming into the shop. I was not sorry, for I would need more practice at home before I could address her in the tones of Lucas Phillimore. I stood in front of the parlour mirror trying to lessen the mobility of my face and voice and when I came back into the kitchen to test my new restraint of tone and look upon my father and Colenso my father would silently produce for me a bottle of some herbal cleanser in which he had faith, and Colenso would advance some theory that made me out to be a kind of mumbling schizophrene with one leg tied to the working class and the other to the bourgeoisie: as these two groups drifted further apart, he said, the effect on my legs and vocal chords was bound to be disastrous.

Oswald and Edgar came to the shop quite often. They did not give their orders openly but waited for Mr Ellicott to be out of the way, then whispered their requests to me. This increased the suspicions of those voters who believed there were sinister changes going on in me and they cautioned Mr Ellicott to nail his counter more firmly to the floor if he did not want to see it carted off to some fresh premises on the backs of Oswald, Edgar and me. I reassured him by saying that Angela was out of sorts and kept sending the boys around with messages of affection for myself and him. This touched him and he puzzled the boys by taking hold of them occasionally and telling them in deep, tragic tones 'Tell her, boys, that the sun does not shine without her. Tell her we count the hours until she is back with us again.' He kept on this tack so often and so long I thought he might have been overdoing the tonic wine.

I made haste to let Oswald and Edgar have all they wanted, and more. This was the only way in which I could keep Angela sweet during our estrangement and I piled on the dainties to make sure that her relation with Lucas would not grow into anything deeper than a device to humble me. The more I gave, the more the fancies of Mrs Lang waxed. I found myself slipping the boys quantities of cooked ham, the rarest silverskin pickles, and once, but not even for love would I have repeated a gesture as passionate as this, a bottled chicken, as cosy in its surrounding fat as a jewel in velvet. I repented of the folly as soon as the boys left the shop. I tried to catch them, with such haste and such a jangling of buckets as I plunged through the entrance that my mental stock went down even further with the customers who were present. But the lads had gone down the street like hares. They were cunning and had noticed my hand and brain fumbling over the decision in the shop; they were giving me no chance to restore the chicken to its shelf. I swore to myself that the next time they came into the shop I would get their heads into focus like a couple of golf balls and let them have it with one of the thick, top-quality brooms that hung near the cash desk.

I gave some thought to love, though no longer in the clean, happy, unbothered way of yesterday. Colenso's words kept walking back and fore in my mind like black ghosts, winking wickedly every time they passed the window and hinting that my obsession with decency and self-advancement might have made me into some futile castrate, a passionless dupe. I could not ask Mr Ellicott for tips in this matter; I knew he kept his whole experience as a lover in a special private museum which was as hushed in its quiet seclusion as a chapel. I knew there could be no revival of interest in him. If his gonads ever rose to the surface of the evening pool in which they lay it would only be to tell the midges to be quiet. So I changed my tactics with the older women who came into the shop.

Some of these elements were as coarse as emery cloth in their conversation and time and time again I had had to reprove them for some open reference to the libido. Not violently, of course, because a too clearly shown purity of heart can often give offence, but I would pretend to gasp and pick up the tin of Flit and begin to spray. But nothing could cure them of the urge to discuss in front of me the most secret details about themselves and their husbands. They would stand at the door and point at some voter going down the street whom for years I had been used to regard as a pillar of laundered piety and denounce him as an unlimited goat who had long since worn down his fur to the canvas. They would give instances of their own contacts with these performers and often in such contexts as religious revivals and trips with the vestry-guild which made me faint with the fear that one day I would uncover the twitching face of foulness behind all the apparently unpolluted doorways of existence.

I learned now to encourage them in their talk, winking away as if I were the very boy who had stood behind the voters to give them the last shove as they tumbled into sin. I developed a way of slapping the side of bacon sensually with my meat-knife when they came out with jokes of a sexual nature so gross they would have had Hadrian Mogg calling around with canaries to test for methane. As they told these stories they would lean over the counter and dig me in the chest and stomach as if the reference now coming up would drag me across the landing and fill the cans of my being to the brim. 'Oh, God, you look so neat and clean,' Mrs Chiddle, the leading story-teller, would say, and she would stand there with her head thrown back in the gesture of a scream though no sound came, and I would stare at the brilliant red of her lower gum which was bare since she lost her denture on a bus trip to the Cotswolds.

Some of the women urged me to add my own bubbles to speed the mill-race of tales but I genuinely had none. So all I could do was stare back at Mrs Chiddle and her friends, looking as informed and suggestive as an old tom, hinting with the fat jocosity of my chuckles that the day would come when Hadrian Mogg, having taken his final certificate, would come along and open a ditch of confession in my mind that would have them racing back into the nearest vestry for a quick faint and a long absolution.

The women also had a way of making the most of any article that had the quality of symbolism and they tainted so many of my commodities by linking them in my imagination with the act of shame that my eyes would blush if they fell upon them in the course of talk with some purely chaste and quiet customer, and the conversation would end on my part in a tattoo of terrified hiccups.

I went through with the whole midnight curriculum of winks, hints and plain provocation lest I should be depriving myself of some vital earthiness or cheating Angela of some ingredient of a full existence without which she might drift into all the mischief of a bitter alienation. But for all the paddling in the mud flats with Mrs Chiddle and her brigade I could feel no naturally easy interest in the topic rising in me; it remained suspect and unattractive. So it was with keener interest I listened when I heard these women, from behind a mask of shrieking gaiety, discuss the various medicines, patent and herbal, appliances and mental techniques which they knew of as guaranteed to bring Blucher rushing in with the reserves to save their mates from some dismal Waterloo of the senses. One of them mentioned the medicinal wine of which Mr Ellicott was so fond.

One afternoon when he was having his nap before tea I nipped into the kitchen where he had half a bottle of the tonic. The shop was empty and I was curious to see whether I would be moved to any change of outlook by half a gill of this concoction. It had none of the bleak insipid taste I recalled from a previous sip. This was bland and inspiring. I returned to stand behind the counter and await the coming of miracles.

As I stood there I nibbled at cheese because I remembered another of the women having said that the incredible stamina of certain Celts was due to their passion for roast cheese. After a few minutes I felt desires creep among the darkened streets of me, each bringing a strengthening light of confidence and with it a libidinous haze as delicate and promising as the mist that hides the coast of Somerset from us in the early hours of a brilliant summer's day. I saw my hand shake as I served a child who came in with an order for broken biscuits, a popular item with voters whose lives were in even more pieces than the biscuits. Then the shop was empty again.

I pondered the philosophic issue of all this. A mere friction of fear and concern was coaxing into being a desire where none had been before. To love, to murder, to make a profit, all was a matter of clearing the ground in the mind on which a preoccupation could land and scratch its legs.

I longed to talk with someone. Then Mrs Chiddle came in. I did not, as I usually did, wait for her to begin the conversation but met her with some daring word-play of my own. My voice in its excitement went sliding about in an uncertain upper register. My hands clenched above the counter as I tried to drag it down into the mature baritone cellarage where Lucas Phillimore's padded about on its confident business. Mrs Chiddle leaned towards me. She was shiningly genial. Her hand touched mine. Her old blouse hung loosely away from her body. She gave out a breath of

— 133 —

something friendly, ancient, assuring. A draught was blowing in at both my ears to nourish the flame that was growing in my head. Here, I thought, was a chance at least to study the chapter headings of the course so that I would not be too clumsy or nervous if Angela really did have an interest in this type of wantonness.

I pushed the board on which rested the remains of a York ham towards Mrs Chiddle. She helped herself to a handful of the still succulent crumbs and I heard her give the low moan she always uttered if her palate found a skilled kiss upon it. The sound stirred me to a higher tension. I nipped from behind the counter and closed the door of the shop, as quiet as fraud. I blushed as I did so and mumbled something to Mrs Chiddle about having a new consignment of coconut matting in the hardware section. She followed me into the corner where these articles were stacked. They were low priced and hard bristled but coloured in rich reds and browns that spoke to the eye if not the hand of a moderate sensuousness. Mrs Chiddle placed herself against the pile. 'Testing the give,' she said. 'Important with matting.'

She leaned back with her full weight. She suddenly said something about being tickled by the bristles and began to laugh. 'And that staring way you look and that pencil sticking out of your pocket is funny too,' she said, and laughed even louder.

There is nothing like laughter, loud, vulgar laughter, to drain the mercury out of a man's thermometer even when it is squeezing hard against the very top of his skull to make room for fresh hallelujahs and a climactic amen. I found myself pressing my knees frantically into the matting, anxious to have its prickles pierce my flesh and set up a fresh pain of sensation that would drown the racket of my embarrassment.

I broke away from her, giving as my excuse that I

thought I had heard Mr Ellicott stirring. 'Oh, don't worry about him,' she said quite casually. 'He's hung his hat on this stand more than once.'

The shock of that finished me off. I served her with what she wanted, burning with shame at the sight of her fixed, companionable smile. One half of my mind was in a swoon from this brush with iniquity; the other was itching to query that reference to hats in this context. As a sop I slid two free boxes of breakfast oats into her basket, feeling, as I did so, a sinister sense of directive power.

As soon as Mr Ellicott came back into the shop I told him that I felt unwell and asked if he could spare me. 'You're pale,' he said. 'You go off home. You're too conscientious.'

I did not go home. I went straight to Angela's, determined to have from her a clear statement on Phillimore and her view on love.

There was no one in the Langs' kitchen. The whole family was in the parlour, sitting around a well supplied table on which the main item was the remains of the bottled chicken. At the head of the table was Lucas himself, huge in tweeds, wearing an expensive light brown suit and a dark brown tie that gave him a melancholy overtone. His whole being as he sat there had a mellow, moonlit, plangent quality. Mrs Lang was bent servilely towards him, absorbed in his talk. Angela had her eyes fixed entranced upon him, watching the slow, sure, self-conscious movements of his mouth and hands as if he were some new and complete revelation of grace.

As I stood at the parlour door I felt the last cockle of my heart come under the heel of a resolution to catch Offa Mogg a clip for having been daft enough to invite Lucas into our lives. I wanted to say something loud, unforgettable in its grieved intensity, and I prayed to God that my voice would pay some heed to my stage directions. In my mind I ran over half a dozen good opening bars. 'State your case, Phillimore.' 'What are your intentions, Lucas?' 'I'd like a word with you, Phillimore.'

Lucas turned his chair around to look at me. Even seated he could give the impression of having you at the bottom of a pit and I could feel my eyes peering painfully upwards into the dark. 'Isn't this the relative of Wilkie who is employed in our dairy departments?' he asked in a voice that was gall's creamy top.

'Yes, yes,' said Mrs Lang impatiently, as if Lucas had just pointed to a roach. 'Please go on, Mr Phillimore. And you actually saw the Prince, our dear Teddy, there at that meet in Leicestershire?'

My heart was saying so much it was hoarse. It said: 'Look, my father *is* the dairy department, Phillimore. Without him there'd be no cows, no milk round, no profit. Without him you wouldn't be able to eat, you lazy, stuck-up bastard.' But my voice said nothing. I cast Angela the sort of look I have seen used by such voters as clowns with septic sorrows and sealed lips on the screen of the Cosy.

'If you have brought anything, Stobo,' she said in about the brightest voice I had ever heard, 'just leave it on the table as you go out.'

'I didn't bring anything.'

'Goodbye, Wilkie,' said Lucas.

I left the house. My inside was grey and swollen, like the clouds that drove over the northern hills promising rain and sadness. I felt a hatred in me like that which I have sometimes seen on the face of Colenso when speaking of those upon the earth who pilfer the genius and toil of others. I felt tricked and tainted by that hatred as I had by that incursion into small, deliberate lust. No one had ever wished more than I to be clean and cool.

I quickened my step and cursed all those who commit the crime of being inept and oppressed, whose desires are innocent and unused to the terrible roads they must travel.

I wished sincerely to see Phillimore dead.

When I received the full impact of that reflection I found myself back outside the shop. The light was on in Mr Ellicott's window. I bowed my head to it in apology for having allowed myself, even for a moment, a thought that did such injury to relations making for trade. But the thought did not leave me. It got used to having my boot in it and just stayed there, seeming to be sorry for looking pained as well as bitter. My mind returned to the thing I had felt in the shop that afternoon when Mrs Chiddle came in. To love or to murder. Clear the ground for a preoccupation with either and it will speed to its fulfilment.

13

Later that evening I went along to Kiprianos' café to meet Offa. The only people in the shop were Offa and two extremely old men with bowler hats, eroded faces and lamenting voices. Offa was also wearing a bowler and a long black overcoat which showed he had been attending some function connected with death. Offa was never flippant in these matters as many voters connnected with newspapers were. The merest mention of some element who might shortly be landing in the Black Meadow would bring Offa out in his bowler to set the right key.

I made my greetings as cordial as I could considering the state of strain I was in. Offa waved me to a chair. The two men with him, cousins, Shiloh and Milton Pertwee, were sadder in their smaller, more mobile way than misty hills. They worked irregularly as plumbers, having little real interest in piped water, and their main activity now was to give weight and dignity to funerals that might otherwise have a skimpy and casual air. They were useful to Offa in two ways. They kept him advised of families in which bereavement might shortly befall and Offa would go along to them and assemble the materials of a short biographical sketch for the *Bulletin*, by the tone of urgent significance in which he spoke of the dying investing the whole event with a glow of dramatic interest that often robbed sorrow of some of its cruel and mutilating thrust. He could mount the wild grief of any widow and coax it into a slow, mellow movement of healing, reminiscent self-confession.

The cousins also helped Offa with his memorial verses which he turned out and sold by the score to those families with which he had got on such good terms during the period of loss. There were some who said that no higher tribute had ever been paid to the stupefying power of grief than the orders handed in by the grieving to Offa for his verses which, his critics said, definitely polished off death as a topic. But I liked them. My father and I often cried as we read them aloud to each other from the In Memoriam column of the *Bulletin* on a Friday night. Friday was also the night when Kiprianos fried his best hake and my father and I always had two cutlets each, and the combination of this fine fish with Offa Mogg on death and reunion beyond the grave always gave us happiness. Colenso often annoyed us by reciting the verses in a roistering, comic way, even the one we had ourselves bought on the fifth anniversary of my mother's death:

> Up in heaven a door'll go slam,
> You'll turn the knob and there'll be Mam.

He would also chant the one I had decided in advance to pick out for my father when he too would be a target for rhyme:

> You're lonely now, but don't be sad,
> Just wait awhile, we're coming, Dad.

I brought my coffee from the counter and sat down when I saw Offa put his notebook away. We said good night to Shiloh and Milton and I hoped for a lightening of Offa's face. I wanted him to reassure me about Lucas and Angela, to tell me that my spasm of hatred had been a stupid self-betrayal, not to be repeated, that I should now begin again to see life in its normal smooth, friendly light. But Offa's expression as he looked right into my smile did not change.

'We'll have to do something about that Lucas,' he said sombrely.

'Why, Offa? I don't suppose he's such a bad chap, really.'

'You're the last person who should be saying that, Stobo. The last person.' His eyes were hotter than my coffee, his look as black as Kiprianos' hair, a typical Mediterranean thatch which Kiprianos kept as well-oiled as his chips. 'I really put myself out for that Phillimore. I thought I saw the outlines of a gentleman there, as clearly as you can see anything since astygmatism became a trademark of this damned place in 1870. I wrote those things in the *Bulletin* praising him as the biggest thing in agricultural science since Jethro Tull and a social figure so laden with *bon ton* as to justify a place on the same mantelpiece as Sir Gwydion Pooley.'

'What's he done to annoy you, Offa?' I asked anxiously.

'I thought I had made a friend of him. I approached him in a very frank way and told him how glad we were that he had broken his exile up there on the hill, and then went on to give him what I thought would be a few useful tips and hints.'

'And coming from you they would be useful, Offa,' I said sincerely.

'That's what I thought, but not Phillimore. I told him that my brother Hadrian, a student of sanitary matters, was worried about the subnormal look of Blakemore's farm and that something might also be done to improve the status and appearance of your father, because as things stood those kids in the Centre to whom he talks about farming as a new life might take one look at his settlement and think farming some kind of Siberian exile, an even poorer prospect than the Remand Home.

'He just stood looking at me, very impressive, very dignified. I thought he was taking it all in and I was eager to go further. I told him that I was your friend and that he would do us all a favour if he didn't encourage Angela's infatuation.'

'Oh, don't worry about that, Offa. I had a chat with Angela. She says there's nothing in it but that her friendship with Lucas will deepen her understanding of life and make her a better wife and a greater actress.'

'Is that so? Don't be so innocent about it, Stobo. If you had heard the way that man turned on me you would revise your estimate of him. He told me that he and his cousin were gentry and that the state of the farm was his business, and that if he found Hadrian snooping around again he would dip him in the gravy and feed him to the dogs. About your father, he said that they had only kept him on because it is the habit of the gentry to be loyal to their older and more helpless servants. Then about Angela he said quite brazenly that he had been a great lover in seven counties of Britain and the only reason he had not set up in practice here was that so far he had not found any suitable subjects. There was a light in his eyes when he spoke those words that boded no good for Angela.'

I went to the counter for two more coffees and took some time over it, chatting with Kiprianos about a new brand of biscuit of which we had just had a consignment. I hoped that when I got back Offa would have come down from his high dramatic hill and started to see things in a more jocose light. But when I returned to the table he looked just the same, like Herod beginning to wonder about the other age-groups.

'He called me a vulgar prying pimp and said that when they had finished the duck-pond he would invite me up to open it.'

'Perhaps he meant that as an honour.'

'He meant that I'd get in there ahead of the ducks.' He tapped viciously on the marble table-top. 'But he'll be sorry he ever spoke to Offa Mogg in that way. I'm not the man to get on the wrong side of.'

'What are you planning, Offa?'

'Nothing specific. My programme always is to collect facts. Pile them up, up. When you've finished they will assume their own creative shape.'

'What facts are there to gather about Lucas?'

'Yesterday Shiloh and Milton Pertwee called on me and said that Miss Elvira Oxenham, who was once a housekeeper up there with Samson Blakemore, was ailing and in need of someone to talk to. So I went and listened.'

'What did she say?'

'What she said was full of drama. I wish our newspapers had a more unbuttoned viewpoint about the truth and fewer scruples about defamation. I'd have the whole vat of tar simmering for Phillimore. Elvira said that Samson has always been afraid of Lucas, as if Lucas had some kind of hold on him. When Lucas went away on that last job as steward in the north he got into a bit of trouble with money, and Samson had to sell a lot of stuff and put himself into debt to keep Lucas out of gaol. Lucas came back and it seemed that his one object was to get hold of all the happiness that ever existed on that farm and wring its neck.

'Mrs Blakemore was ill at the time but the three sons were a great help to Samson and they were not doing so badly. Lucas got a young girl up from the town to help Elvira with the housework. He exposed Samson to this girl. Samson, a very full-blooded voter and direct as a dog in these matters, had been an outcast sexually since his wife's illness and he fell in love with the girl. She kept him at arm's length and Lucas told Samson that this was because she was already being fully attended to by the two youngest sons.

'Lucas did a lot more to blacken relations between Samson and the sons, telling him that the boys were robbing him blind and wishing him dead so that they could modernise and make more out of the farm, and telling the lads that the old man would use them as cheap labour for ever and a day and then make a second marriage that would sink them without trace. The oldest boy, Martin, that big, gentle one, had all his work cut out trying to keep some sort of peace.

'Then Lucas persuaded the girl to give in to Samson, and one night they were having a to-do on the landing of all places. Are you following me, Stobo? There's a very glazed look on you, boy.'

'It's a terrible tale, Offa, but for your sake I'm listening.'

'Well, there they were and at just the right moment Lucas arranged that Mrs Blakemore and the two younger boys should burst in from different quarters and discover Samson *in delicto*. Samson, a sincere lover and an inept dissembler, was caught with all his defences down. This shock helped Mrs Blakemore to her end. There was a terrible quarrel between Samson and the two younger sons. They left, never to return. Martin found out where they had gone and was actually packing to go and fetch them back when he collapsed with that peritonitis and died.'

'All this sounds too rich for the blood to be true, Offa. What if this Elvira has some grudge against Phillimore which she is working out of her system in the form of lies?'

'A woman as near death as Elvira and who in her late middle age has gone back to the prickly shirt of chapel morality would not lie. The shadow fell over Blakemore's farm then. Lucas would fetch whisky up for Samson and he would drink himself savage and sullen talking to the ghosts of his wife and Martin and seeming to get answers and taking turns with Lucas at outraging Elvira who seems to have been quite fond of them both. During these brutal sessions in the kitchen Lucas kept the key of the door in his pocket. One night they were too much for Elvira and she cried for help. Your father, Stobo – listen to this, boy

– your father who was having a late sitting with the cows came in through the window to see what was wrong. Samson and Lucas beat him senseless, finding as much enjoyment in this as they had in Elvira. Often after that they would find some fault in your father's work and cuff him without mercy. Elvira asked your old man why he stood for it, why he didn't let them have one back with the milk stool or the manure fork. And do you know what he said?'

'Something reasonable, I bet. It takes a lot to goad him.'

'Too much, boy. He said, "Mr Blakemore is my friend; he is in grief; he is trying to scorch his grief to the dry bone of acceptance. If beating me and cursing me off will help him speed up the job, so be it." Honest to God, Stobo, I don't go all the way with Colenso Mortlake; I wouldn't dream of indicting a whole society, a whole class, on the basis of a few follies discovered in the lives of one or two loons; but I think your father's too much of it and should be cured.' Offa drained his coffee and fixed his eyes on me like a pair of suckers. 'Now we come to the real question, Stobo. What are we going to do about all this?'

'Do? What do you mean?'

'Your father outraged and your lover betrayed.'

'Oh, come on, Offa. Don't overload the course, boy. I know the news has been a bit thin lately but don't try to slip me in as a meat-cube.' I was itching with embarrassment at the load of tense implication that Offa was trying to lay on my shoulders.

Offa stood up, his face so hot with indignation that Kiprianos moved back from his tea urn, unable to stand the double blast.

'Stobo,' said Offa quietly, 'Man and nature both suffered betrayal and great hurt when your father consented to be such an accommodating and spineless character. I'm not going to let that happen to you. So if in the next few weeks you have an odd feeling in your rear, it will be me starching your backbone.'

'Don't worry about me. I'll fight for my rights.'

'You are coming with me tomorrow.'

'Where to?'

'To the bedroom of Miss Elvira Oxenham. It will make your hair stand on end to see her eyes blaze when she talks of the depravity of Lucas Phillimore. To think of that man exchanging as much as a word with Angela. Miss Oxenham, in her twilight, is very religious and she thinks she'll have to concentrate on godliness time and a half if she is to be forgiven for having associated with such an impious pair of oafs as those cousins.'

I had no wish to go to Miss Oxenham's bedroom. I wanted to concentrate on life and made a poor sick-visitor. I did not want to talk to her. I did not want my hatred for Lucas fed. I wished she had had the tact to drop down dead before she began to nourish Offa with this saga of Blakemore's farm.

'We're going to treat the old lady subtly,' said Offa.

'What for?' I spoke brusquely, as if begrudging Miss Oxenham anything but a quick jerk of her bed which would land her on the hard floor of truth and silent resignation.

'I want to worm out of her the secret of that hold Lucas has over Samson. There must be some dreadful facts rotting below that surface to explain Samson's acquiescing in such antics. She must know.'

I thought to myself bitterly that if she did not know now, she would as soon as Offa started to pump her. He seemed to stimulate the old girl more than religion.

14

I was to meet Offa at seven o'clock the following evening, and when the time came I was not sorry to leave the house. My father's friend, Leo Watham, had decided to take a hand in the education of that young element from next door, Wally Fletcher. He put Wally in a chair facing my father who, on instructions from Colenso who was stage-managing this tableau, was to stare at Wally with a look of smiling candour to encourage him to believe in the good life. Wally, who was a friendly, responsive boy, if in a fog ethically, would smile back at my father, and there were the two of them looking like a pair of runaways from the open air school.

The books that Leo found from which to read selected passages to Wally contained some of the most repulsive material I had ever heard. The purpose of these excerpts was to convince Wally that crime does not pay and to my ears, sensitive to any propaganda in favour of decency, they made crime move about bare and bankrupt, looking for a client. If the readings did not ram the moral home to Wally, who never paid enough attention to get the full point, they had a powerful effect on everybody else who called in to our kitchen. Leo stuck to books that showed the terrible end to which criminals came, books with titles like: *Secrets of the Guillotine*; *A Walk at Nine: My Life as a Hangman*; or *Never Again*, by some lag of eighty who had finished his last stretch at seventy-nine and now lacked the strength to challenge the police or anything else. While Leo was putting a lot of dramatic force into these recitals to persuade Wally that he might as well listen to Ventris Lee and stop acting the goat, Wally would be spreading happiness among the company by handing out packets of cigarettes and sweets which he had probably lifted an hour before from the shop of Thorold Wigley.

Leo's purpose was to terrify Wally with his untiring record of voters being hanged, and I agreed with Colenso when he told Leo that his approach in this matter was altogether too negative, that he should try to give Wally a happier mental frame than a mere urge to dive into the hedge at the sight of anything that looked like a gibbet. The effect of the readings on me was black, especially when they started to ferment inside the strange disquieting thoughts I was beginning to have about Lucas.

My dreams were drenched in Newgate showers. I could see myself luring Lucas into the shop and watching with sickened eyes as he gaily and Mr Ellicott feebly alternated in the possession of Mrs Chiddle, who would often in mid-dream lose her stout shapelessness and come to look like Angela. Then I would take some of the rat-poison from the warehouse, test Lucas and Mr Ellicott for tail, slip the stuff into two tumblers of the tonic wine and serve it to them. The scene of their writhing and dying would dim into one in the condemned cell with Melancthon Mills reading tract after tract to me and spinning with shock as the warder broke in and said that Wally Fletcher had made off with the rope and that Royston Angove had been seen about the town with a load of firewood that looked very like gallows board.

Or I would see myself in some terrifying climactic

— 147 —

quarrel with Angela. This was a dream that usually came after cheese, done in the Dutch oven with bacon, and very rich. As I raged at her my body grew until I towered over her. As I did so, my body cast off my ordinary working clothes and put on either a military uniform or hunting scarlet, and as my fingers closed round Angela's neck her mother would come up to me, grin approvingly at my new gigantic size, finger my new costume with pride and glee and tell me that I was now something like a son-in-law, one of whom Lucas was but the shadow. I thanked her with a salute or a tally-ho which always interfered with the work I was doing on Angela. I never got to the point in my dream where I choked her, but I could feel the urge to do so in my fingers all the time.

These dreams worried me to a point where I found myself calling in at The Thinker and the Thrush for a glass of stout and a serious, reassuring talk with the licensee's husband, Hugo Farnum, a leading clerk with the Council and a man lucidly censorious about most things on this earth including the drink trade with which he had only accidentally become associated on marriage.

But Leo could be reading fairy stories for all the effect they had on Wally. He would chew away at his toffees and nod his head cheerfully at round after round of Leo's epics of detection and snapped spines. He seemed greatly interested in the hangmen, inquiring after their names and habits, and asking how long exactly the job took them and what it paid. 'A short day,' he said when Leo gave him a rough estimate.

'Look boy,' said Leo angrily, 'just fix your mind on the voter on the trap who is expiating with his neck just the kind of flippancy of which you are the local trademark. Never mind the hangman. He's just the knell of doom.'

'I was just thinking he gets a short day. Look how tired my old man gets, and you and Mr Wilkie. And still you're mostly short of fags. How could I get such a job as this boy with the noose?'

'You could go to that element Jethro Patton on the Vacancies Counter at the Labour Exchange and, after explaining to him your bias against productive labour, tell him you fancy hanging people. Jethro would then short-circuit you to the County Mental and I can't say that would be such a wrong address for a rodney like you.'

'Have a butterball, Mr Watham,' said Wally holding out a paper bag and sounding very earnest.

Colenso was most interested in the shattered look with which I had been going about since my break with Angela. He spoke to me softly in a corner of the kitchen. 'I'm glad,' he said. 'That Mrs Lang, Stobo, is a maniac and a menace. There is a seam of pure Bovaric waste in the mind of the under-privileged and that woman is the very heart of it. Psychologically she's been riding to hounds for the last twenty years and she's been using poor old Lyndhurst as her hired horse, which accounts for the wan, tired look you see on that voter. Just think what it means to be working on an ashcart or that macadam plant and then having your wife plant her mouth on your ear and blow rhapsodies of aristocratic longings into it day in and day out, moaning that some trick of seminal chance has put her in the wilderness where she has no right to be, where she stays only because her marriage to the poor serf, Lyndhurst, has nailed her feet to the foul ground of exile.

'Logically and fairly such delusions should induce a quick and deadly poison in the veins of the poor bats who harbour them. But with that boy Lucas on the scene some crisis may well be provoked that will shake the opium out of her teeth.'

'Crisis?' I asked, not really wanting to know but asking all the same.

'I saw her last night,' said Wally, who had the gift of sticking his ear into two or three conversations at the same time and listening to what one was quite privately saying. Leo at that moment was talking with force about the murderer Landru whose career, although on a plane of grim thoroughness which Wally had not yet attempted, had its root in the same kind of pilfering as was committed thoughtlessly by the young. Lyndhurst and my father were simultaneously feeding Wally with supplementary material about some voter in Bandy Lane who had started off quite innocently taking stuff from the handier counters in Woolworth's. He left the store after his first raid so laden with loot he had needed two people to help him through the door and was caught by some old voter on a crutch when the alarm was given by an assistant who discovered she had nothing left but the till. This performer wound up on a landing arguing with his father, a man full of texts and recriminations. The landing was small and the texts bitter; to get a bit of peace he pushed his father down the stairs and ended up being turned off in the County Keep. Wally's only answer to this was that Woolworth's wasn't on his beat. As for the episode on the landing, the staircase at his home was too narrow for any debate and in any case his father was on the torpid side and never argued with anyone. But despite all this talk from Leo and Lyndhurst, Wally had also been able to follow what Colenso and I had been saying. 'I saw her last night,' he said.

'Who?' asked Colenso and I together.

'That Angela. Your girl, Stobo.'

'Where?' I asked, and I was conscious again of

falling into two separate halves, the one cudgelling Wally into silence with masterful brutality for having dared to trespass into an estate of private longing, the other half doing business at its forlorn old booth of vulnerable ordinariness. 'Where, Wally?'

'Coming out of The Thinker and the Thrush.'

'There's nothing in that,' said Colenso. 'Angela is a friend of Mrs Farnum.'

'She was with that bloke who talks to us about foxes and wars, Phillimore the farmer.' Wally sucked at his toffee, moaning with delight as loudly as Mrs Chiddle as the sugar pressed against his palate. 'There's a soap pill for you, that element. A noble. Very lah-di-dah and no messing. A voice that comes right up from his boots. A soap-pill.'

'Where did they go?' I asked.

'Up that lane behind The Thinker. I see a lot of people who come out of The Thinker go up that lane.'

I crouched over the table, making a terrible racket with my teeth on the dry toast I was eating, serving notice to all the people in the kitchen that I did not wish to be spoken to. I could still hear Wally calmly telling Leo that he had already heard the story of John Lee, the man they could not hang.

I finished my meal, washed and dressed. Colenso asked me if I would like him to come out with me and discuss what should be done in the matter of my tangled personal affairs but I had sufficient self-control left to tell him that I did not want to get my affairs more tangled and I should be grateful to have him nowhere near me.

'Take me or leave me,' Colenso said, 'but I still think it would be the best thing on earth for your kidneys if you told Angela and her mother to go and jump in one of the deeper eddies of the Moody and then took a torch up the mountain and connected with the shirt-tails of those farming cousins.'

'Colenso,' I said, 'every time I ignore you, it is a victory won.'

I went out. I met Offa in Bandy Lane Square. We set off in the direction of Miss Elvira Oxenham's home. He kept saying that our main task would be to worm out of Miss Oxenham what the hold was that Lucas had over Blakemore.

'What exactly would you do with this information if you had it, Offa? What we want is a hold on Phillimore.'

He made no reply. He just looked masterful in a sly way and it struck me that there was in Offa very little of that ordinary urge to use his knowledge of people to promote an increase of changed traffic between him and them. He peered into their closets because he was interested in closets. He liked the startled, then dependent look of people who glanced up and found Offa standing right under the light of their sacred reticence. 'It's amazing,' he said. 'Practically any fact you uncover about people rattles their bones.' And he looked delighted at the prospect of taking one more step into the savage thicket of Bandy Lane's interlocking privacies.

When we arived at Miss Oxenham's the house was full of voters of a respectable, earnest kind, all members of a fervent sect in Bandy Lane called the Rousers, friendly and very vocal. They had large premises with a great white lantern outside on which was written: 'God is Love. God is Light. Keys next door.' And on the other facet: 'Death is Silence. The Enemy is Silence. Make a Glad Noise.' These people set great store on hymns of a happy kind with a small, easily grasped moral and emphatic gestures.

Their chief organiser was one of our local

undertakers, Pandolph Treasure, a brisk voter and so blithe as to be altogether out of character with his trade. He had been stung by charges of having a stake in death and cleverly manoeuvring people into the Black Meadow when dividends were down. So he had brought the Rousers into being to keep the dying amused and defiant and, if nature decided to drop off anyway, to sing the victim on his way to the Meadow in a way that would give a certain grace to bereavement and banish the muffled, oppressive muteness of our average funeral party.

The very first time they tried that tactic nearly finished off the Rousers as a new sect. It was the funeral of Shiloh's brother, Pwyll Pertwee. He, like his brother and cousin, had spent many years as a plumber fixing washerless taps and incontinent pipes in a remote, fey, pixie-ridden valley to the west, in which occupation he had acquired a gift of prevision in the matter of death so accurate he made doom sound like a bus service with this boy in charge of the timetable. He had been one of the first to join the Rousers but without any conviction that anything could really be done to chip or whittle the marble melancholy that forms in the inmost heart of man. One winter he foresaw his own death and counted so many prophetic corpse candles leaving the house that he resigned from his section of the ARP because these air-raid wardens are against unmasked lights. Then after a gruelling experience in an attic with some voter's cistern he collapsed and was certified as dead by a doctor who had long ceased to be fussy about the deeper, more essential differences between life and death. For this element if you were not up singing and working you were for the box.

The funeral was arranged. Pandolph Treasure said that, although his business was so bad that he might as well be running his own tapes over it, he would escort Pwyll to his last resting place with a heavy heart. It was a golden day for Milton and Shiloh and they allowed themselves to do what they had always wanted to, march right in front with the undertaker. From the word go, Pandolph had the entire body of mourners singing, especially when they reached the gates of the Meadow where the damp chill of the hillside and the continuous drip of moisture from the cypresses threatened a climax of helpless misery that drove many voters to outraged, defensive protests. Then the people heard a kind of steady drumming. At first they thought it was Pandolph giving them the beat and they were glad. Then they noticed that Pandolph had no wood to be beating on and that the drumming did not correspond with the rhythm of their song. They brought his attention to the sound. Their ears drew them to the hearse. Pandolph got the lid off and there was Pwyll, worn out but still alive. He was hurried home and restored to fair health but with a more passionate objection to the dark than before.

Miss Oxenham was in the front bedroom. There were Rousers crowding the landing, the stairway and even the front room. This was one of the most wanton bits of sick-visiting I had ever seen and I told Offa that it was distressing that with a very ill woman upstairs these voters should be cluttering up the house and carrying on as if they were on Bandy Lane station waiting for an excursion train. Pandolph Treasure explained that one of the functions of the sect was to scare away the ravens of gloom and fear by organising festivals of song at the very bedside of the stricken until disease had gone or death had come. Offa whispered to me that in some of the small brittle homesteads of the town the sect's singing had been so loud and so good that the sick and dying had been shuffled off before time by sheer vibration.

Pandolph rapped on the banister rail to prepare his followers for the down beat and took them at a breathless tempo into 'Come Lasses and Lads' sung to words of a religious bent written, Offa told me, by Pandolph himself. This arrangement of the old dance measure went:

> Come, banish death's sting,
> Come forth now and sing!

'That's subtle,' said Offa ironically. ' "Sting" and "sing". I bet Pandolph kept his head on ice for a week after coming up with that rhyme. Just listen to the racket these Rousers make! I admire Pandolph, but he can say what he likes, this isn't in good taste. Impending death has as much right to be treated with a bit of gentility as anything else.'

All the people round us were going full out, bringing their bodies closer, making a sweeping gesture of the arm to signify banishment and then raising the arm on 'Sing'. It made the little house shudder with the noise and seem painfully crowded. Offa winced. 'You ought to see Elvira,' he said, 'so small, so frail, like thistledown. With the volume of breath being driven up the stairs by Treasure she's probably being bounced against the bedroom ceiling like a ping-pong ball.'

They sang for an hour, then left us in peace. Miss Oxenham was propped up in bed, wearing several layers of bed-jacket, pink, white and blue. She had been excited by the singing and was smiling gaily although she was, as Offa had said, little more than a wisp and her eyes were as faded as the bottom bed jacket, an old article.

Offa explained that I was interested in her

experiences as housekeeper to the Blakemores in the old days and when he said 'the Blakemores' he winked at her and made it sound like a suburb of the jungle. She went over the ground that had already been covered by Offa but seemed to be throwing in details that had not been there before. Except when she cried, or sang to us in a voice thin as an eggshell songs that had been favourites with Martin Blakemore, she seemed to derive a lot of happiness from her recital, and I could see that having a confidant as smooth and patient as Offa had done this woman more good than any tonic. 'We have been wondering,' said Offa, in a voice softer than the crimson silken counterpane, 'what could have been the secret that enabled Lucas to be tolerated for so long in the Blakemore home?'

Miss Oxenham blushed and turned her face to the wall. I found myself looking at a pile of women's magazines on a bedside table. On the cover of the top one was a picture of an old lady not unlike Miss Oxenham, grey, neat and precise, and underneath the words: 'What was Old Nannie's Secret?' I stared at this for so long that when I returned ny eyes to the bed I almost said, 'Out with it, Nannie.'

'I couldn't bear to tell,' said Miss Oxenham. 'It was too terrible.'

Offa did not press his demand. He smoothed out some creases in the counterpane. Then he fixed a little metal table over her legs, mixed a yellow glucose drink and unwrapped a bar of chocolate. Miss Oxenham made a gesture when she heard the tinfoil being torn. Offa, quicker to understand than I, snapped off some of the chocolate for us. I chewed away, my normal cautiousness buried, almost suicidal as I contemplated how my whole life was being made as varicose as Mr Ellicott's legs by all this intrigue and uncertainty.

Then Miss Oxenham turned deadly pale, her face

pressed into the pillow, blown into shrinking by some wind of pain or fear or regret and I was gripped by a realisation of the crass autumnal banalities of life in its further, quieter reaches. I would have wished to give a quick consoling clasp to the small insignificant hand that appeared moving in fitful helplessness above the counterpane. I would have wished to take it in the sudden assertion of sympathetic love that was trying to find a path for itself inside me, the kind of impulse that had grown blind and oafish since my mother's death. But I made no move, frozen in my embarrassed solitude, wishing myself dead or back behind the counter with nothing more poignant than the profit margin to crochet a black shroud for my heart.

'I wish Mr Treasure were still here,' said Miss Oxenham. 'He and his friends make me feel so happy.' She began to sing in the tiniest voice you will ever hear this side of the wainscoting:

> And when our songs are on the breezes blown,
> I am no longer afraid, no longer alone.

And she glanced at us as if to say that after the high anaesthetic winds of Pandolph Treasure and his crew she found something muffled and disquieting about the way we looked. I tugged Offa's coat to tell him that I wished to be off. But all he did was bend over, doing a bit of tender fussing with the bedclothes; then he spoke to her in a voice which equalled for throbbing urgency anything I ever heard from the voters who often speak in this way from the screens of the Comfy and the Cosy.

'Miss Oxenham,' he said, 'do you know my friend Stobo Wilkie?'

'Oh, yes, I know Stobo.' The eyes she turned on me

were so faded now they looked as if they were hanging on consciously but not fanatically to the last of their light. 'I know his father Wyndham Wilkie who is still employed as Mr Blakemore's milkman. He had a kind way with the animals.'

'You can help Stobo,' said Offa. 'A lot in this boy's life depends on it. We sense something dark and menacing in the lives of those two up on the hillside. It has soured Blakemore to a point where the only thing that gives him refreshment is to torment Mr Wilkie. Also Phillimore, to whose lecherous tendencies you have more than once made reference, is now taking a serious interest in Stobo's girl friend, Angela Lang, an actress of promise and a flower of innocence.'

Miss Oxenham looked at me in a strange worldly-wise way. She blinked her eyes. 'What I have to tell is too terrible for your ears.'

Offa blinked too and smiled as if this were going to be even better than he had thought. He put his finger to his lips as if to suggest that we would not press her and nipped down to prepare a light supper for her. I stared at the magazine, feeling curious about the serial to which the picture of the lady like Miss Oxenham belonged. I was just going to pick it up and start reading when Offa returned with two poached eggs puffed up to the size and quality of meringues.

Miss Oxenham ate them with what I took to be a gross and inappropriate haste. Then, after wiping her mouth with the air of making a final preparation, she said, quite plainly: 'I was the mistress of both Mr Blakemore and Mr Phillimore.'

I went in my mind through some possible ways of answering this statement. 'Oh? No! Get away! Well, well!' None fitted and I gave up.

Offa was nodding away and looking at Miss

Oxenham with compassion as if to say that it is the fate of beauty to be exploited.

'In their way, Mr Mogg, both those men loved me deeply.'

'I'm sure they did.'

'I was always patient with Master Lucas. He was so young, always the wild devil, the lover who would come for you on a white horse, if you follow.'

'We follow, Miss Oxenham,' we both said solemnly.

'And they both...?' said Offa.

'Both. But the child I bore was Mr Blakemore's. Master Lucas was away at the time taking his mare Jezebel to the different county shows.'

'The child?!'

'A rare mare, Jezebel, full of fire and fight, a she-devil.'

'The child?' said Offa again and I could see that he felt as I did that we would get the gist better if Miss Oxenham would stop lugging horses into her tale.

'Oh yes, I paid the full price for my soft, tender nature.'

Offa patted her pillow. 'You're a woman who has suffered, Miss Oxenham. It is always the loveliest who are laid lowest by life.'

'That's a nice saying, Mr Mogg.'

I knew that Offa's saying came from Thorold Wigley's calendar about flowers which bloom but briefly, but I was glad that Offa had thought of it and that we were finally coming close to some black revelation about Lucas.

'Where is the child, Miss Oxenham? If there is anything we can do...'

'Nothing. Nothing, now. The child is dead. My boy is dead. Mr Blakemore wished him to live...' Her voice was now a whisper. Its life seemed to have drained away to feed the returning brightness of her eyes.

'But Lucas said no. He was always the cruel, hard one, was Master Lucas.'

'What happened, Miss Oxenham? Tell us, please. We want justice. We are justice. We must know.'

'It was when Mrs Blakemore was ill. When she found out about my condition she rose from her bed to drive me from the house. I can see her now at the top of the stairs, standing there in her nightshift, pink like mine now. Her mouth was twisted, her hair black and hanging. She tried to scream at me but the sound did not come. All she could do was moan and lift up her shift showing how thin she was with grief and pain. Oh, it was terrible. Master Lucas came in and saw her. He laughed. Martin came in and rushed at Lucas. He stepped out of the way and sent Martin senseless to the floor with a blow to the neck. Mrs Blakemore fainted away and I rushed up the stairs to help her. The little life inside me was fluttering and throbbing with fear.

'Mr Blakemore was sitting at the table doing his accounts because he had given up paying any attention to his wife who was now very queer. Your father was there too, boy. He saw it all. He knows. As I ran up the stairs as fast as I could Master Lucas shouted to Mr Blakemore and pointed at me: "A few more trips like that Samson and she'll drop before her time and save us a lot of trouble." A hard man, Lucas.' She put her feather-light hand on mine. 'Save your girl from Lucas, my son. He will destroy her. Save her from him.'

'I will, by God I will.' I felt the drama of my mood bursting its seams. 'As God is my judge I will.'

'And the child?' asked Offa.

'It was kept secret. I had no help to bring it into this world. It was not allowed to live.'

'You mean those two... killed your baby?'

— 160 —

'It was not allowed to live.'

'What did they do with it?'

'It was buried.'

'Where, Miss Oxenham, where?'

'You know the very big apple tree behind the farm?'

'I know. The cookers.'

'At its foot. Find it. Give it my love. Tell him...' She was crying bitterly.

'Oh, this will be a pill for Phillimore! This will save Angela. We'll dig up the evidence, Miss Oxenham. The warrant will be out for both of those rodneys.'

'No!' she said, her arm at full length pointing at Offa. 'Never!'

'What do you mean? Do you want those two to go unpunished?'

'For as long as I live silence will rest on what I have said. Swear!'

'All right, we swear.' Offa was winking at me but I thought it was very out of place and in any case it was clear that with Miss Oxenham's awareness stretched like a tuned harp nothing escaped her. If Offa had gone up on the roof to wink, the hint of mockery would not have been lost on her.

'When I am dead,' she said, and her voice grew shrill, 'charge! In the meantime, fetch me the Bible.' I fetched the bible that she indicated and she joined Offa's and my hands upon it. She was trembling violently with excitement and I could detect little misery in her attitude. 'Silence!' she said.

'Silence,' we repeated.

The neighbour who was her only nurse came in, whipping us with her tongue when she saw Miss Oxenham in tears. She drove us away.

'By God,' said Offa as we walked away from the house, 'this will rock Bandy Lane. And it will cure

Angela of the urge to have truck with anybody but you. And it'll show Lucas. Do you know what he called you, Stobo?'

'No.' I tried to sound as if I did not care. These taunts are driven into the mind like pegs and before you know it you are using them to rig up some fresh tent of obsession.

'He called you the bastard with the buttery chops. Imagine your old man keeping his tongue still on those secrets all these years.'

'He must have been daft,' I said bitterly.

'No, no. Loyal. A fine, lovable fault. The cement between master and man. Without that, Stobo, we'd be right in the clay.'

'When do we go into action, Offa?' I had not liked the complacency of his last words. There is a time to be speaking to the Chamber of Trade about the need for social cohesion and a time not to. 'I want my hands at the throat of that sneering sod. I want to see the look on Angela's face when I shout the news at her.'

'Patience, boy. I'm not saying that I don't believe Miss Oxenham. But you've got to go through this life, Stobo, feeling that death and a libel suit are the two great certainties.'

'All right then. Let's get tools and go up to that apple tree.'

'All that that would get you is a summons from Blakemore for trying to make off with part of his orchard.'

'Look Offa, I'm getting to know you, boy. It doesn't seem to matter to you that those two elements up on the hill might have committed the supreme offence, that they've treated my old man like dirt, that at this moment Angela is in danger of losing her diadem. All you want is information to whisper about. Well that's not good enough. I want to shout, I want to draw blood. If you're not going to dig for that proof, I am. Tomorrow evening I'll go up there and confront Phillimore with the gruesome relic.'

Offa nodded agreeably as he heard these phrases which were honoured features of the *Bulletin*. Then he frowned. 'Listen, Stobo, I hold sacred the promise we gave Miss Oxenham. When she put her shrivelled hand in ours on the Good Book, that was one of the most moving moments I've had in my life and I'd cut my right arm off and as much of yours as I could get hold of before betraying her trust.' We were under a lamppost. He waited for a slow-moving man to pass, then drew himself to his full height, which made him taller than me by the depth of his hair. 'If you betray a promise made to a dying woman, I'll hound you out of this town like a dog. For God's sake let's have a bit of reverence around here. When Miss Oxenham is dead we'll take our lamps and we shall find out how dead the past really is. Until then, not a word.'

He left me.

I walked about without making in any particular direction. I had no wish to go home. I would have questioned my father about his years at the farm, but I did not wish to do that in front of Colenso who would have lost no time in goading me about Lucas and whipping me up into some kind of mischief. The moon had risen. I walked up the broad, beech-lined road that led up the hill that lay on Bandy's western flank. The road was still and lovely but not soothing to my nerves which were being grilled by my longings. The shadows were full of competent lovers, some of them motionless and groaning, some of them coming out with words of sharp joy in the fullness of their union. I recalled something that Colenso had told me about Bandy Lane being, at all levels of activity, one of the most articulate places in the history of speech. Hearing those lovers I agreed with Colenso and ached to be uttering the same words under the same impulsion.

I ran down into the town towards Angela's house. There was a light in the front room and the sound of music. I did not knock but went straight in. Angela was at the piano. She was playing very softly the accompaniment of a song called 'Thou'rt passing hence, my brother', a very sad piece and a great favourite in Bandy Lane which was, psychologically, in a constant state of seeing someone off. Her father was standing by the piano, his hands on his lapels, singing. Lyndhurst was dressed in his blue suit and I could see that he had been to The Thinker and The Thrush. Oswald and Edgar were sitting on the mat by the fire, playing with the maimed remains of a meccano set. They hummed a vague accompaniment to their father's singing and when I helped them out with my own unassertive but accurate tenor I felt the whole atmosphere become warmer, more secure.

Angela turned from her playing and smiled at me. I touched Lyndhurst on the shoulder in an extreme fit of affection, encouraged by her smile. 'She has seen through Lucas,' I thought. 'She has seen the white line on the water where the rock of peril lies. From now on, Stobo, you'll burn with a brighter flame, boy. If it's excitement and romance she wants, you will supply these articles.'

When the song ended Angela got up from the piano. She told her father and brothers that there was tea on the hob but old enough now to darken the stomach of a graven image, and some bread pudding and toast in the pantry. She put her arm on my shoulder as she often did. I was so relieved I could have cried directly into her bosom, though I knew I would have found such a manoeuvre hard to perform with any ease or accuracy. 'Is it all right now, Angela?' I whispered.

'What do you mean "all right"?'

'With you and me. You know.'

'No, Stobo, it's not. I'm going away with Mr Phillimore. I've had enough of all this, of you, of my mother, well, of all this, and don't ask me to explain why all over again. I'm going off with him, first chance.'

The hottest speech of all time was under my tongue, making my whole head wince and rock. Whole sentences from Elvira Oxenham's narrative were in my mind, ready to move to the exposure of Lucas. But into my mind came the face of Offa Mogg, his brows right down, dandling the thunderbolts he would let fly at me if I allowed my malice to make unprovable charges and stir up unseasonable scandals.

For the second time that week I left Angela's house as if I had been blown out.

15

The following days were hard to get through. Business was brisk. Many people came into the shop whom I had not seen before and they looked at me in marked, significant ways, some with curiosity, some with sympathy. The increase in trade and attention to myself did a lot to ease the pressure which, unrelieved and suffered in solitude, would have put me through the doors of the County Mental like a bullet. Since hearing the news from Angela I had barely exchanged a word with anybody. With the customers I maintained a minimum of courtesy and as soon as closing time came I escaped from the shop, had a hot pie and a pot of tea at Kiprianos' and slipped out of the town.

I took that climbing road up the western hill, through the thick flanks of beech and oak. I fed my demand for some dramatic climax on its silence and shadows. At the crest of the hill, the land fell sharply away on the other side, forming a small valley, dyked some years before to form a reservoir. The water gave a heart to the night and as I stood there alone and looked down on it I cursed the civic zeal which had kept me too busy at the Social Centre with Melancthon and Dunkerly to bring Angela up here more often. Feasted on beauty as serene as that, our relations would soon have advanced beyond the point where they could be broken by the intervention of such a man as Lucas.

A wide sweep of white motor road embraced the lake on its southern side. Halfway down the slope to the water's edge was a tavern, The Kindly Light. It was an old house, quiet, cool, little frequented, whose windows in winter cast their rays, lovely in their solitariness, over the lake. I often finished my walks in the bar parlour of The Kindly Light, talking with the landlord, Rollo Treweeks, a very interesting and useful man to be with at moments when life seems intent only on finding your thumbs in order to hang you by them.

Treweeks was a well dressed, cultivated man who did a lot of reading, whose mind, to me, seemed to have taken on something of the green, tranquil richness of the little valley in which he lived. He owned the hillside on which his tavern stood and was partner in a sawmill at Bandy Lane which dealt with the trees felled in the woods surrounding The Kindly Light. He was glad to see me come into the tavern for he was busy only during the summer months when coach trips brought him a full house.

My talks with Rollo during that period were just what I wanted because with him there was no danger that I might be lured into any explicit, dangerous revelation of my trouble. Treweeks's weakness, which came out in all his conversations, was concern about the shrinking of the earth's fertility and the reckless increase of man's issue, especially in Asia and the eastern half of Bandy Lane. That theme robbed him of sleep. When I made some observation about fertilisers, he tut-tutted. The only reliable source, the horse, was dying out and he reckoned from watching some horses in and around Bandy Lane that even these were growing more niggardly on a conscious, anti-human basis. Chemical substitutes he denounced as leading to all sorts of new organic diseases so repellent that the life-force might just as well shut up shop and have done with the whole confusing business. But it was superfluous breeding that made him, towards the end of an evening, lyrical and prophetic, and when I gave out a quiet hint one night that the perfidy of my sweetheart might now make it impossible that I should marry, he gave me a sort of respectful salute and handed me a light ale on the house.

'Those people in India and China! Good God, I've often denounced our own prolies for their idiot habits and fancies: football, darts and Sunday papers of the shallower sort. But better that than the way those Asiatics carry on. Seven times a day, that's what I was told by a man who stood just where you are standing now and he was still blinking when he told me. Give me darts any time. Consuming the whole earth with our great, damned, dirty, carious, insatiable mouth! I'm getting on; I may never get out of here. But if you do, Wilkie, tell them to stop it. Tell them that continence is more than one half of wisdom.'

'I'll tell them that, Mr Treweeks.'

'Thank you, my boy.' And he would shake my hand, moving his head with great relief as if I had taken some monstrous weight from his mind.

Four days after the thunderclap from Angela, Rollo offered me a job as his assistant barman and clerk to the various scattered elements of his business interests. The latter part of the offer took my fancy and I thought it would be a good, attractive gesture at that moment to immure myself in the tiny secure valley, but I never could have stomached being a barman. Basically I am not at ease with people who are either drunk or high spirited. A rather slow witted, earnest world would suit me well.

I never started back for Bandy Lane from The Kindly Light until about ten, and by the time I got home my father and Colenso were in bed and I was spared the need to discuss anything with them. But Colenso was not inactive. I found from the glances and odd remarks from customers in the shop that the affair of Angela, Lucas and myself was being built up into an arresting plot. Helping Colenso, but not consciously, was Dunkerly Dodge who in the long round of his visits as a club collector found any item as dramatic as this grist to his mill. He held people so spellbound as he talked to them about Angela that they often found at the end that he had covertly guided their fingers through a signature that committed them to another club contribution.

Dunkerly's line was to depict Angela as an eaglet of talent. It had only been a matter of time before her wings grew so wide they would burst her cage and take her off to the sky where the full force of her beauty and genius could soar unshackled. She had been destined from the start to outgrow all the small, squalid impediments that had reduced her progress so far to a crawl. I heard that Dunkerly had, in some quarters, included me on the list of impediments, and I noticed some of his clients, inspired by these narratives, coming into the shop and bending over the counter as I served them to see if I was as small and squalid as they had imagined.

I regarded these remarks by Dunkerly as treachery and resolved that I would settle with him. But just after making that decision I found myself talking to his wife, a woman of such fragility and distinction that I was ashamed of the sawdust on the floor. She had just come in with her customary large order and as I parcelled up her goods I spoke of Dunkerly more flatteringly than ever before, glad to wash the strange momentary spleen from my mind.

To Colenso the whole business was meat and drink. He pictured me as being at heart a rebel who had been tempted to take on an artificial colouring by a quirk of historical development, the emergence of a local bourgeoisie eager to exploit the disillusion that had attended the collapse of the old syndicalism and social fractiousness. When he used those terms on me I got the wind so badly I had to rush out to Kiprianos' and get a glass of hot peppermint, treble-strength. He made out that I was idling away on the butter counter gifts that would have shown to better effect on the barricades, and he showed me rough plans of these articles in case I should ever swing back to normal and decide to put one up under Sir Gwydion Pooley's nose.

I had, he said, tried for years to be a lick-spittle, and

there were few things in Bandy Lane that were not a lot cleaner for my diligence in that role. I had even, in my efforts to make my spine agreeably soft and my flesh acceptably flavoured to such toadies as Melancthon and such pundits as Sir Gwydion, allowed my own father to become the chopping block of two degenerate moujiks. But, in the heart of every proletarian lad who has been exposed for even an instant to the true creative doctrine of social change through class advance, there was a flint from which fire would be struck under the impact of the right event. In my case that event had now come in the form of Angela's betrayal by Lucas. (Colenso and Leo Watham left me in no doubt as to what was going on in that lane behind The Thinker and the Thrush.) I would now be seen springing into action like a panther, small in the body but long in the claw, battering the heads of Blakemore and Phillimore with a rain of pickle jars before moving in for the final blow with a whole Caerphilly cheese.

In these prophecies Colenso made adroit use of the area's immediate and regrettable past, slipping the stitches out of wounds that had stopped throbbing many years before and making the decent-thinking people of the town wish they had used a stronger thread or used the needle directly on Colenso. People who had been reasonably quiescent under a tumulus of political and industrial compliance for a whole decade were seen to stir and finger away at the clods when they heard Colenso's references to me as a revolutionary spirit and one of the most harassed moments of my life was when I was approached by Nestor Nicholas, one of our policemen, a slow talker who specialised in looking around corners suddenly and fixing you with a stare so full of implications it would have made a side of ham feel guilty.

Nestor looked in at me several times before he finally came to the counter and said that he had discussed my case with his inspector and that it would be as well for me if I guarded against being dragged into the schemes of that Machiavellian mole, Colenso Mortlake.

'Good Lord, Mr Nicholas,' I said, offering him a chocolate cream, 'do you think I'd ever do anything like that? If Mortlake even says anything that's a bit over the mark, I'll be down at the station to tell you like a shot.'

'Thank you, boy,' said Nestor and he put his great hand into the bottle of chocolate creams as coolly as if he were doing it in his sleep. The he laid his slow, sad, suspicious eyes on everybody in the shop and rattled the spike of his helmet on the festoon of buckets over the door as he left.

When I got home that evening Colenso, watched by my father whose face was fixed in a smile of admiration, was repairing an old wireless set on the table. Seated on the sofa were Wally Fletcher and Royston Angove. Their faces showed as much pleasure at the deft manoeuvres of Colenso's hands as my father's. 'What are they doing in here?' I asked spitefully, looking for some reason to fly into a rage.

'Wally says he found the wireless in an ash bucket and he wants to have it fixed up for that old widow who lives in the house that looks like a chicken-cot.'

'Where do they say they found it? An ash-bin, did you say?' My voice was bulging with disbelief and I was glaring at the two boys like one of those prophets whose names are unknown because they burn themselves out before they can leave anything in writing. They just smiled across at me. After Ventris Lee they found me as easy to manage as a toffee.

'Yes, I'm going to believe it,' said Colenso. 'Most of

the parts were rusty or shattered.'

'Probably broken when they tore it out of the owner's grasp.'

'Oh no. Put some tram-oil on your nerves, boy. They are screaming. Don't be so uncharitable. These lads are doing a Christian act. Mrs Enoch will find the wireless as incredible as Marconi would have found her.'

'When giving advice, Colenso, I think I know as much about a man's Christian duty as you do. What's more, don't go spreading any more talk around this town of what I'm going to do to Lucas Phillimore. Please understand that much as I care for Angela I care even more for law and decency.'

'What's been happening now?'

'I had a visit from Nestor Nicholas. He looked at me as if I were some kind of hooligan. Told me he has his eye on me. Took eight chocolate creams to get his gall back to normal. That's what your wild daft talk gets me: watched by the police!'

'Don't worry. If Nestor had a telescope he'd still be like a bat.'

'Just mind your own business.'

Colenso put down his pliers. 'I will,' he said quietly. 'I've given up trying to find the answer to your case, Stobo. But I'll be really sorry if you do nothing about this crisis. Quite apart from the fact that I would like to see Phillimore on his butt and your father repaid for all the mucking about he's had to take from those two moral dwarfs, the effect of doing nothing about all this is going to be bad for you. At the moment your mind is full of keeping your nose clean at Ellicott's, of keeping in well with such conformists as Melancthon Mills and Nestor Nicholas, but if this Lucas goes off with your girl, the fact will grow into you like a thorn and ten, fifteen years from now, when she'll have come a cropper and your father'll be too dead to create a problem, you'll be rushed into the hospital with a septic heart.'

'Oh, go to hell!' I shouted and made for the door. I came back and stood in front of Wally and Royston. 'Forget you heard me say that, you two. You see what you've made me do, Colenso. I've used bad language before lads I'm supposed to be an example to.'

Wally and Royston were both looking full of sympathy. 'Don't worry about us, Stobo,' said Wally. 'We're bloody hopeless, Royston and me.'

I left the house. Dusk was feeling about the town for a grip. I saw Angela boarding a Birchtown bus. I broke into a run and called her name. She turned as she was climbing the stairs of the bus but made no sign of recognition. I began the beloved walk through Bandy Lane park on to the mountain ridge and The Kindly Light. I needed the comfort to be found in the easy, well nourished despair of Rollo Treweeks. I loved the sufficiency of his establishment, the smooth infectious delight with which he spoke of the world's inevitable devastation by hunger, martial folly and undisciplined gonads.

A drizzle started. Rain on such a night was the stopper on a bottle with me inside. I turned back and made my way towards The Thinker and the Thrush. Fears like a shirt of wicker formed across my chest. In the shadows of the roadside I could see my own pressed body and chalky face lying in wait for Lucas to deal him the blow which by some quirk of suggestive pressure might still be my final comment on the matter. A hundred yards from The Thinker I paused, wondering whether it might not be better for my stomach and my morals to go to the Centre and talk about ethics with Melancthon Mills or about rates with Odo Mayhew. But I decided that just then either piety or astuteness would sicken me. Making this decision, I slipped the first of my few instincts off the leash for a little private hell and anarchy.

I went into the best lounge of The Thinker. It was empty except for Hugo Farnum, looking respectable and choked in a collar made for a dachshund. From upstairs came the first movements of the glee and discussion groups. Hugo was reading a book called *Fuel, The Key* and he was pursing his lips over his large teeth. He was second-in-charge on the administrative side of the Bandy Lane Gas and Electricity Department and he was a voter who gave a lot of thought to fuel.

I ordered a shandy and was glad when he began to talk to me and take my mind off my sombre unwanted thoughts by explaining to me the thesis of his book. It was that all the materials that make man warm and keep him in motion have lately been tickled into annoyance by the thoughtless drive of man's fingers into their bosom. They have therefore decided to take a good look at man and they do not like what they see. They have now decided to dwindle. By the time they finish, men who want any kind of cosiness will wind up by burning each other. They have done this before, but then it was for pleasure; now it will be scientific and we will have charts showing which men burn best. This theory, coming on top of Rollo Treweeks's talks on our impending famines, filled my head to stretching. I had the feeling that the little anxieties of my own heart were impertinent with all organic life lined up at the door of a vast icebox fiddling with the knob.

There was a wave of laughter from upstairs. 'Listen to them,' said Hugo. 'After what we've just been saying, they laugh. No understanding, no subtlety.'

'Sledges, every one of them. I'd like you to deliver a

few pellets to these boys in the Discussion Group. Too glib of any sense.'

'You're right. The valves of humanity's heart can be stricken, leaking, whispering, the way hearts do. What do these voters say to it? They nip into the glee club and make such a hell of a racket humanity's heart could be calling louder than the hooter of the steelworks and they wouldn't hear a sound. Anguish, by and large, gets a very poor audience when you consider the trouble it goes to.'

'You're the boy for them, Hugo. They want to cut their teeth on something grim, something fundamental.'

Hugo was beaming at me with pleasure now. It was not often he had the chance to come out as a prophet. His wife Felicity, the daughter of Tridwr Vaughan, was an earthy girl, of maximum bounce. Her ideas were largely those of Tridwr, blithe with a sardonic lining, and she would have liked to see Hugo less pensive and a lot more open at the front. She had a mezzo-soprano voice with a tremendous sentimental shake in its bottom register that had a fine effect on men in their beer. She never had any trouble getting the customers out on a Saturday night. At five to ten she stood on a box behind the bar of the sawdust lounge and sang 'When you come home, dear' and the voters crept out, many of them crying, all of them feeling as if they had just been sewn up in a shroud of temperance tracts.

'Man is an improvident loon,' said Hugo. 'Look at the people about here. What do they do when work is brisk and pay high? Do they get a nest egg to stave off the disgrace of camping out on the Social Insurance? No. They buy pianos and God-knows-what faldelals. As if music could ever be a substitute for the fine sturdy independence our parents had.'

Colenso, carrying a half-pint glass half full, had come to sit at my side. His eyes were wandering about the room but he had caught some of Hugo's remarks. That was how Colenso was. He was like those butterflies and moths that come thirteen miles through the dark in search of a mate but in his case it was something controversial that started the vibration. You could go down a two thousand foot pit-shaft just to have a little peace and quiet in which to say something comfortably reactionary and provocative and within minutes you would see Colenso, with or without the cage, come floating down to take up the issue with you. 'True enough, boy,' he told Hugo. 'But the only fine sturdy thing about your parents was their bone structure, and they were clearly shedding bits of that during the years they were keeping you at school. What the hell is wrong with buying a piano? My old man bought one for me as soon as he had finished paying for his father's crutches.'

He stood up and sauntered out again. Through the open door we saw Lucas Phillimore who was standing in the hall looking around imperiously. Colenso looked from Lucas to me, smiling subtly, as if he had just arranged a link between two significant currents.

Lucas came to the door of the lounge and glanced in. After my first glimpse of him I kept my eyes fixed on Hugo, hoping Lucas would go away. I would have left the room myself if I had been able to get up from my chair, but I felt as if Colenso had fixed me to the cushions with his pliers.

'Why didn't you deal with Colenso?' I asked Hugo. 'Who does he think he is, insulting you?'

'I'd have floored him with ease for two pins.'

'Why didn't you, Hugo? Colenso's nose needs a stay on the lino.'

'Oh, it's my wife's fault. She's got some sort of soft

spot for him. We're having the place rewired and she asked him to come in and look the place over and give us a few hints so that we can fence a bit with those electrical contractors. Perhaps we can get them to let us have it with just the top teeth or the bottom but not the whole set.'

'A good move that. I'm glad that's the explanation. I didn't like the look of the way he came nosing in here. You can never tell what mischief that element's got at the back of his mind.' I dropped my voice. 'Is Phillimore gone?'

'No. He's coming in now.'

Lucas began walking around the room very slowly. On the walls were hung some prints which I considered the most toney and tonic things in Bandy Lane. Hugo had got them for the best lounge as a kind of protest against his wife's mania for decorating the place with pictures of old Bandy Lane rugby teams that had shattered the maximum of bones and old debating teams that had shattered the maximum of beliefs. The prints that Hugo had bought showed groups of people in Africa and India armed as if for war, their feet as often as not resting on some animal they had just slain. Lucas was chuckling with admiration for these people and praising the various types of gun he saw being handled. 'Oh, look at that one. By God, if it isn't the old ·02. Can't beat it. Bring down a rhino at twenty feet.' Remarks like that which were bound to be full of flavour in an area where the only dangerous sports left are: playing catty and dog on the steep slopes where there is a clear chance of a hernia in the longer leaps; and making love in full view of an inflamed deacon.

Then Lucas seemed to notice me. He came to sit beside me. He was quite genial. 'Hullo there, Wilkie. What are you drinking?'

'Shandy,' I said, but Lucas made no move to get a drink for me or for himself. I was not used to the culture of best lounges. For all I knew there might be voters who went round making surveys of what other people fancy. The silence was awkward. 'What are you drinking, Mr Phillimore?' I asked.

'Plain beer, old chap.'

I brought him a glass and he pulled his chair closer to mine after he had taken the first sip. He seemed anxious. His face was drawn and for the first time I felt a pity for the man, an interest in him. I had the feeling there was something personal he wished to discuss with me, some load of reflections he wanted to throw off. After a while he spoke bitterly of the ill luck that had prevented him from developing his full talent in estate management. He grimaced with hate as he spoke of the meanness and incompetence of Samson Blakemore. His tone was quite passionate, his voice loud. 'Oh, God,' he said, 'if only I had my own farm. Have you any money, Wilkie? Would you like to be a partner if I could buy a holding? There seems to be good peasant stock in you and your father.'

'I have a little money, Mr Phillimore.' My mind was full of such comments as: 'Why should I help a treacherous bastard like you? The only reason I didn't poison that glass of beer I just bought you was that I can't afford both beer and poison on a Thursday night.' But the tongue with which I spoke was as gravely decorous as a vestry. 'I have a little money. Saved for a decent time to get it. I'm going to buy a business.' I tried to make my tone very significant here. 'I had hoped to persuade a certain young lady to share my business and my life.' But Lucas was not affected by my reference. He was out on his own bleak hillside of meditation where wry winds were blowing too hard for him to hear me.

A little later he began to talk of Angela. He praised her beauty, her voice, her bearing. Her family he drily dismissed. 'A damnable lot. They'd bore the berries off a hedge, the whole set of them. She'll be well quit of them, by God, she will. She's lovely. She's bringing a cool hand to my brow, Wilkie, when I most needed it, when I thought I'd never know such a thing again. In some ways it's been the greatest passion of my life. Physically speaking, of course.'

'What's that?' I asked in a voice just like the creaking of my wicker chair. I felt my face go the colour of cream-washed walls.

'Physically, of course. It's been hard going in certain respects. Not as young as I was, you know. Kept pretty fit, of course, but this kind of tempo can be terrific after forty.'

'What do you say?' I could see Lucas's lean form nude and detailed in front of me engaged in nameless antics with Angela, a pantomime of vileness. I fought hard to keep down my beer and my disgust. He laid his hand on my knee and laughed.

'Don't look so green, Wilkie. We are men of tact and knowledge. And thanks for doing the preliminaries, old boy. I hate the untried, the embarrassing commitment, the pioneer stuff. Thanks for saving me the trouble, boy. She's a tonic. Oh God, if only I could lay my hands on some money...'

I got up and left him, my spine a solid icicle. I left The Thinker and the Thrush. I went over to Kiprianos' and ate a sandwich while I listened to a clown on the wireless who was performing a round of vulgar buffoonery about his relationship with his wife. 'Turn it off, Manolos,' I said. 'That kind of talk hurts me.'

'True,' said Kiprianos. 'That is no way to talk of love.' He switched over to some funereal music which

I found to my taste and in my mind I walked behind the dead body of Lucas. Kiprianos, not knowing the quality of my visions, asked me if there was anything wrong with the sandwich.

I went home. Neither Colenso nor my father was there, but a few minutes later my father came in with a bag of chips, humming in a subdued, friendly way. I did not allow him to unpackage his chips. I took them from his grasp and threw them onto the table, making it clear by this gesture that I thought such a package a very poor article to be trespassing on the mood that was ravaging me. I took him by the collar and shook him as I had seen voters do on the screens of the Comfy and the Cosy when they are trying to extract confessions from their fellows. 'Now then,' I shouted, 'the truth about Phillimore and Blakemore, for God's sake! Tell me the truth. How many of their crimes have you seen with your own eyes? We'll expose them, we'll flay them.'

'My chips are getting cold, Stobo.'

'To hell with your chips. You're a fine father. Here am I on the topics of life and death, my heart jet-black with grief, and you worry about your chips. Tell me, which of them killed Miss Oxenham's baby? Where exactly is it buried?'

His shoulders moved. He was very strong for a man of his age. He shook himself free. He sniffed at my breath. 'You're drunk or daft. You've been listening to Mogg or Dodge. There was no baby, no burial.'

'That's what you say. They've kicked you up hill, down dale, and now you've no guts left. You're afraid of them. You're afraid to talk.'

'Oh, I don't know,' he said, placing his chips in front of the fire and going to the pantry to cut some bread and butter. 'Now and then they've been good to me. Blakemore gave me a job when jobs were hard to get.'

'So now you feel loyal to them and want to protect them. But I'm on the warpath. I'm going to shake the sugar out of that Phillimore and make Blakemore sorry for every harsh word he's used to my old dad.'

'Don't talk such nonsense,' he said. 'Have a chip sandwich.'

'No.'

'In any case, it doesn't matter any more.'

'What do you mean?'

'Mr Blakemore is selling the farm and getting rid of me.'

'Getting rid of you? Who told you that?'

'He did. After Lucas went down to the town tonight he came into the shed and had a chat with me. He sounded as mad as you. He said he thought Lucas was trying to shuffle him off, putting stuff like ground light bulbs in his tea to get rid of him and get hold of the farm. Also Dolly and Daisy have been off colour lately and there's been something in the papers about anthrax. He doesn't want a sick herd on his hands. So he's selling out, and after next week you won't have to worry about the way they treat me. My only worry will be finding a new job, at my age I mean, and being out of practice with everything but cows.'

'Does Lucas know about this?'

'No, I was the first person Samson told. So he told me, anyhow.'

I felt a strong need to be seeing and hearing Colenso, who at least created the impression of being able to stick both his questing fingers in life's eyes, for curiosity's sake or for simple gouging. Then I heard his footsteps on the concrete gully. He appeared carrying a large bottle of lemonade. He often drank a half pint of this stuff before going to bed because he said it gave a buoyancy to his dreams. I stepped up to him at the moment he came through the door and shook him by the hand. He fell back and watched me warily. 'I'm with you, boy,' I said.

'What are you talking about?'

'I'm with you on your march to the new day, the red dawn. Against oppression, snobbery and all that stuff you've been talking about for years.'

'I never thought you'd listened. What part of the procession are you in?'

'With you, boy, at your side. I've heard the way you've been branding that Phillimore and I'm with you. Go up that hillside, Colenso, and take the sneer off Phillimore's face, You'll find Stobo Wilkie right beside you.'

'At my side but tending to slow down at the gate of the farm.' He turned to my father. 'What's the matter with him?'

'He's had a little ale and he seems half off the hinge.'

'I want to see the end of Phillimore,' I said. 'Nobody does what he's done to my old man and gets away with it.'

'He's probably given someone too much change,' said my father sympathetically. 'That always upsets Stobo.'

Colenso laughed and pushed me into a chair. He handed me a cupful of lemonade. 'Take this. A two-way traffic in gas and your kind of thought will do you a world of good.' He opened my father's packet of chips and helped himself to one. 'You're a bright one, Stobo. You've had your head shoved into a furry little private warren for years and the silences down there must have been peculiar to have you acting like this when you suddenly get your ears full of stuff they've been hearing all the time. Your old man has been a footstool for years, but what did you do? Tell him to break the churn over Lucas' head or kick Blakemore's farm from under him? Oh no, be loyal, you said. Think of your job, Dad.

'Now you find that Lucas has hurt you, has had knowledge, as they say, of your precious Angela. And you want to lead a revolutionary phalanx up the hillside.

'Nothing doing. In this phase of the moon I'm sticking to electricity. Get Dunkerly and Melancthon and Odo to put on the red berets and start the flood. I can see all tyrants giving up the ghost at the approach of those elements. But as far as I am concerned, going up there and trying to vent your own personal rage on Lucas will do no good at all. If you feel strongly about it, go ahead. It will be an interesting encounter and will coax you a few inches out of that cave you've burrowed yourself in at Ellicott's.'

'He said something about those two killing a baby of Elvira Oxenham's,' said my father. 'To me he's got a finger on the latch of the hatch.'

'You'd better go to bed,' said Colenso.

I said no more. I gave them one last look of defiance, helped myself to some of the vinegar-soaked fragments of fish-batter from my father's plate and went to bed. At the foot of the stairs I turned to them and said: 'I'll surprise you all yet. Nobody treads on the face of Stobo Wilkie.'

'No more than four at a time,' said Colenso. 'Good night, Stobo.'

16

The next day was again full of waxing and ulcerating crises. I finished at one in the afternoon and walked over the ridge to The Kindly Light to have an ointment of long-term anguish laid on me by Rollo Treweeks. Then a return to Bandy Lane prompted the feeling of some urgent business impending there. I spent a few minutes in Mr Ellicott's parlour, explaining that I would do tomorrow the few little jobs of tidying up which I had left undone on my quick departure earlier. I was put on edge by the ominously harsh tone in which he commented on Angela's affair with Lucas and my failure to bring her to supper. He spoke of her graspingly as if she were part of the air he needed to live. He dropped a hint as plain and heavy as a lead ball that without Angela he might begin to view me a lot less favourably than before. I left him in a raging hurry and banged my head against the damp side-wall of the house. I hammered in my temper against the rough-cast stonework, hurling curses at Mr Ellicott but keeping my voice down.

Then I went along to the Centre. I could not bring myself to go in. I went around to the plantation of oaks at the back of the building and walked along the paths that had been driven through it by the labour of the members. The sound of the wind in the trees' ancient, feeble branches matched my own wild mental music. Through one of the lighted windows of the Centre I could see Angela and Dunkerly on the stage rehearsing some scene, and by craning my neck I could see the heads of Lucas Phillimore and Odo Mayhew deep in talk. Lucas was wearing the velour hat that had briefly belonged to my father. It was an affectation of Lucas's to keep his hat on indoors, his excuse being that it was fatuous for an essentially outdoor man to observe the same conventions of courtesy as an essentially indoor man.

I walked away from the Centre in the direction of the Constitutional Club where Offa was often to be found making contact with the town's leading citizens. On my way there I thought of Miss Oxenham and of how my field of action would be cleared if she were no longer on earth to seal my lips and Offa's about the stock of skeletons in the closets of Blakemore and Phillimore. I went down the side street where she lived.

The hall and stairway were full, as I had seen them before, of choristers from the congregation of Pandolph Treasure. I worked my way in and, standing at Pandolph's side, joined in their singing. Pandolph explained to me, 'It's the harmony that does it. This old girl hangs on by a thread. In a way we all do. It depends on how well the thread is encouraged to stay in one piece. We do it with harmony. Death is merely the climax of many avoidable discords in the life of a man, discords within himself, discords within the universe.'

I moved away from Pandolph and started trying to disrupt some of the four harmony lines that were reaching a full liveliness around me. Pandolph and his friends spotted the tactic and with as near an approach to swing as these elements allowed themselves, escorted me out. But as I left the house I heard a man called Tennyson Dunne, an associate of Pandolph's and very knowing about death, tell him that it was doubtful whether Miss Oxenham would last another twenty-four hours.

I found Offa Mogg in the snooker room of the Constitutional Club. He was playing a game with one of the town's doctors, Wilfred Poinsette, a deep-voiced, irreverent old voter. Colenso and I had, as boys, done a lot of jobs for him, such as exercising and washing his four dogs, two spaniels and two setters, as aloof and eccentric as the doctor himself. He had taken an interest in us both, had given us huge meals in days of meagreness in the airy little shack at the bottom of his garden where he did most of his living, where he kept a large part of the library that fascinated Colenso. Around the shack he had a large plantation of mulberry trees which he kept not for the making of silk but to strike a note of sweet contrast in a zone so full of sackcloth.

The doctor had grown more silent with the years but he was still full of the most caustic remarks about life. He often described the broad masses as being pecked to death by flights of charlatans and rogues and professed to be even more amazed by the stamina and stomach of the peckers than by the patience of the pecked. He spoke of the rich and the professional classes with a frankness that robbed some of the snooker balls of their roundness and had brought on strokes among members of the Con Club committee, a very cautious lot intellectually who insisted that an idea should be fifty years old before payment was made. It had been suggested that Dr Poinsette be asked to leave the Con Club and join one of the overtly radical clubs in the area, the '1848', the '1917' or the 'Keir Hardie', but he was too popular to be annoyed and in any case he liked the Con Club beer.

Although his remarks sometimes made Offa rock with rage and shock they were often seen together, for the doctor was a busy culvert of revelations about Bandy Lane people. Dr Poinsette for his part treated Offa with a flat contempt, referring to him as 'Pooley's poodle' on account of Offa's great regard for the steel magnate, and he said that Offa was the only journalist he knew whose heart and thoughts came to an even finer point than his nib.

I watched the game listlessly. I was not very interested because my snooker career had stopped when I found that with the cue in my hand and the powerful lights in my eyes my arms would begin to tremble violently. After one or two experiences of finding my cue under the cloth rather than over it, I was warned by the billiard-room stewards to stick to public service and making a steady profit. When they had finished I went over with them to the small bar in the corner. The doctor was handed a glass of warm milk by the steward's wife and into it he poured a fair ration of rum from a glass. He sniffed and stared at it with a Caribbean glow on his broad, wise face.

'I've never seen two boys look so eager and dedicated as you. You confront life like a couple of terriers. Let's hope the life force turns out to have the kind of lamppost you like.'

'We represent a new spirit, Dr Poinsette,' said Offa and I was glad he was making his tone so clear and formal. 'A generation ago it was the badge of honour in this town to worry about humanity. Now we worry about ourselves.'

'It'll get you into exactly the same kind of clay. It delights me to see anyone look as cunning as you. Offa, I remember you as a baby. Just the same. You used to look at your rubber comforter as if you had just been reading the latest quotations on the second-hand rubber market. Personally I still find people who give a thought to mankind less tedious than the other sort. There is nothing more repellent than a full-time preoccupation with one's own perishable guts.'

We drank in silence. The argument into which the doctor was inviting us was old territory. We had travelled there. We had come through with dry feet. We had answered the questions and turned our backs on them. We existed compactly inside our dark serge suits.

My drink was shandy, but in view of what I wished to do later in the evening I had asked the barman to make it particularly weak. My mind was perfectly calm. The news of the sale of Blakemore's farm had convinced me that Lucas would now act swiftly in the matter of leaving the town. I intended therefore to go to Angela that night with or without Offa's consent, whether Miss Oxenham was alive or dead, and beat her over the head with the facts I had about him. In the house, waiting, I had some packages of the best Austrian sausages which I was going to take along to create as relaxed an atmosphere as possible.

Offa left us to have an interview with the club chairman and Dr Poinsette suddenly said: 'I suppose you're hoping to get Ellicott's shop?'

'I'd thought of it, doctor.'

'You deserve it.' He added thoughtfully: 'He's in a pretty bad way between one thing and another.'

I gulped down my drink and got another.

'Do you know, Stobo,' he said as I returned from the bar, 'as a doctor I've often felt like doing a little research on your old man. He might provide some crowning evidence for a theory I like propounding: that in the face of such mass beastliness as wars and persecutions, the active force is less significant than the passive. The promoter of filth and injury is normally more than half mad but the receiver of same is normally more than half sane – so the balance of responsibility is his. As long as there are those who will hold out their flesh to be beaten, life will remain an academy of bruises. Your father is a prime example: a malleable, pliant monkey. Your mother was the same. I'd like to have a specimen of your hormones. No, don't get up, not now. I'd like to know how, coming from such a pair, you are capable of even coveting Mr Ellicott's goods.'

'I don't covet, doctor. And my father's grown the way he is because he wanted to help Blakemore. There have been terrible goings-on up there.' I had dropped my voice to a whisper and brought my head close to his. He was listening intently but looking quizzical. I was sure that he with his shocking, free and easy ways, would, in the next few minutes and with only the tiniest urging from me, come out with something undeniable about Lucas that would leave even Miss Oxenham's confession in the lurch.

'Oh,' he said. 'Such as what, now?'

'That Lucas is degraded, a proper... ' I fished around for some term that would have the sophisticated, medical ring, but wound up with: '...a proper ram.'

'Most men are. Properly organised there would be no need for it to appear on the charge sheet.'

'I heard that he gave Miss Oxenham a child.'

The doctor rubbed his head against the back of the settee on which we were sitting. He was nodding approvingly. He finished off his milk and rum and spoke quietly into the glass. 'She lived and will die a virgin,' he said. 'Without question the most blameless woman in Bandy Lane until I advised her to start living.'

'Living?'

'By lying. And I'm delighted she's managed to find someone to believe her. About two years ago I found her dying of drabness and humility. There is nothing that so dries up the bloodstream as meditating non-stop on the fact that one's days have been unflavoured by the excitement of sin through no real wish of one's own. I got Miss Oxenham to join Pandolph Treasure's outfit which goes in for singing and rapture. I weaned her away from penal acceptance of the authentic horrors on which she had been nourished and interested her in the healing powers of fiction. In no time at all she had, mentally, been ravished on a broader front than Africa. She had been fancied and overcome by every upright male in Bandy, from Sir Gwydion Pooley to that little voter who walks about with a leftward crouch collecting pennies from gas meters. Theoretically she had led a faster life than Pompadour without any of the wear and tear. It did her more good than liver extract. She's Bandy Lane's only novelist and she gets no cramp in her fingers, no dislike from rival writers.'

'You mean she's just a liar? And I thought...'

'It's always happening, Stobo. You find a patch of existence that you think solid, against which you feel you can press with some passionate assertion, and you find it's just another silly fiction, high-quality marsh and nothing back on the bubbles when you go under. That's probably the source of most evolutionary fictions. Call it a taste for uncreated truth. An ape probably once said, "I am becoming erect, I am becoming hairless. This matted stuff on me is just teatime shadow and a bad blade." Out of a mass of apparently crazy assertions and assurances comes the ground-plan of a new reality. In the case of Miss Oxenham it was undertaken too near the grave to be of any real use, except as an aid to the heat given out by her tiny gas fire. In the case of humanity it is an act of the highest consequence. Now I've got to slip over to see her before the evening's out. Goodbye.'

As he left me, Offa returned. 'You are looking very comatose, boy,' he said. 'What did the doctor tell you?'

I gave him a summary.

'Now you see, Stobo, just how careful you have to be. Cats have no law courts and look how gingerly they walk. That Miss Oxenham, sitting there in an oxygen tent of whoppers, luring us boys onto the offensive against Lucas. If we had come out prematurely with the story Samson Blakemore could have had us put away in the County Keep for life for such a libel. I've often had the feeling that if a man could really speak from beyond the grave, as the spiritualists say, he should shut up till then. Safer.' He bustled off after a committee man.

I left the club. I walked again through the street in which Miss Oxenham lived. There was a small group of choristers outside the house. Pandolph Treasure was speaking to them, looking very grave. He told me that Miss Oxenham had passed away as quietly and unforcedly as a sigh at the beginning of the third verse of 'When the Roll is Called Up Yonder, I'll be There'. 'Our tempo might have been a little too savage,' said Pandolph thoughtfully.

I moved away from the choristers. I went home and picked up the peace offering of sausages which had just been noticed by my father and which would have vanished within minutes if I had not called in. I walked towards Angela's house. At the opening of the street in which she lived I found myself walking behind her and Lucas. He had his arm around her and they were laughing in the happiest way. They went into her house. I walked on, wishing to keep an eye on the place until Lucas left. He was not long. He came out alone. I could see him clearly in the light from a street lamp. His body looked stooped now, his laughter a million miles away, his face worried, sad. He walked away, slower than the night.

I went around to the kitchen door and knocked, wishing to keep my manner cool and formal. Through the lighted window I could see the whole family sitting around the table. Angela was knitting, her emphatic brows pulled down low over her task. Lyndhurst was reading a thick book and nodding his head in pained desperation as if the words had just forced him to listen to something he had been trying for fifty years not to hear. The two boys were on the sofa, copy book in front of them, looking crazed by some cloud of tap and tank problems. Mrs Lang was watching them with a smile, seeing in her mind the flesh of some new achievement growing on the wasted tissue of her wishes. 'Who's there?' she called.

'Stobo.'

She said something to Angela, who shook her head in refusal. 'Come back tomorrow,' said Mrs Lang.

'I've got something for your mother,' I called out to Angela.

'What?'

'Sausages.'

'Come back tomorrow.'

'What sort of sausages?' asked Mrs Lang.

'Those Viennese ones. The best.'

'Come in, Stobo, my boy.'

I went in, my neck drawn into the collar of my overcoat, giving myself deliberately a crippled, pitiable look. Angela took me by the arm and led me into the small garden behind the house. We leaned against the wall and stared for a few minutes in silence at the moonstruck mountain ahead of us.

From beyond the wall came a surge of simple scents from a plantation of fruit bushes. It was the sort of compact, assured smell that makes one touchily aware, that invites the senses in its kindliness to go out on the march. From the open door of the kitchen came the fragrance of the Viennese sausages now being fried by Mrs Lang. It was a beautiful appetising whiff and I carefully registered the thought that Mr Ellicott could raise his price on them threepence in the pound and still keep his sales. Angela at my side must have sensed the relaxing of my mood, the swift recession of my tears. 'Often,' she said, 'on nights when there's a moon, I stand here and watch the mountain.'

'It's a fine mountain. Very quiet. Nice to walk on.'

'When the moon is full you can see the white line of the road that leads up the ridge over to the lake.'

'I've been up there a lot lately.'

'Somebody told me.'

'That Rollo Treweeks is a nice man to talk to. He's got his fingers in eight businesses in Bandy Lane. Doing well. Drink, building, transport, cattle-cake, undertaking. Steady lines.' At that moment I wished I had taken that job he had offered me, so that I could have boasted to Angela of my connection with such a man. She ran her hand over my head, affectionately, and laughed.

'Poor old Stobo,' she said, quite detachedly, as if she were standing over my grave.

'What's the matter with me now?'

'You're such a funny old thing sometimes. Everybody laughs at you.'

'They do, do they?' I tried to make it sound like a challenge but there was no hardness in my voice. 'I've got a steady job, Angela, a good future, a good future.' I repeated it because I had the feeling that the phrase had gone into a deaf ear, a threatening night. 'Angela...'

'Yes, Stobo?'

I looked suddenly at her face. It was happy, smiling, but clearly on account of the moon, of her own thoughts. 'Have you changed your mind now?'

'About what?'

'Phillimore.'

'Why should I?'

'Blakemore's putting him out. He's selling the farm.'

'That makes no difference to Lucas. You should know him better, Stobo; he's a wonderful man, the sort of man I've always dreamed of. Always the right word and the right way of saying it. Better than Dunkerly Dodge, and Dunkerly won the Pooley elocution award last year.'

There was a silence. The fruit bushes seemed to produce extra waves of pungency to help us over our embarrassment. I wondered whether I should lay on a barrage of lies about Lucas to create the advantage of a momentary confusion in Angela's mind, but my mind was tired and I could see the truth nodding at me from behind its bandages and urging me for God's sake to give it a rest. Then, 'But he's not even got work,' I said.

'Don't say such things about Lucas to me. He only stayed with Blakemore while he was willing to try and make a go of the farm. He's been talking of leaving for the last three months; now he's made up his mind.'

'He'll never take you away from here.'

'Is that so? Well, just listen, Mr Know-All. He's got a big job with a firm of tractor manufacturers. He's starting as clerk in their head office, then he goes on the road.'

'What's the name of the firm?'

'What's that got to do with it?'

'Because they'd need a factory of tractors to pull the truth out of that man, any man, it strikes me, though I seem to be pretty normal. I've come up against a lot of lying lately. Miss Oxenham, a liar. Offa Mogg, very offhand with the truth, seems to think he can take it or leave it. Lucas, probably leading the pack. I only hope he was lying when he told me about his friendship with you. It shook the last nerve out of me. What's the name of the firm?' I was as nearly the masterful bullying lawyer as I shall ever come to it with my unreliable voice and my general lack of force. 'Mankind may fancy being waltzed around by falsehood in its hot old halls, but Stobo Wilkie stays out in the porch, cold but ready to wait there for the facts until he freezes.'

After some hesitation she gave me the name of a manufacturer. I entered it with care in the little diary issued by my association which gives the costs of grocery items from 1700, and if you study this list you will see that not even the highest human hopes have been raised as steeply as prices. That is because hope perishes but food endures, and even as I stood there by that wall, my heart feeling like a side of bacon looks up there on its hook, I was happily conscious of the delight being spread in the kitchen by those genuine pork chipolatas.

'When do you think you will go?'

'Next week. Thursday, Friday...'

'Will it be to London itself?'

'Oh yes. Lucas says he's sick of the provinces.'

'What about your father and mother?'

'My father is too wrapped up in himself to notice. It will do my mother good to be without me for a bit.'

'I could tell you things about that Lucas...'

'Everybody around here can. He's above them. They bite his toes. It doesn't hurt and I won't listen. So long, Stobo.'

I walked away. At the kitchen door I heard grunts from food-packed mouths which told me my gift was going down well, and the knowledge helped restore my balance.

17

The next day Mr Ellicott had a faint in the middle of the morning and I gave him a dose of sal volatile so strong I could almost hear his heart telling me not to go to extremes. When he recovered he was livelier than I had seen him for years, staring at the till with eyes that burned right into the figures and turned the entrails of debtors to ash. In his glances at me I noticed the sullen unpleasantness which had lately crept into his expression was more marked. It concerned me, put me on edge. At closing time I stayed on to do some stacking and tidying that had got behindhand in all the turmoil and vexation that had been brought into my life by Lucas Phillimore. I went into Mr Ellicott's living room just before I left. He was sitting by the fireplace reading a book on Biblical prophecy. He had read me some extracts from this book when he had seen me going around looking too sanguine and I could not understand why a man with such a bad heart and weak legs should read a volume so depressing. He did not look up from his reading, so I mumbled goodnight and asked myself what exactly had come between us.

I went for a short walk along the banks of the Moody, a stream in which you get the quickest alternation of shallows and deeps, calm and fret. On its further shore were some blocks of tidy houses, some looming adjuncts of the steel plant and two or three farms hanging on to some scurvy scraps of pasture land. The sound of water was good in the ears with the disturbing smell of the Moody on my right and the squall of conflict from the packed futureless houses on my left putting beauty on its back and kicking its secrets back into its mouth.

I found my mind full of the remembered sight of Lucas' face and body, sad and uncertain, as he left Angela's house the previous night. I was moved by a slant of moonbeam on a placid stretch of the Moody's surface, its dark pollution eased into a kind of muffled loveliness by the shadow of the pickle factory. I felt that my troubles might have been brought to an end if I had made that lurching misfit some shrewd charitable gesture, if for example I had gone up to him in the gloom as he slouched along back to that miserable little farm from which he was shortly going to be booted and presented him with, say, fifty pounds, with happy hands and laughing mouth, saying, 'Mr Phillimore, a helping hand for that fine dream of yours for a holding of your own. From a friend, though a man you have bitterly wronged.' That might have had a double effect: it might have driven him from the plan of a job in London which would take Angela away from Bandy Lane; it would also have caused Lucas to see me in a new light as a rather fine liberal young voter, his hand and wallet in the right place, and he would have regretted having tripped upon my personal happiness by attracting Angela with his fly-blown sophistication.

I looked up at Blakemore's farm, its meagre farmhouse and barns, grey and carious. I tried to spur myself to go up there at that very moment. But I turned the idea down, telling myself that I feared a rebuff from Lucas; actually because the sour look on Mr Ellicott's face that evening did not encourage me to whittle down the savings on the size of which depended my ability to make the shop mine.

The house was empty when I got home. Colenso, to take my father's mind off the worry he felt about Blakemore's announcement, had taken him to an operatic concert two towns away and I hurried off to bed, knowing that when they returned there would be a lot of intensive singing in the kitchen. My father, whenever he was knocked bow-legged by some splinter of calamity, could always be thawed back to joy by music of any sort.

When he came into the shop next morning, Offa was big with news. Mr Ellicott gave him a harsh look as if to say that next to an outbreak of flies on the ham he could think of nothing worse than Offa. But Offa outstared him as if his position as high priest of Bandy Lane gossip had given him a certain immunity from criticism. He just stood there and let his eyes bore through Mr Ellicott and from the look of him I would have said that even about Mr Ellicott he had some slab of revelation waiting to be lowered into place if Mr Ellicott ever gave him any real displeasure.

Just then Mr Ellicott was called to the door by Tudwal Parker, a solicitor and so foxy he would stand still for hours rather than reveal in which direction he intended to go. This Parker had been trying for years to persuade Mr Ellicott to sell his business and live on the proceeds of investments that would be suggested by him. But fortunately for me Offa had been able to dig up the story of several voters who had entrusted their savings to Tudwal Parker, and if Tudwal, in his role of broker, had been armed with a dowser's rod especially adapted for the finding of shares that were shortly going to pass into a mortal fit, he would not have put these voters more quickly in touch with them. It seemed as if Tudwal had only to mention in the lowest voice that a little Bandy Lane money was making in the direction of a certain enterprise for that enterprise to turn up its eyeballs and call for the box. So far these stories had worked a spell on Mr Ellicott who was willing to discuss the game of bowls with Tudwal but pocketed the kitty and marched away as soon as the conversation turned to money.

Offa began his announcements as Mr Ellicott went out into the street. I cut him a piece of the madeira cream-slice of which he was very fond. 'You know Wedlake Roper, the estate agent?'

'Oh, yes,' I said. 'Mind like a knife, Wedlake.'

'He has, too. He's arranging the sale of Blakemore's farm. And he told me in the club yesterday that he was glad to see the end of the deal. Like Ellicott, Blakemore doesn't trust banks, so he wouldn't take a cheque from Wedlake Roper's clients. The hundred pounds deposit was paid in cash and Blakemore has got it up there with him in the house, now. And the quarrels between Samson and Lucas have been terrible. Samson has been accusing Lucas of wanting to kill him and steal the farm, and every time he mentions that the farm has now been sold and is therefore inaccessible to Lucas he winks, laughs and then bends his legs so sharply he almost disappears into those tall trousers of his. A terrible sight, that, says Wedlake, who has seen this turn now several times.'

'Those trousers are very tall, Offa, but for God's sake tell me how all this matters to me.'

'Samson told Wedlake that Lucas had made attempts on him. A few shoves at the top of the stairs, and one or two electric bulbs have vanished at just the same time as Samson has noticed a lot of very gritty sugar in his tea that he can't spoon into dissolving. This, he says, is the bulbs being fed to him by Lucas, and he told Wedlake that if Lucas succeeds in slipping him a bit of filament as well all he'll need in the new house he's going to buy down here in Bandy is a switch fitted into himself and he'll be able to flood the whole place with light.'

'He's off the hinge, that Blakemore.'

'The world is off the hinge, Stobo. We are just the separate creaks. And Lucas is in a very queer state.'

'How? How queer?'

'The poor chap is at so many crossroads he's spinning like a top. Last night at that big pub, The Rand, there was a meeting of Territorial Officers. Lucas was one of them once and they invited him along. He was in his element. The booze flowed wide and deep and his tongue wagged like a bell-clapper. Wedlake Roper was there and after a few jars he got very loose lipped himself. He told Lucas what Samson had told him about Lucas wanting to be rid of him by means of ground bulbs and so on. Lucas said he had never considered it but if he ever did he would reject powdered glass as being too pleasant for an element like Samson. He asked Wedlake if he knew where Samson was keeping the hundred pounds in cash. Wedlake knew where, but he was so drunk at the time he can't remember whether he told Lucas or not.'

'Did he say anything about Angela?'

'Oh yes, I'm coming to that. A couple of these officers were pulling Lucas's leg about it and telling him how lucky he was to have a nice bit of stuff like that, free of charge and off the hook so to speak, here in Bandy Lane where they have to go and pay top rates in Birchtown for a whore of the second class.'

'They said that?'

'I'm only quoting Wedlake Roper, an accurate chronicler as well as a good estate agent.'

'What did Lucas say to them?'

'He laughed so much they had to prop him up. He gave them a little sketch about Mrs Lang and Lyndhurst and the twins that had them in fits. He said Angela was like a hot coal for him from the start.'

I did not dare pick up that reference to coal at once. I felt a warm burst of loyalty towards the Lang family. Lucas's action had touched some obscure little chord of tribal solidarity in me. 'What was that they said about Angela?'

'He said some terrible things about her altogether. He said he's going to take her to London for a few days and the last big blow-out of his life. Then he's going to leave her to cool because by the time he's finished with her it'll be months before she's cold enough for anyone else to handle.'

'Is all this true, Offa, or are you trying to goad me into a rage where I will kill Lucas just to provide an item for the *Bulletin*?'

'Honest to God truth, every word of it.'

'So he's going to take her to London and leave her?'

'That's it, and don't ask me to go over to Angela's and repeat this because she'll just think we're making it all up to get our own back. Lucas also said that when he's had his unlicensed honeymoon and given Angela a taste of real life he's going to settle down. He has plans.'

'I know. He's got a job as a traveller for a tractor firm.' I was glad to be able to tell Offa something for a change.

'Nothing like that. Ten years ago there was a very

beautiful woman in Birchtown called Ursula Bendall, a real flash girl. She was very fond of Lucas and he told Wedlake Roper last night that this Ursula still streaks his memories with a strong gleam. She married a rich farmer about twenty miles west of this. Lucas cried when he spoke of it. Tears are often daft but it's always important to note in which direction they flow. I made some inquiries about it. It seems that this rich farmer is now dying... and Ursula will need a good farm manager.'

'Lucas?'

'I hear that she's been making a few little queries about him, how he's placed and so on.'

'All right then. There's our solution. Let's go and tell Lucas that this Ursula still longs for him and if he slips over to her place and gives her husband's bed a good shake, she and the farm will be his.'

'Life's not cheese, Stobo. It can't be sliced as roughly as that. Be a bit subtle, man.'

'Who wants to be subtle? All I want is for Lucas to vanish and Angela to stay here.'

'Right. But Lucas has his pride, although he's got no more principle than a roach. The initiative will have to come from her.'

'What about Angela?'

He patted me on the shoulder as if he were preparing me for the reception of a terrible but necessary bit of truth. 'Look, Stobo, you've got to prepare yourself to be humble where Angela's concerned. Dunkerly and I have been talking things over. We think it wouldn't be such a bad thing if she went away with Lucas. After such an experience Angela will come back to us with that little bit of extra depth that distinguishes the really great dramatic actress from the run-of-the-mill sort.'

'What do you mean, depth?'

'The rub of life's file over the soft surface of the heart. With you, Stobo, she might have known a feather-duster, but not a file.'

'Well, if you want me to be a pig for a change...'

'No, you'd never achieve the scope, boy. Evil of the right creative kind needs training and inherent aptitude.'

'You're making this very complex, friend.'

'Existence is a blind horse, Stobo. You need a cunning hand on the halter.' He gave me a wink. 'What did you say the name was of that tractor firm Lucas is supposed to have a job with?'

I told him, in a voice as dead as the bacon hanging on my left. He walked out of the shop as Pandolph Treasure came in. Pandolph was as gay as a cricket and rubbing his hands in a way I thought unwise in a voter whose trade has to do with death. 'Good day, Mr Treasure,' I said. 'What can I do for you, sir?'

'Ah, Stobo, my boy, there you are. I've got the order here for Miss Oxenham's funeral tea. She always insisted that the order should be placed here.'

'She always spoke highly of Mr Ellicott's lines. It gave us pleasure to be praised in such terms by a woman of refinement, Mr Treasure.'

'Keep up that way of talking, Stobo,' he said delightedly. 'The polished and balanced sentence is just what we need in a town that puts out its words with as little ceremony as it puts out its ashes. This is going to be a real tea, Stobo. Thirty guests, and ham and tongue for all. A real four-slicer, a premier interment. Between you and me, Stobo, I've had offers, tenders from caterers in my own little religious group, but to me the requests of the dying, especially about food, are holy writ. And Miss Oxenham was fanatical about Mr Ellicott's ham.'

Normally I would have risen to the bait of

Pandolph's suggestion and hinted at a rebate if he would increase the order by so many pounds. But my talk with Offa had filled me with iron filings, and I merely stood ready to start serving.

18

I met Offa in the Constitutional Club that evening. He left me early to report a meeting of the Club's social aid group which helped shuffle the more embarrassing cases of distress in the town out of view. Dr Poinsette was there too and he persuaded me to join him in a game of snooker on condition that he would pay for the cloth if my cue ran amok. As he played he told me that he had observed several symptoms of megalomania in me, and that I would either end with Mr Ellicott's braces and a whole chain of shops or I would jump right over a cliff when the combination of scheming and Bandy Lane weather brought me to the day that was too long and sandy to cross. He expected me to be amused but I was as glum and impassive as the balls.

We went into his favourite corner. The steward handed him his warm milk with its infusion of rum. His voice when he spoke again was weary. 'In the days when I cared, Stobo, in the days when I cared, I was the finest engine of pity on this earth. I had my fingers near the heart of truth feeling for the fatal leaking valve. With more time I might have done something for the mother of that girl of yours.

'God help people like Mrs Lang who find reality indigestible. They become poor shaking maniacs whom we treat with scorn or fun, never as what they are, grim, unfailing signposts to the fact that reality is not what it should be, that our days groan beneath a burden of outrage made palatable only by our fiendish gift for comedy. There are none predestined to be maimed. For every year we spend trying to heal the mutilated we spend just a second on trying to quarantine the things that mutilate.'

'Some people you can't help. Some people are out on their own, unwilling to be touched.'

He did not hear me. 'I did what I could for Mrs Lang a long way back. I tried to give her the sort of psychological aperients needed to excrete desires that have grown dark in the cloisters. I tried to point out the fine positive tasks she could fulfil as the mother of promising kids and the wife of a man who at least wasn't a monster, although he could never earn more than just enough to keep the breath in and the bailiffs out. A fine line of moonshine. It might have worked in a less well dentured society. She was gradually coming round. She was sealing up the fissures of longing for the glories she had glimpsed as a skivvy, the cracks of wanting that chapped her heart and made it too sore to touch on the days when the winds of current facts were too cold to bear. Then Lang went sick for months on end. There is no task that requires greater co-operation from society than the simple one of keeping sane and Mrs Lang didn't get it.

'And that Lucas Phillimore is another one. Prometheus junior, having his guts nibbled out by a flock of crows convinced they could have been eagles if things had turned out a little better. You'd like to see Lucas dead, wouldn't you?'

'Oh, no, nothing like that. I've given papers at the Centre on law and order and the sporting spirit in the game of life.'

'You can give a hundred more and you still wouldn't be able to prevent that little black moth rising from the cupboard at the back of your mind. And the moth will tell you that the presence of a certain person on this earth is an ache and an outrage.' He had almost finished his drink. The amusement in the glance he gave me was now quite brilliant. 'Lucas has always headed for an end as grotesquely absurd as the shabby useless life he's lived. He might well land in some preposterous scheme of vengeance set on foot by just such an artless little voter as yourself, Stobo, and the Sunday papers will look at you in the dock and talk about your neat suit, your gentle look, your tidy tie, and they'll ask: How? Why?'

'Oh no, doctor, nothing like that. Oh God no.'

'Well, you'll be pleased to know that Lucas is not at all well. Years ago his kidneys gave up trying to understand him and he's been having mortal trouble with them ever since. Wouldn't surprise me either if he'd made contact with the ailment mentioned on the posters. He knocked about with at least two women who might have inspired the posters.

'And another thing: in his early days as a lover Lucas was renowned for his fertility, with a talent for begetting that would have got him into the first chapters of the Bible. With what he paid out on his brood he could have re-equipped the family farm. If he's still up to standard it wouldn't surprise me to see your Angela ending up with the issue of Lucas on her hands.' His lips paddled luxuriously in a fresh drink. 'I can see the interest gleaming in your eye, Stobo. Your mind is racing with a dozen dandy little possibilities. Poinsette doesn't like Lucas, you will say. He will not want to see Angela being debauched, possibly diseased by this snobbish reactionary fool.

Under guise of treating Lucas, he will shuffle him off, thus freeing Stobo from a load of fear and worry.

'Well, in the days when I cared, Stobo, I might seriously have pondered such a drama. But now I am no longer inside the victims who are affronted. I stand behind the reality as it lurches on its way. I do not direct it by as much as the pressure of a thumb to some selected target. Now, Stobo, I am interested to see what brew will result from the fusion of two such chronic and lightweight dreamers as Angela and Lucas. I am delighted that Lucas is bringing his forthright brand of amorous mischief to bear on the shirt-tails of a busy little climber like yourself. You're not too much of a spectacle really. Being a victim on a large scale might do you a world of good. Speaking offhand I would say that you have about one hundredth of the goodness and natural nobility of your old man. Chemically considered, you are a bit of pure waste. Good night.'

As the doctor went through the swing doors Offa's face appeared excitedly and he beckoned me. He led me into a small card room where we were alone. The doctor's last words had left me flattened and I sat inertly as Offa spoke. 'Just been to Wedlake Roper,' he said. 'If you ever feel your world is shaking, he's the boy to go to. He'll hoop it tight and trim for you. He rang up the offices of that tractor company, the local office in Birchtown. Lucas hasn't got a job with them, there or in London.'

'What's he going to do, then? What will he do for money to take Angela away?'

'That's the point. When a man is at the end of a rope and his legs kick, watch out. He went to Wedlake and tried to borrow fifty pounds. Wedlake said no and he saw a very dangerous look in Lucas' eye.' Offa sat there delighted, his fingers clearly pleased to be stroking one tentacle of possibility after another. 'The whole thing is opening up like a rose. Lucas may drop a mattock on the head of Blakemore. He may nip over to the place where Ursula lives and I can see those two at the foot of her husband's bed trying to rattle him into a faster and more sensible tempo of departure. Honest to God, there are times when life is almost too interesting, though from the blank look on your face at this moment, Stobo, I wouldn't say you agree.'

I said nothing. My hand had dropped away from the needles. I was just waiting to be knitted.

'Do you know what's just occurred to me? There's a bit of the bandit in Lucas. Watch the way he sways when he walks. There's a defiant, predatory tread in it.'

'That comes from dodging tumps and slopes up on the hillside,' I said. 'It gives a very springy measure to a voter's movements.'

'It's more than that. In the days before such things as Parish Relief, dole and properly organised police forces came along to chill a man's urges to be free and easy, Lucas would have had a lair up there on the mountains, and he would have come roaring down with his band, looting and burning. And that would have been a good trade for such a man. Those fearless eyes, telling life to charge itself with passion and poetry for pity's sake. And think what it would have done for the *Bulletin*!

'One night in the Centre we were talking about one of those films where a gun-moll is shot to pieces in her lover's arms. He is a gunman in flight from a bank robbery. And I said, "Isn't that a horrible thing? These lovers condemned to live like foxes and finding their marriage consummated at last by slipping into a ring of pure lead." Angela was there.

She said no. She said that after twenty-four years of Bandy Lane such an end struck her as a Sunday School trip. When one has known the best of love, she added, it is better to have death press it into a book where its colours will never fade. Did you know there were such thoughts in her, Stobo?'

'She talked to me about gun-molls. She asked me if I had the impulse to go loping through life like a wolf, snapping at what meat I fancied. That's a fine way to go talking to a young provision merchant. And that scene you described: the lovers, the posse edging through the belt of trees, the machine guns, then dead in one another's arms; she's got an advertising still from Banfield Marsh the manager of the Cosy and it's hung up in her front room.'

'There you are, then. It's obvious.'

'What is?'

'That Lucas will suddenly break out. He sees himself as a lion beset by squirrels. There are some lives that mature from a single scream in the night. They spend years in a state of nodding, muffled tolerance. Then the scream. Angela and Lucas could do a fine duet. They have a fine stock of silences they will want to break.

'What if Lucas now decides on some great act of rapine with Angela at his side? Can't you see the two lonely, brave, murderous figures? They might even stage a job here. They enter the offices of the Bandy Lane steel works, planning to do more damage than anything since the Merthyr riots or the last slump. The defiant cashier. The contemptuous shot from Lucas. The chase. Then Angela singing something along the lines of "I've known one night of love" but stronger and more dramatic because there's theft and murder thrown in, and that in a place where larceny stops short at Wally Fletcher and wife-beating is done with such care it never ripens into a chargeable offence. Then she dies in Lucas' arms.

'We could drop a hint of this to Lucas. We could tell him that life has cast him for the role of taker and shaper, a Robin Hood who will form the first fully individualist answer to the rot of the welfare state. There'll be no radical nonsense about robbing the rich to help the poor with Lucas. He will rob the poor as well as the rich to join the rich.

'The trouble is that Lucas, as an officer and a gentleman and arguing off and on with all the militant rodneys who have given him offence in this division, has an almost unnatural repect for property. Even about the noblest of men these days there is a hint of the eunuch. Lucas would probably faint at the thought of doing anything to a bank manager except touch his hat to him. When shabbiness slips into the heart and you find yourself choosing one brand of torment rather than another because it keeps you warmer, that is the essential gangrene.'

'Offa,' I said, 'all this talk of yours is playing hell with my bowels. Stop it, please. I've made up my mind what to do.'

'What's that?'

'I'm going to make a fine gesture. There'll be none of the blood-and-thunder stuff you're after. I can see my role now. I'm the quiet man of character who slips out for matches every time the girl he loves wants to burn her wings and rub the ash in his eyes. A bit of a rag mat really but the pattern is strong and the quality first-rate. I'm going to make Angela a gift. I'm going to give her the money she needs to escape with Lucas. I've got some money saved and there's no hurry now to reach the purchase price set by Mr Ellicott for the shop.'

'Are you mad?'

I tried to give a short, tragic, distracted laugh to tell Offa that on the quiet I thought so. 'I only wanted the shop for Angela's sake. If she never comes back I've been offered a nice job by Rollo Treweeks at The Kindly Light and I can see a future for myself in the quieter reaches of the victualling trade.'

'What kind of spineless chatter is this, Stobo? Life can't go on if men won't go out and fight for the women they love. You want life to go on, don't you?'

'At this moment it's going on over my neck and I wouldn't be offended if it stopped. In any case, Offa, when Angela is left stranded in London by Lucas and has to come back, she'll feel an awful fool. She'll come to me before I go to her, and won't that be something to hold over her head?' We looked at each other, half smiling, excitedly rubbing our rough lumps of cunning and hoping they would not chafe our fingers to the bone.

'That's a point. But all the same, this is a tame, timid way out of the problem.'

'Dr Poinsette explained it. He said, "Stobo, you're pure waste." All right, I am that. You remember that lecture we had at the Centre from Prothero Wilce about the nitrogen cycle? Here am I, reporting for my turn of duty. I'll go to the bank tomorrow and then I'll seek out Lucas. It'll be a fine scene. I'll say very quietly, trying to keep my baritone, "Lucas, the wind of hope has died in my heart. My house is desolate." You notice, Offa, that this is a kind of noble, Red Indian way of talk. "The shutters are down and its peace for ever broken. But my first thought is for Angela. You are financially in the pan and the furthest you could take her on your own steam is a twopenny bus ride out of Bandy. She wishes to taste a type of life with you different from what she will know with me. My money would have

— 211 —

been hers and what is hers is yours. Take this, Lucas, and God go with you." '

Offa shook me by the hand, very moved. 'Yes, that's got its own sort of beauty too. If you want me to write some extra material into it, let me know.'

'I think it will do.'

I had a last shandy and walked over to Angela's. She was alone in the kitchen, washing two large piles of dishes in a small tin bath on the table. I had often helped her with this task. I stepped to her side and did so now. We said nothing. As my fingers probed into the warm water to catch some floating bit of cutlery I took her hand in mine. I squeezed it and said, 'It will be all right, Angela. It will be all right.' With that kind of mood in my mind, those words in my mouth, and suds up to my wrist, it was one of the best moments in my life.

I wiped my hands and with a wise patient smile left the house.

As I got to the end of the paved gully at the side of the house, I passed Lyndhurst. He had been to an adult class run at the Library and Institute by Melancthon Mills on astronomy. This was one of the most complicated classes ever run in Bandy Lane because Melancthon was not a trained star-gazer but had stumbled across four books containing flatly opposed views about what would shortly be happening to space, and each theory in turn had caught him a sharp clip across the neck. When he spoke to you of impending occurrences beyond our gravitational field his eyes became blank and terrified as a starless night. When he was lecturing on the topic he ran between his alternative theses like a hungry mouse between four high-grade cheeses, for each of the propositions had the kind of vicious implacability favoured by Melancthon in all things that lay outside the range of his own quiet kindly life. He insisted upon doing it because he felt that the mental life of Bandy Lane had been ravelled by too nattering an emphasis on such transient issues as wage levels and international disputes. He felt that if the place could have its clucking head dipped for a while into the quaking possibilities of woe inherent in every innocent twinkle in further space, there would be a more serene and complacent view of things all round.

I did not want to stop and talk to Lyndhurst. I was enjoying the full-cream content of my attitude. In any case I knew that he had long ceased to be interested in Angela; that he was indeed in a vague way sympathetic to any scheme that got her away from the place.

'That Melancthon,' he said. 'If that boy isn't hanging out on the line I'll eat my heart and that's no dish for the teeth of a man. Last week the universe was a shrinking bag. Once it was crisp and ready to keep us baffled on a permanent basis by staying so. Then it saw men getting so much sleep on the job and generally talking so much nonsense about fulfilment in such a vast trap of emptiness it decided to sag. Then this week Melancthon changes his mind. That's his way. He hands you one bit of despair. You get into the way of wearing it jauntily in your hat and then he says you look better bald.

'This week he concluded that the outer lining of the universe might keep its rigidity. But the consciousness of the people will get sharper and will one day pierce the lining. Through those punctures, Stobo, and stop fidgeting for God's sake, the air that sustains the whole circus will quietly flow. So if you hear a quiet hissing going on out there, don't blame God or erosion or faulty fitting. It's all the people who've made senseless daggers of their minds ripping away all the serenity of life in general in their efforts to find a little peace and security for themselves.'

I made no answer. Lyndhurst's talk was always so fundamental you felt at the end of it you were doing sentry-go in an upright coffin. At that moment I could with pleasure have dropped him and Melancthon into the Moody for I felt that between them they were creating a volume of fuss and bother in human thought that would do life no good at all. He forced me to lean with him against the short iron gate in front of the house.

'Really,' he said, 'there's no problem. True, it is an outrage to be here in this situation but the worst betrayal is to make a fuss about it. Nine of us in ten are saddled with wives, parents, children who are much more bewildering to us than the stars and planets. You find me a man who will talk about the universe as a shrinking bag and us as a covey of chips waiting for the salt and I will show you a man who is tormented by some unease about human life to which he will not give voice. There is no problem. The stars grow tired like us. They get up early and try to go to the grave late, just like us. They get tired of mooching about and never getting to the valley of sunlit orchards which is their desire. So they stand still and stare.' He dropped his voice and sounded quite disturbed. 'It's a staring match. We worry each other, so we stare. They stare at each other. They stare at us. We stare at them. Have you ever heard of such a hell of a hobby as that?'

'What for, Mr Lang? What do they expect to see?'

'They are waiting to see who will drop first, us or them. In a fight like this nobody gives in.' He ran his fingers through his hair. 'That notion sickens me. I wish I had never had it. I want to be earnestly rational but between the universe and those bloody foremen on the Council my mind is like a crushed roach. What's your theory of the universe, Stobo? Tell me something calm and reassuring, for God's sake.'

I was glad Lyndhurst had asked me that, because I had been thinking of that very question in the light of my recent experience. I was ready for him. 'The stars,' I said, 'are bright because they are the souls of those who have been proved and tested by suffering.'

'Oh, Christ,' he said, and left me.

19

The next day was time to make the withdrawal of money from the bank and make my offer to Lucas, all with a margin of minutes wide enough to provide me with a pleasant meditation on every step taken. I asked Mr Ellicott for the day off. I was shocked by the way he took my request. He glowered at me and muttered, quite unlike his usual self. I could see he wanted to intimidate me, with his frowning and grimacing, into saying that it didn't matter, that I would withdraw my request. But I was in no mood to truckle to him any more, so, firmly but with my usual courtesy saying that it was our slackest day and that he could manage for one day without me, I took my leave.

On my way to the bank I thought much and bitterly about Mr Ellicott. During the years when his legs had been so bad he would have had to give up if it hadn't been for me. He had had me on a round-the-clock basis giving him all the diligence and loyalty in the world, and that for a pound a week less than the least he would have had to give a manager. And that was the reward I got: a snarl at such a reasonable request. If he had not made me that promise about the shop's ownership passing to me on his retirement or death I would not have stuck with him for a week. As I walked I felt moments of malevolent impatience with him which I tried to forget by evoking the thought of the many fine evenings I had spent in his parlour with Angela. Then I began to remember the way in which he had sometimes looked at Angela, and what Mrs Chiddle had told me about him, and my spite redoubled.

I set out on the path that led to the hillside farm. I leaned forward to keep in touch with the bulging wad of notes in my inside pocket. In the few minutes I had been carrying them they had become part of my heart. Half-way up the path I turned round and ran back down into the town to Kiprianos' café. I drank hot tea, making noisy gulps to provide a great anti-thought pantomime and touching my notes with a growing sense of deprivation and rage in my fingers. Kiprianos watched me from behind an urn and cautioned his wife to keep near so that she could keep an eye on the trade if he suddenly had to vault over the counter and put the grip on me.

In the afternoon I went to the Cosy where there was a performance given specially for the Old Age Pensioners. Banfield Marsh told me I was very young to be in on an event of this sort but I told him recklessly that I had been sent along by Melancthon Mills as a social scientist to watch the reactions of the pensioners to the cinema. The old people, some of the most willing in Bandy Lane, heard this and put on a lot of different reactions to keep me busy.

By the time I left the cinema the last of my desire to help Lucas was gone. I felt that my fingers would have dropped off if I had gone through with the ceremony of handing over anything of mine to such a man. The film I had seen was full of blood, a tale of vengeance executed without guile on a man who looked a bit like Lucas and who, like him, had been presumptuous, handsome with October overtones, and unproductive in a way that galled the peasant hero as much as did the former's theft of the latter's girl. There were many sounds of approval from the old people in the audience who were busy comparing this sonnet of simple butchery and its rounded finality with the tooth-worn untidiness and thread-bare bathos of their own lives. Half deliriously, as I left the hall, I promised some of them a few tingling emotional decisions in the near future that would bring the life of Bandy Lane up to the same nourishing standard as that laid on for the old-aged by Banfield Marsh.

I thought of going to the Centre for a talk with Odo Mayhew who with a few of his heavier paragraphs on local government finance would have driven Cleopatra into nursing. But I was led on by the feeling that despite the deflation of my scheme about the money there were still positive things I could do in the matter of Lucas.

I went along to the Constitutional Club, guessing that Offa in his own way might have brought life a bubble or two nearer the boil. On my way there I saw Dr Poinsette. He was walking along in deep conversation with Wally Fletcher, Royston Angove and another lad called Orion Ellis. Orion was carrying a cardboard box almost full of tin-foil tops from milk bottles. This load was part of a campaign started a little while before when Melancthon Mills had been on the point of washing his hands of the young delinquents and there had been some long, desperate talks between them, him and Ventris Lee.

Wally proposed, wishing to bring Ventris and Melancthon back into their normal position of eating out of his hands, that they save the tops off milk bottles to make a little holiday money but on the basis of social service. They had started saving immediately, and once they had persuaded Royston that he was not supposed to take the tops off bottles that were still standing, full, on doorsteps, all was well.

They made an arrangement to sell the tops to the local Technical School which found it could process the tinfoil for some useful purpose. The money they got they were going to give to a home for crippled children in the county. The boys' parents had not been able to stable the collection and Dr Poinsette had made a shed in his garden available to them, and he said that if the pile got any bigger he would have to move out on to the kerb to practise his medicine.

The boy Orion Ellis was eleven, about a year younger than his companions. He was black-haired, pensively bright and one of the easiest, most pleasant talkers in the zone. Dr Poinsette took an interest in him and had now appointed him to be washer and minder of his dogs and weeder of his garden, the jobs that Colenso and I had once done. He had at first found Orion to be wild, inattentive, and unreliable, with a tendency to let such botanists as Wally and Royston into the garden where they would work earnestly and leave all the wrong plants standing. Then the doctor had turned the boy loose on his books and Orion, whose home mentally was a wilderness, had gone at them like a dog at a bone. The doctor had also guided him into mathematics, in which he was himself beginning again to take an interest, as a means of muting with the cool litany of endless measurement and reckoning his urge to pour scalding indictments on the encrusted idiocy of his fellows.

Orion's background was shady. His father was a piercing tenor and nimble sinner called Theo Topliss who had slipped out of Bandy Lane as a minor music-hall turn before marrying Orion's mother, Dolores Ellis. A great, laughing, friendly girl, her laughter died down utterly when her father, a diabetic, passed away with worry over Topliss's flight and Orion's arrival. She had looked after the child as well as she could, giving him good food and decent clothes. She managed to keep him company, too, for as long as she kept her job in the Bandy pickle factory, but her temper there ravelled as the motionless acridity of the pickles in the vinegar kept on reminding her of her relationship with Theo and she left.

Then she became a barmaid at the Bandy Lane Station Hotel and her absence each evening set Orion to wandering about the streets where he had first come to Dr Poinsette's attention. He had been fiddling with the handle of a van containing toys, the property of a bilious, vindictive voter named Edgar Timms who had just been visiting the doctor for a prescription that would give him the sort of blithe look which one would expect from someone connected with the toy trade. Coming out of the surgery this pill saw Orion apparently trying to take the back door of his van off its hinges. Deciding to give his natural temperament one last fling before starting on the course of Franciscan bonhomie that the doctor had recommended, Edgar banged the boy's head against the van with a force that knocked him senseless. That was how the doctor met him.

For myself, I had come across Orion because he and his mother lived near Angela's and Dolores had had a few fierce quarrels with Mrs Lang, whose assumption of fine airs when she passed her neighbour drove her half mad. As often as not Dolores, especially if she had just come with sore feet from a busy afternoon serving at the hotel, would bawl a couple of home truths at Mrs Lang. Mrs Lang, who set a high price on wedlock, would from a safe distance mutter something about Topliss and Orion and refer to Dolores as riff-raff, dissolute, a scandal and other things that made the chapel doors smile broadly and the pious to rest easier. After encounters of that sort Dolores would sometimes get drunk and she would see the world in the image of Topliss and the double torment of her father rushed into his grave by his diabetes and an outraged morality. Twice she had lost her job. Dr Poinsette had intervened to get her restored, with the result that some watchers had been set hinting that Orion was the doctor's son.

This had surprised the doctor whose wife was dead and whose son was in Africa, somewhere silent along the Congo, and either not able or unwilling to write. But the doctor had taken it in good part. He put a notice in the *Bulletin* saying: 'Dr Poinsette is perfectly willing to step into the breach of any disputed or dubious paternity, especially that of the loose-tongued who have started the latest stories going around about him.'

When I caught sight of Dr Poinsette and the three lads he was telling Orion: 'And don't forget to wash those things. That milk fat is a bonus for the germs. When you deliver them to the Technical School, they'll have to be as fresh as the dawn. Off with you.'

Wally and Royston took their leave of the doctor with a fine courteous gesture that rose the caps right off their heads. This training was due to Dunkerly Dodge who believed that with a veneer of good manners no man can possibly be as depraved as he otherwise might be. He had given these boys a veneer so thick they had barely been able to move for weeks and now they would surprise one by coming out with routines worthy of the old Southern colonels. Orion's leave-taking was very polite too, but he was hampered by his cardboard box.

I tried to avoid meeting the doctor for he looked thoughtful and the first glance he gave me was one of disgust and I had no desire to be receiving any philosophic X-rays from him. The bones of my dilemma were already clearer to me than pikestaffs. I was too slow. He took my arm and made me walk back with him along the pavement I had been travelling. 'Come on, Stobo, walk with me. Just a little stroll. There is a tendency to paralytic stoppage in your thoughts and I would like to promote a more dramatic flux.'

I was embarrassed and moved reluctantly. I knew all about Dr Poinsette's little walks about the streets of Bandy Lane. They were his substitute for surgery hours which he considered degrading. He always said that the greatest fillip to disease since the organisation of social ignorance was the string of little hutches alongside doctors' premises in which patients were invited to huddle, bringing their septic spots to ripeness in shabby desolation and waiting for their little dab of the doctor's rationed time. Dr Poinsette, through most of the day, moved through the streets and if he saw anyone look sick or forlorn he would ask them to stand still a minute. Either he would send them on their way with a reassuring pat on the back or tell them, 'You're behind with your health, friend. Your ash-buckets are full,' and he would give them the precise time at which they were to come to the front door of his house.

'What's your father going to do when he finishes with Blakemore's milk round?'

'He'll find something.'

'I'm sure he will. We'll all find something. By God we will.'

We came to a short street standing in crumbling isolation on a hillside. The split, scaly stonework of the houses, the incipient rubbish dump that had formed on the sloping ground immediately in front of their doorsteps, combined to give the place an effect of maximum drabness. At the street's far end ten or so children were playing a game that kept them in a conspiratorial huddle, a habit for keeping up warmth. The adults in sight, moving slowly in a sort of sullen greyness, seemed stupefied. They nodded their heads at the doctor but their greetings went no further than that.

'One of the first streets laid down by the first Pooley when he started his first foundry,' said the doctor. 'In a place like this one gets one moment of clear consciousness and then is out for the count.' He looked at the thick seam of rubbish on the slope. 'One day the tins will have the sense to stay inside and the tenants will be out on the dump. The liveliest elements left this street fifteen years ago. To live publicly, longer than one's grace, one's usefulness, that's hellish for a person, but for a place, ugh! Stones and earth are more to be pitied in this complex of mutilation than flesh. Up the human sleeve there is always one astonishing last card.' He stopped and shouted: 'Does anyone here want Poinsette?' There was no answer. The children looked up from their game, laughed and down went their heads again. An old man in a torn cardigan smiled and turned away from us to empty the contents of a big brown paper bag onto the dump. Further along a solitary boy was throwing stones without interest at a cat which stuck obstinately to a salmon tin. He counted each stone as he threw, as if that were the whole point of the exercise.

Dr Poinsette buttoned up his fawn overcoat and pulled his green slouch further to the front of his head. 'Nobody here wants Poinsette,' he said. 'Of course at least twenty of them do. But they turn their back to me and fondle their diseases like jewels. In too many lives getting ill is the most creative thing they ever do.' He put his hand on my shoulder, friendly. 'At this moment Stobo I'm even prepared to be tolerant with you, to say that you might have the root of the matter in you. Living with steady self-assertion even on the most vulgar plane is almost saintly. I must go along to The Thinker one night and have a hell of an argument with young Colenso Mortlake on that theme.'

He turned again to look at the little street. He pointed at the stone-thrower who was still singing out the number of each stone. 'Look at that lonely little zany there. The odd genius out. Huddled in his corner with murder and mathematics winking at him in turn. Do you ever feel the shower of questions that comes at you from every human being, Stobo? It blinds the mental panes. Look at that kid, now. Will he kill the cat? Who or what will kill him? The cat stays there. Is it looking for salmon or death or both?'

'I don't care,' I said. 'The mountain should fall on them all.'

'Oh, the good little merchant,' said the doctor with a laugh. 'If the account is botched, close the ledger and have done with it, eh?'

When we arrived at Kiprianos' the doctor led the way in. Kiprianos, a great admirer of Poinsette, who had been treating him for years for two of the flattest feet in Bandy Lane, took us into his kitchen and we sat down in fireside comfort to drink our coffee.

Kiprianos' children, five of them, wanted to play with us but the doctor, who looked tired, waved them away. Kiprianos led them into the garden behind his premises and set them to one of the endless tasks of sweeping that crop up in catering.

'Thank you, Manolos,' said the doctor. 'I like your kids but there are times when one is raw and the fingers of kids thrust too strongly.' When Kiprianos had gone, he said: 'When those kids were younger they nearly drove Manolos mad. His wife had gone back to Greece to see a dying parent and she left Manolos to cope here. She almost had a double funeral on her hands. Trade was heavy and the kids devilish.

'Manolos told me that he was standing behind the counter one night feeling as oppressed as if the ceiling had come down on him. His kids had just come in to ask him if they could set the kitchen alight. He had no insurance at that time so had to say no. They went out the back and reduced some of his stock to ashes He suddenly found himself saying: "My heart is now going to break. I can stand it no longer. My heart is going to break." Then he heard a strange sound and felt himself being let down to a lower level. This, he said, is it, the breaking heart. But it wasn't. The arches of his feet had fallen and he was so flat in that quarter before I took him in hand he could, with a little meths in his navel, have done service as a spirit level.'

'But he's all right now,' I said. 'He walks all right. His kids are quieter, thank God. His trade is brisk.'

'True.' Dr Poinsette sucked his coffee in noisily to bring my attention more fully on himself, for he had seen that I had made those remarks about Kiprianos in a mechanical, apathetic way. There was nothing that interested me less than Kiprianos' feet or his kids.

'I met Wedlake Roper at the Club this afternoon,' he now said. He looked at me as though he thought the news would be important to me. But my mind at that moment had returned to the remark Lucas had made about being grateful to me for having found Angela broken in. This was a black, terrible point to me still. I wondered if Poinsette could give me any information about it. He repeated his remark about Roper.

'Wedlake is doing well,' I said. 'He's got a good business. Worked it up from nothing.'

'He's doing all right. I've been watching him with interest. These chaps who come up from a well of unqualified poverty and make their mark always fascinate me. It's like watching the surface healing of an operation about which you are in doubt. Wedlake's father died of the dust. He was given a chance to study accountancy by an aunt who was a bit of a snob and cut down Wedlake's relations with his father to a minimum. This suited Wedlake who was in his own astute way a nitwit, and he never went to see his old man during the years when he was building up his real estate business. Even when his old man was dying Wedlake made great play of the fact that he was just going off on his first holiday to the south of France.

'When he got back, his father was dead and buried. Sometimes these contradictions can be assimilated or excreted. If so, good, you have another self-assured lout to provide another link in the armoured coat of our ruling group. If not, watch out for the terrible screamed apology that the victim is always making for some piece of crassness that can no longer be apologised for. Wedlake, I think, is apologising via the bottle. He can never get over the ease with which he made his money. Every time he makes a deal as an estate agent he sees his father's weary penurious old face looking at him out of every note and coin. So he rushes to get rid of them. Most of the time now he is fuddled and I find his talk very interesting, if you follow.'

'No, I don't. Wedlake goes to the club so much because it helps him in his business.' I tried to sort out the personal implications with which the doctor might have intended to vein his talk. 'What does it matter anyway if you don't help to carry your father to the grave?'

'Not much, I suppose. But when it comes to pointing out the witches on the roadside of men's dreams, Stobo, gibbering out their prophecies and their regrets, let me be the guide. Wedlake could probably do as much business outside the Club promoting crafty deals for the godly as he does inside. Within us all is some undischarged act of generosity. It's in Wedlake, the act he owed to his father. And now at odd moments it aches and glows in his little night.

'This afternoon, for instance, he felt he wanted to be generous to Lucas Phillimore of all people. He knows that Lucas has been trying to find the deposit money that Samson Blakemore has hidden away in the farmhouse. Wedlake knows where it is. He told me. It's at the bottom of an old brown riding boot in Samson's bedroom. Wedlake would never have slipped it out to me but I worked him to a tearful peak with some elegiac references to his father, and besides he was in a rage with Samson who has changed his mind three times already about some of the purchase details covering the outbuildings on the farm and is coming down at five tomorrow afternoon to sign a supplementary contract.'

'What are you telling me all this for?'

'I don't know exactly. You never know what knowledge is good for until you spread it abroad and see to what uses it is put. It must be a comical sight up there in that farmhouse. Samson does no more work. He's leaving that to the new owners. He just stands guard over his little treasure, tormented despite himself that he's now going to leave Lucas destitute, and almost hoping that Lucas will try to steal the money from him so that some climax can be reached between them.

'I've got to be off now. So long.'

As soon as I heard the shop's front door shut I hurried over to The Thinker and the Thrush, hoping to find Lucas there. He was indeed there. He was talking in the basket lounge in a quiet masterful way with Hugo Farnum. I was in a mood of optimum vigour and cunning. My indifference to Lucas was as complete as his to me. I went to sit in a corner.

I was sorry that Lucas and Hugo did not look at me for my expression was of confident knowledge. I checked it in the mirror on the opposite wall and made it more intense. As I was practising these grimaces Mrs Farnum looked in and told me it would do me the world of good if I went upstairs and had a session with the male voice party as an alternative to being so introspective. Then Wedlake Roper came in. He was exuberant and gave us all a loud greeting. He had a pink, full face and always wore white collars with long wings that gave him the look of starched tremulous insecurity you see on the face of an aging choirboy.

Lucas turned around and looked at Wedlake malevolently. Wedlake went pale and made a gesture as if his head had been jerked by a forceps of ice. He picked up two drinks from the bar and brought them over to my corner. He was only slightly drunk and gave the impression of having only just recovered, and too quickly, from some shaking ordeal. 'Glad to see you, Stobo, boy,' he said. 'Glad to have the privilege of drinking with you.'

'Good luck, Mr Roper,' I said, not sure whether to smile to show I was abreast of his irony and wondering how anyone came to be so desirous of my company as Wedlake was at that moment.

'Glad to see you've stuck up for yourself. Glad to see you've refused to be sucked down. Get in the swim, Stobo, and stay there. They've tried to get Wedlake Roper down before now,' he stared at Lucas and Hugo, 'but they don't succeed.'

'Good luck,' I said, not knowing if one finished saying this after one sip.

'This is a big day for me.'

'How is that, Mr Roper?'

'The political committee at the Con Club called me in to ask me if I'd like to stand as the Independent candidate for the Central Ward.'

'What did you say?'

'I said yes, of course. Always been an ambition with me, that. It was something my old dad wanted for me, always. "I know you'll make money, Wed," he'd say, "but what I want for you most of all, Wed, is for you to speak for the people, for the little, helpless people like me." And by God, Stobo, that's what I'll do.'

'That's a fine thing,' I said, 'speaking for the people. I bet that was a great moment for you, Mr Roper, being called in like that and told you were the chosen one.'

'Of course it was. There's been a lot of talk and slander against me. I've put up for the nomination three times before. Always a lot of big-mouths and die-hards against me. Malicious. False as hell, the lot of them.' He put down his drink and laughed with delight. Hugo and Lucas looked around. Lucas said something bitter that made Hugo smile and they resumed their talk. 'But I clinched it this time,' said Wedlake. 'I know I've got enemies on the committee because off and on I come out with some home truths, real humdingers, about the way my old man suffered with the dust and got palmed off with a medical certificate that said he had inherited bronchitis. There are some in the Club who say that I'm a bit of a Red behind a blue rosette even though I've done so well in business.

'Well, this week I showed them that it can be wise to be a bit of a Red. You know the old mansion beyond the Pooley place? Lovely house, thirty acres of good fine ground, modern equipment. Used to belong to old Flaxton, the railway director. Mad as a hatter last going off. Thought he was Watt and wanted to sue the GWR for infringement of patent rights. But a fine old gent. Real Christian. Private chapel. Prayers every morning, hymns every whipstitch. Own organ. House came on the market last month. I was the agent.'

He stood up to replenish our drinks. 'Now imagine what has happened,' he said.

'You pulled off a tremendous deal. Cleaned up, as they say.'

He looked down at me disappointedly and went to the bar. 'You are no brighter than some of the rodneys on that committee,' he told me when he returned. 'I bought it myself. And I'm going to give it away. Know what for? As a convalescent home for dust-sufferers, silicotics. And on the big gate in front I'm going to have a plaque put: "Given to those afflicted by the scourge of pneumoconiosis by Wedlake Roper whose old dad would have loved to see him make this gesture." '

'Oh, that's beautiful, Wedlake.'

'Not bad. And can you see anyone in the Central Ward voting Labour when they hear about this?'

'Good God, no. These Socialists talk. But what have they got to give?'

'Too true. And this will be a slap in the eye for Charlie Chiffley.'

'Mr Chiffley the architect?'

'That's it. He's put up a toilet or two, the sod. "It is only one," says this Chiffley, "who speaks with the aplomb and the authority that come from a good background from birth who can wean the voters away from the illiterate cult of class envy. Roper is tainted by his origin in the slum. Roper is not wholly one of us." That's what I overheard him saying one night and if I hadn't been in the middle of a bit of business with him I'd have pulled him right out of his collar. Why shouldn't I have these thoughts about my old man and his Calvary? When I knew he was dying, wasn't I the first man in Bandy Lane ever to take a plane trip all the way from Nice to hold him in my arms as he died? And to sing to him the songs he taught me as a kid and that he wanted to hear once again?'

'It must have been a beautiful scene, Wedlake.'

'It was.' He wiped his eyes and I could hear a huge sniff of disgust from Lucas.

'Will you change the name of Flaxton Hall?' I asked.

'Oh, yes. It will be Roper Hall, after me and my dad. That's not conceit, is it?'

'Not a bit of it. It'll be sweeter for bearing the name of a man whose money and sacrifice went into it. And let's hope Bandy Lane will never forget.'

'It won't end there. Practically all the house selling business in this area is in my hands now. I'm going to set aside a certain percentage of the houses at easy rates of purchase, pie-easy rates, for the families of dust-sufferers who might be in need of better accommodation.'

'Damn it, you're a saint, Wedlake.'

'It's going to make a few people sit up, I can tell you.' He hummed into his glass. He was excited with happiness. I edged nearer to him.

'Tell me, Wedlake, what was that black look Lucas gave you just now?'

'Oh, him. He's another! This morning we were having a few jars and he was almost crying with worry. Blakemore is putting him out on his butt and he's got that Lang girl on a string. I mentioned that I had bought Flaxton Hall and before I knew it he had me by the lapel, breathing into my face and telling me this was the chance he had been waiting for all his life. A place like that: good land, good equipment, a house fit for a gentleman. Stuff like that. And do you know what his offer was? That I give it to him without any deposit. Give him five years to make a payment out of profit. That was Lucas! A poor daub that couldn't even make a go of the Mint. I laughed so much I couldn't see, and when I opened my eyes again he had gone.'

'Serve him right. Imagine him saying that when you had such a scheme for Flaxton Hall. Enough to make a donkey laugh.' We guffawed in harmony and in the middle of it Wedlake, as was his disconnected way, fell into a serious silence and left.

His place at my table was taken by Dunkerly Dodge, who did some insurance business with Mrs Farnum. After Dunkerly had his drink – a cherry brandy, for Dunkerly has a refined taste in these matters – I asked him if he had heard about Wedlake Roper's splendid gesture. Dunkerly nodded sombrely. 'I hope he gets all the fun he can just talking about it. Because it won't go any further than that.'

'But he told me he had it all fixed up. Made the gift. Changed the name, written a plaque about his old dad. God knows what.'

'Wedlake dare not go through with it. His wife wants to make a trip to America this summer to visit her sister and Charlie Chiffley has found a buyer for Flaxton Hall who'll give Wedlake a profit on the deal that will break the back of the expenses. She told Wedlake this afternoon she'd beat his brains out if he didn't put through the deal for Chiffley's friend.'

'Does Charlie get a commission on this?'

'He doesn't need one. He's been giving solace to Wedlake's wife for the last year, ever since booze moved up to first place in Wedlake's curriculum, although I would say that a man would feel like a stonemason giving solace to such a hard-faced bitch as Mrs Roper. She's from one of the town's ruling families and she's never stopped rubbing it into Wedlake that socially he came from three feet below the cellarage and was born in a house that the Council condemned under pressure from the mice two wars ago.'

I told my thoughts to drop into the slowest walk. 'This Chiffley,' I said, 'is Wedlake's opponent for the nomination in the Central Ward. Now you tell me he's seeing Wedlake's wife.'

'Not seeing, more servicing.'

'That then. He must be a monster.'

'No, just an architect saddened by living in a town that builds only to keep off the rain.'

'He wants to destroy that wonderful scheme of Wedlake's to bring new life to the sick. If that goes bust so does Wedlake's nomination for the Council and he's got his heart set on speaking for the people. He promised his old dad.'

'It's already gone bust. My wife was with Mrs Roper late this afternoon. She said Wedlake saw the light after the first burst of rhetoric from his wife. She told him that if she caught him pouring thousands of pounds out of his pocket for the sake of winning a municipal halo she would either shoot him or procure his ticket for the County Mental. That was after she had threatened to leave him. She's an awful bitch but that frightens Wedlake. His life for all his bounce is very poorly riveted and she's one of the few things that gives him any sense of being properly held together.'

'Well, I think it's a shame. That wonderful thing that Wedlake was going to do for his old dad... What if we drop a hint to Wedlake about Chiffley? That would enrage him, stiffen his spine a bit.'

'Look, Stobo, don't overdo the guile. Life isn't as malleable as all that, you know. The odds are that Wedlake knows. His only answer to Chiffley is money. So he has to make money. At this very moment he's probably on the phone to somebody who's offering top price for Flaxton Hall, somebody who's never heard of the dust or of Wedlake's old dad.'

'But he told me...'

'Of course he told you. His last kick before sinking back into his own appointed pool. So he gets the penny of a dream and the creamy bun of profitable fact. You live best when you mix the flavours. We love the horse but travel by train.' He looked quite pleased. 'Are you following all these references?'

'And I was going to go on to that Lucas and madden him by saying that Wedlake was going to give Flaxton Hall to sick miners. Oh, that would have given him a shock. He wanted the place for himself. Think of that.'

'I'm not altogether against Lucas. There are too many of our fine old homes going for shabby new causes.'

Colenso came in, wearing the large bow tie, black,

which showed that he was attending a rehearsal of the glee group upstairs. 'What's the matter with you?' he asked.

'Why?' I asked.

'You look dead. Did Hugo slip a foxglove into your last gill?' He and Dunkerly stood over me. I knew that I was now going to get from these two a set of axioms that would cover me like a headstone.

'Stobo has found,' said Dunkerly, 'that there is as much underweight and short change in truth as there is in trade.'

'The lies of the stricken,' said Colenso, 'are the stirrings of the future.'

'Would you two wise-looking bastards file off and leave me alone?'

'Come upstairs with us,' said Colenso, 'and put those little passions of yours out in the ashbin for God's sake. Dunkerly is going to give us a few lessons in how to interpret a requiem. We need it. The way the boys sing now you'd fancy that voter was off for a week in Clacton.'

'Leave me alone.'

They left the room. Lucas came over from the bar, his lips loose with displeasure. 'Wilkie,' he said, 'I've heard my name being bandied about more than once in this corner. Any more of that and your teeth will land in Birchtown.'

I half stood, praying for an extra foot of height and a new team of muscles and reflexes. There was no change in me. I could hear fulfilment snoring and refusing to budge. 'I'm sorry, Mr Phillimore.' I dropped my voice so that not even the straining Hugo at the bar could hear. 'I was only telling Mr Roper how much I'd like to help you. You should have had Flaxton Hall and Angela should have been your queen there. By God, a fine pair, Mr Phillimore. I'd have carried your groceries up that long drive myself just for the honour of your patronage, the prestige. It's terrible, the way you have been treated. But you're proud, Mr Phillimore. You're hard to help.'

'Quite right,' he said, wanting to turn away but held by the urgency of my tone. 'What are you getting at, Wilkie?'

'You shouldn't be needing help. Especially with that old Blakemore gloating over the money he has in that old brown riding shoe he has in his bedroom. At least half that money belongs rightfully to you. He's been picking your brains for years. My father's told me that a dozen times.'

Lucas blinked but said in a quite flat tone: 'Samson just sits there like a hen with a sore anus.'

'He's coming down tomorrow afternoon to Wedlake Roper's office to get a few more pounds for the outbuildings.'

A rough sacking of silence came upon us and I was glad to slip out of the room.

Without pause I sped up the road to Blakemore's farm. Night had fallen and for that I was glad. I could gesticulate all I wanted and I could disperse in that way some of the embarrassment I felt at my speed and intentions. From The Thinker and the Thrush I heard a bellow of sound as the boys upstairs started on the requiem. Then, faintly, the voice of Dunkerly crying them to a stop, a pause for thought about the essential quietness and rest of death, and urging them sharply to ponder for decency's sake the distinction between a dirge and a spree.

I banged at Blakemore's door. His head appeared at a lighted uncurtained window. Behind his head I could see the farm's main room, shapely but gaunt. He was holding a small, clean shotgun in his hands. 'Who's there?'

'Stobo Wilkie.'

'If you've come to plead for your old man, clear off. He's been driving the milk off-key for years. If you don't get away I'll be doing as much for you.' And for some reason he laughed at that.

'I'm not here for milk or for my father.' I was conscious of putting things into the order of importance I thought would appeal to Blakemore. I was aware slightly of a certain betrayal, but loyalty can often be a hindrance.

'What do you want here?'

I told him that Lucas knew where the money was, that on the following afternoon when Samson would be down at Wedlake Roper's he would probably make an effort to get it.

Blakemore did not make a reply. I watched him go back to his seat at the fireside and sit there, thinking, with his gun across his knees.

I returned to the town. As I reached the main road my legs were shaking so badly I could swear there were children around me dancing to their beat and in a moment of sickened illumination I knew that the world has not yet plunged utterly to hell because villainy is, by and large, more exhausting than virtue.

20

Angela came into the shop the next morning. She looked happy and hummed one of her contralto tunes at Mr Ellicott as she paid her bill.

'Did you see Lucas last night?' I asked her.

'Oh, yes. He came over.'

'How was he?'

'Bright as could be. He'd been a bit worried. But he said we won't need to be packing sandwiches for the train tomorrow. It will be the restaurant car, three courses. How does that sound to you, Stobo?'

I looked at her earnestly. I tried in what I next said to strike a note of horror that would move her to sorrow or regret. 'Think of it, Angela, think of it. Going away with a man and not even married.'

'Would you like us to get married?'

'No, no!'

'Well there, then.'

I nodded my head and began to understand that there may be a basis of acceptability in the most monstrous flippancies of living fact.

As she left the shop, although I knew I might never see her again I did not say goodbye or wave my hand. I remembered Mr Ellicott telling me that emotion in a grocer is the worst possible thing for the butter and cheese. In a panting, panicked world the distributive trades must keep cool. And Mr Ellicott stood by his cash desk watching me and the tub of Danish with eyes like leather washers.

I met Offa Mogg at Kiprianos' during the lunch interval. I felt ashamed and confused by what I had done. All he did was go sh-sh-sh and wink and by the time he had been doing this for about half an hour I felt worse than ever, like a match being used by Offa to set off a monster firework.

'Oh, by the way,' he said at last, 'you know that farmer that Ursula Bendall married? He's in a worse condition than ever. So do you know what I did? – and don't forget I did it to save Angela from a fate worse than Parish Relief. I rang up Ursula. I said I spoke as one who was one with her in her grief and that her old friend Lucas Phillimore would have been at her side giving her strength and courage but he himself has been stricken low and is eating his heart out for her, quietly, of course, a nibble that respects monogamy. Over the phone she sounded fine, quite excited, as if she enjoyed having grief barking at her from all flanks. I suppose that kind of feeling comes from having your husband feeble from the start. She said, "Poor Lucas, poor Lucas", and she's going to try to dash over in her car to see him.'

'What's the point of all this?' No gladiator to the death could have approached his opponent more cagily than Offa.

'The odds are that Lucas will draw the line at stealing that money. Don't forget that he went to a good school and a good regiment where the precepts are very moral, if simple. Last night he had a few drinks in him and if the school and regiment spoke at all it was *sotto voce*. Today he'll be sick and frustrated again, desperate at the thought of being led off to London by a girl so much his junior. When you're broke and middle-aged and romance seeks you out, the best thing to do is to hide and try to throw it off the scent. Not hard to do. A blind, defective thing, this urge to love.' And Offa tapped the side of his bowler and left. He could flick himself on and off like a light.

What happened during the rest of the day I got from Offa. The events of the evening I saw for myself: reality, moving fast and sweating freely, with a strong smell on it.

Lucas spent part of the afternoon in the Club, then passed an hour or two hanging about the street that led to the hillside path. About five he saw Blakemore come down. He went up and entered the farmhouse. Blakemore, sly and covert as a fox, regained the farm. He slipped into one of the outbuildings where he had hidden his gun. Then he entered the house.

Then, according to Offa, who claimed he had gone up to the farm seeking a statement from Blakemore on whether having cows permanently on a slope might lead to any particular bias in the milk, there was an outburst of angry voices. Out of the house came Lucas and Samson. Samson had laid down his gun. They both caught sight of Offa and this seemed to throw them into a temporary, ramshackle unity. They drubbed the senses out of him, and as he limped down the hill the only thing that kept him sane was the sight of a fire down in Bandy which gave him the promise of at least one exciting item for the paper before the day was out.

Lucas and Blakemore went back into the house. The little peace brought on by their brush with Offa might have served to take them around the corner of their spite. But Lucas must have made another attempt to get the money, because, half an hour after Offa had left the scene, out of the farmhouse staggered Lucas, shot. He lurched off towards the stables and Blakemore, without making any attempt to follow him, to finish him off or to help him, locked himself into the farmhouse.

It happened that my father went up to the farm that evening. Some of the metal hoops in the churns had worked loose and Leo Watham, an amateur metal worker, had managed to borrow the equipment to make a repair if my father got the churns to him quickly. Colenso had suggested ironically that my father should do this. He had accepted the suggestion quite seriously and meant it as his final benediction on the head of his former employer. He went up the hillside and worked by the light of a faint moon. He got the churns on the cart, backed Jolly between the shafts and started down to the town.

He told me afterwards that as the cart came jolting

down over the stones he thought he heard a groan coming from behind but as life to my father always seemed sad when he was about at night he thought it was the globe trying to express that it too felt the same way. At the bottom of the path he met Hadrian Mogg, and Hadrian, in his fussy way and to provide the kind of macabre companionship that seems to come easily to people who keep an eye on our hygiene, told my father that he was going to inspect the state of the cart and the churns. My father said it was too dark to do such a thing, but Hadrian said he would use only touch and smell and treat the venture as a kind of eisteddfod test-piece in professional sensitiveness.

Hadrian went on the cart, sniffing so hard my father kept his finger on the lid of the churns. Then he heard a groan and he told my father that this was the first time he had come across a vendor peddling milk that was so old even the churns were complaining. Then he submitted the cart to the test by touch, feeling the churns for any sign of ingrained greasiness. He gave a shout. His hand had touched a head of hair and Hadrian, being one-tracked in these matters, thought he had encountered the fungus of some new and terrible neglect.

My father told him not to talk nonsense, that he had scrubbed the cart out that very morning. Hadrian led Jolly into the light from a lamppost. In the cart they saw Lucas, huddled in a corner behind a churn and looking paler than a curd, badly but not fatally hurt. Hadrian's first reaction was to read my father the clause in the rulebook that makes it illegal to carry passengers in milk-carts, but my father had dashed off for help.

Bandy Lane sprang to life. A stretcher was obtained for Lucas and as he was being carried off to the First Aid Post Angela came running up, looking horrified. As she was on the brink of pouring out her grief she was pushed violently out of the way by a tall, beautifully dressed woman who knelt at the side of the stretcher sobbing so loudly that the stretcher-bearers, a touchy pair of voters and out of practice with this article, thought that Lucas must be dead and came to a halt. This woman was Ursula Bendall, dressed in clothes so dear and fashionable, her face so flawlessly lacquered and creamed, as to cause as big a sensation as the situation of Lucas himself.

Lucas recognised her, gave what was almost a yelp of joy and wept without control as he pressed her fingers to his lips and kissed them with vigour. The bearers took one look at this and started off again, telling Ursula to keep it down a little.

'Ursula, Ursula,' said Lucas, 'at last, at last.'

'Are you hurt badly, Lucas, my dear boy?'

'It's nothing, Ursula. Whatever I have lost has now been given back to me.'

The women in the crowd were now crying as badly as Ursula and even Banfield Marsh the manager of the Cosy said, 'I've seen worse second-feature films more than once.' Then Offa and Hadrian marched up with every policeman in Bandy Lane. Dunkerly Dodge arrived too, and by some miracle of stagecraft he had got hold of half a dozen torches and flares and up the hillside went the procession of flame.

They advanced boldly on the farmhouse door until they were brought to a halt by a shot from Blakemore that carved a shallow furrow in the top of Offa's bowler. 'Searchlights!' shouted Offa. 'The man's desperate. He'll fight it out to the last!'

'And some laughing gas, too,' said Colenso, who had joined the group. 'This place could do with a damned good chuckle.'

'Come out, Blakemore!' shouted Hadrian Mogg,

who had never been happier. 'You're caught like a rat in a trap!'

The police told us to put a stop to these slogans because we were bringing the whole apparatus of social vengeance into disrepute. Then a window of the farmhouse was thrown open and we heard Blakemore's voice.

'What happened to Phillimore,' he said, 'is a private matter. Alive or dead, he's of no consequence. But now I'm going to sprinkle you silly bastards with buckshot purely as a protest by me on behalf of the marginal farmer everywhere. A mountain of ferns, that's what I've got. Who wants ferns? Who in hell plants them and why is it made so easy for him? Now I'm going to give this ill-clad boulder of a mountain some real fertiliser: some fine dead democrats. Here we go!'

And the salvo commenced. We dropped down. Dunkerly Dodge did a lot of needless peering over the shoulder of the man in front. Then the firing stopped. We advanced with care. The light in the farmhouse went on. We looked through the window. There was Blakemore forking three or four fried eggs onto a plate. Offa, when he was not showing the ridge in his bowler to everyone near him, was for storming the place out of hand. But the leading policeman said: 'No, let him get his fill. It was no doubt hunger that made him act so queerly in the first place.'

So we watched Samson have his supper. He ate slowly and with a certain hauteur. When he had finished he came out and joined us for the great dramatic march down the hill.

21

The next morning I expected to see Angela black-eyed, black-robed, howling out her grief like Cassandra, but she came into the shop with a greater buoyancy and zest than ever. When Mr Ellicott, in the sniffling, diffident way that had of late become habitual with him, asked her about Lucas all she did was give us a fine pantomimic impression of how Ursula Bendall had carried on when she had been asked to leave Lucas in peace at the hospital. Angela arranged to meet me that night outside the Cosy. She winked at me as if her intention from the start had been no more than to have a private joke with me. If this world winked less I would not have suffered from the loss.

About my conduct in the weeks that followed I can write only with admiration. The thing to do was to bury what had happened under drifts of new action. Lucas vanished from Bandy Lane in the care of Ursula. Blakemore went to gaol for two years after having a hard time proving that he was mentally using the same handbook as the judge. He convinced the court that the only truly mad thing he had ever done was to become a farmer in an area where even a goat would have had to badger the government for grants.

Dr Poinsette managed to get Mrs Lang into a good convalescent home for a month and she came back walking with a firmer step on reality, tapping cautiously with her foot now and then to feel for the odd board that folly might have eaten hollow, but greatly improved. Lyndhurst found temporary respite from his neurasthenia in the prospect of once more knowing a predictable, normal relationship with his wife.

I persuaded Dunkerly to put on a whole week of plays at the Centre with Angela in the chief part in each one. Offa prepared a tremendous publicity billboard with pictures of Angela in all her roles. This gave her great happiness and I could hear the little upsets of the past being stroked back into peace inside her.

Mr Ellicott became more deliberately sad and even truculent. He complained more and more about his legs. I tried to tell him how much happier he would be if he retired to one of the pleasant resort towns to the west along the coast but he startled me by turning on me in the depths of a mid-afternoon hush and saying he could never live away from the parlour in which Mrs Ellicott had lived and died. I saw that he was never without a broached bottle of tonic wine, hoping that life would take the hint and quietly drown him.

Offa got my father a job with a big new milk combine that had set up in the town, but he lasted no more than a week with that firm for he found the discipline strange and the demand for smartness exacting. The supervisors were young and ruthless and insisted on a spruceness in the distributors which would have astonished the cows if they could have seen it. The milk was delivered in a kind of handcart with tricky hydraulic brakes which my father could not get the hang of after the comparative simplicity of Jolly. For the few days he was employed by the

combine one of the queerest things in Bandy was to
see this load of milk come roaring down one of the
steep side-streets with my father being dragged
behind, his feet more often off the ground than on,
shouting to all he passed to tell him what the hell
hydraulic meant.

Then Banfield Marsh had a small silver-painted
dome erected on the roof of the Cosy and renamed
the cinema the Taj. I persuaded Melancthon Mills to
have a talk with Banfield and explain to him that a
cinema with such a fine top and a name like that
should have a commissionaire, a new departure in
Bandy Lane where the sense of ceremony was found
dead against the outer wall of the Exchange years
ago. At first the proposition had to be spelled out to
Banfield who, apart from his inspiration about the
dome, had always lived on the lowest plane of cinema
management. Dunkerly Dodge waded into him with a
speech about how disgusted he was at the way in
which admission to the Taj and to our other cinema,
the Comfy, had been compressed into a mere
plonking down of money, the impaling of the ticket
on a rough, sharp-pointed wire in the hands of an
usher who, if you were slow in plunging down into
the waiting darkness, did not scruple to let you have
one in the back with his spike to help you on your way
and keep the aisle clear.

While Banfield was thinking it over I persuaded my
father to do some silent propaganda on his own
behalf because I knew that this job would bring him
just the kind of narcotic self- importance his withered
ego needed. I had a hard time of it. He was out on a
dark meadow of memory with those cows and he had
made himself a psychological tomb as watertight as
those marble articles they use in graveyards. We got
him to hang about the portals of the Taj, impressing

Banfield with the correctness of his person and doing a little quiet ushering on anyone who tended to fumble too long at the cash desk.

My father's carriage at this time was not all it should have been. He was bent in a way that suggested that despair had made the meal of all time on the base of his spine. Shafto Pinfold, the Physical Training Instructor at the Centre, who himself was just a clothed muscle and had cleared all thought out of his system a decade before to make way for deeper breathing, took him in hand and gave him exercises in standing erect that would have cured the dead. He taught him to hold his breath and he must have driven dozens of people clean out of the foyer of the Taj by suddenly coming to the end of his tether as a breather and starting to gasp with the force of a bomb.

He had a way too of emphasising the new erectness of body that he had learned from Shafto by giving short stiff salutes to people who were not expecting it, and Banfield twice rang up the police to say there was a rigid maniac on his premises with a military phobia. Constable Prangley came along to deal with my father and accuse him of putting on ironical charades for the Peace Pledge Union. Fanshawe Prangley was a gentle giant, a man of controlled strength and a great asset to the police, a pillar at the Social Centre and the bringer of a brand new type of pensive tenderness to the police station which has often, in Bandy Lane, been on the superficial side. Fanshawe understood when I explained to him about my father wanting to find a job that would take him out of himself and bring him a new confidence, a job that would be local, unskilled, unlaborious and a total change from cows. Fanshawe was helpful. He pointed out my father's fine posture and stride to Banfield and the result was that he got the job.

While he was about it, Fanshawe taught my father some special grips that would paralyse trouble makers in the queue with a single jerk of the right arm. This worked for as long as I could go around at the same time persuading the trouble makers to hand my father's arm back every time he tried the jerk.

Melancthon wanted to fit my father out at once in a fine military uniform, with many brass buttons and lengths of gold braid and a cap with a tremendous poke. But Banfield wanted nothing military and he almost wrecked our scheme to bring my father in from the scrub and back to a full genial citizenship. Ever since he had read the article on the Taj Mahal in the encyclopaedia Banfield had been gone on the Indian motif and if the dome had fallen on his head he could not have been more beyond argument. He spent half his time looking up at the new electric sign he had rigged up calling attention to 'The Taj Mahal' and singing 'Pale hands I love beside the Shalimar' to the girl in the cash desk, Miss Pauline Ffoulkes, as slow, swarthy and deliberate a cashier as you could hope to find and in whose life arithmetic had beaten the lyric urge to death. If my father wanted the job, said Banfield, he would have to dress up as a Hindu.

We managed all right for robes, some white curtain material which, with its colour, hang and my father's general stiffness, made him look like a target for Pandolph Treasure. For a turban Dunkerly had a few yards of some muslin which he had used to procure an oriental effect in a play called 'North of Hong Kong'. Dunkerly wrapped the muslin around my father's head. At first he overdid the height and had my father looking as tall as the dome on top of the Taj; then when he got it at the right level he swathed the stuff so carelessly all one could see of my father above the shoulders was a ball of muslin with my father's face out of sight, and that was just as well for he was blue from lack of air.

When Dunkerly Dodge made a turban he was thorough. But once he had got it correctly round my father's crown he was too influenced by our demands that he make it not too tight, and often when my father was standing in the porch of the Taj, creating something like a sacred hush among the boys in the queue, looking as impressive as that ruler Asoka, the whole headpiece would slip down round his neck. Some of the more helpful patrons would take hold of him in his blindness and lead him down to the rival cinema, and he would be directing the traffic there until he was booted back to the Taj by Hughie Thwaite, the manager of the Comfy, who thought commissionaires needless and snobbish.

These periods of confusion in my father's life were not helped by Colenso who would come up to him in the foyer and put to him such questions as, 'Tell me, Aga, what evidence of the caste system do you find in Bandy Lane?' or 'Do you think, swami, that yoga could really do anything to ease or solve the problems of over-production in this type of society?' It was a relief when Banfield saw sense and decided that my father was losing authority in his Indian get-up and gave him the sort of uniform Melancthon had suggested in the first place.

It was green with yellow braid, the trousers very baggy and the coat right down to his boots. But the best thing about it was the epaulettes. Banfield threw in these as a sort of birthday bonus and if he had dipped him in adrenalin he could not more quickly have hoisted my father onto a higher plane of self-assurance. Children were told to follow him respectfully down the street to get a whiff of the picturesque and a hint of travel. Wally Fletcher,

Royston Angove and Orion Ellis hung about him as if they were the aides-de-camp of an emperor. From the minute he stitched the epaulettes on he was like Napoleon, only thinner and fussy in a kindlier way. They sloped upwards, making his head look enclosed, small but very significant, and I did not see one nuisance in the queue at the Taj who was not silenced as soon as he saw my father give his torso a shake and bring the braid into play. In shadow he looked like one of those elements you see in comics landing on earth from another planet with some tremendous bit of listening equipment growing out of his back.

Things might have settled down from this point into a tolerable pattern. As Mrs Lang improved I could see hope growing in Angela's eyes that soon she might be free to withdraw from full-time household duties and do something more varied and profitable. By that time I was sure that Mr Ellicott would have vanished, leaving no problem except the duty of a decent remembrance. One evening I made a slight slip. Wearing a leer of full knowledge which probably angered her from the start, I stood in front of Angela in the parlour and, as formally as I would have asked for credit in the bank, I made a request for the full rights of a lover. Dunkerly Dodge was always using that phrase and I considered it cool and nice in such an ardent context.

She laughed. When I repeated my request her eyes blazed with annoyance and she caught me one on the side of the face that loosened a tooth.

I returned, not without relief, to my former mouse-like quietness in this field. I was quite happy. I could see a good future ticking towards us. But a day will come which sticks a finger right under the heart of the most reasonable expectation. This day was a flawless one in June. The results of the scholarship examinations to the County School had appeared a week before. Oswald and Edgar were plumply at the bottom of the list, with marks in arithmetic that got a footnote in a Ministry of Education pamphlet and put Prothero Wilce in a teachers' rest home for three weeks. At the top of the list with a wide margin of thirty marks between him and the next boy was Orion Ellis.

The effect of this on his mother, Dolores, was instant and remarkable. Her face lost all its tetchy hauntedness and became serene. Her walk down the street was no longer sporadic, as if she were being pursued and was wondering where to run, but became slow and assured, relishing her presence on earth. The flesh that had been torn from her self-esteem years before by the defection of Theo Topliss had now been restored by the achievement of his son. Orion himself moved about unchanged but at his side Wally and Royston, when not awed by the distinction of their friend, glared around as if challenging the world to treat him without respect.

But the effect on Mrs Lang was terrible. Her two boys curled up out of sight in a corner and she visited no displeasure on them. It was the sight of Dolores Ellis in the street one afternoon that set her off. She went at her in a fury of spite, shrieking out charges that had not Dolores been the concubine of Dr Poinsette, Oswald and Edgar would have had Orion's place on the list. For the first time in the long series of quarrels, Dolores made no effort to defend herself or answer back. Mrs Lang had to be dragged away. Angela got her into bed.

Thinking it might act as a sedative I took my father over to tea the following Thursday afternoon. I took four bottles of stout, hoping they might nourish Mrs

Lang's nerves away from their crisis. We coaxed her out of bed and she took her place at the table with a queenly air that was not made less by a coronet of vinegar-soaked brown paper which she wore to relieve the migraine. Unfortunately as the evening wore on Lyndhurst produced a monster bottle of parsley wine which he had been maturing in a cool corner of the pantry for seven years.

Lyndhurst and my father drank this stuff at a good rate. Their shrouds dropped away and in no time they were howling with laughter on the coarsest plane of satire I had ever heard outside Colenso. They gave their ingrained bitterness the airing of the century. They promised to bring the evening to a joyful close by dumping father's finery onto the Council incinerator which Lyndhurst had a free pass to use whenever he liked. Lyndhurst, riding a gale of conscious and malign derision, recalled his wife's ambition to put the two boys into Sandhurst. 'And the poor little daubs came bottom in the scholarship. No brains to get them through the front door. No wealth to get them in through the side door. Poor little daubs. Bottom, bottom, bottom!' While he was speaking Mrs Lang sipped her stout, stared stonily at Lyndhurst and gripped the edge of the table.

'But we'll give you a taste of glory,' said Lyndhurst. 'Without thought of expense we have here General Wyndham Wilkie for the passing out. Stand by the door, General, and take the salute.'

My father did so, almost as green with parsley by this time as his uniform. He was grimacing away with deliberate clownishness. They made Oswald and Edgar parade past them, using their best Boys' Brigade rigidity, back and forth, giving my father one of the longest salutes since Kipling. Then Mrs Lang screamed at Lyndhurst: 'They have been corrupted by your seed, Lang! My seed was good, was fine, the best there was. But yours was of the slum and it ruined them.' She whipped open the table drawer, took out a bread-knife and would undoubtedly have taken bits off Lyndhurst if she had not tripped over the mat and stretched herself out, weeping and helpless with her brown paper coronet askew, on the floor.

She returned to her bed. Angela tried to restore her own spirits at the piano but suddenly banged down the lid in the middle of a song. 'Oh God,' she said. 'Isn't there any way out of this?'

'Let's go over to Mr Ellicott's.'

We walked over towards the shop. Half-way there she stopped. 'One way and another, Stobo, I don't think I can stand much more of this. Who do people think they are when they have the use of others?'

We had a good supper and some fine music at Mr Ellicott's. The distraction eased from Angela's face and I was glad. Mr Ellicott did not mention the business, which I thought strange for he usually found some detail of the work he wanted to discuss, whatever else he was thinking about. It was when we were leaving he let the fireball drop.

'I've decided to sell the shop, Stobo. It isn't final yet. They want my decision in a month.' He mentioned the name of a big chain store and the sum for which he was selling out, thousands more than the purchase price he had intended me to pay. 'But we'll stay good friends, won't we, Stobo?'

I made no answer.

'Won't we, Angela?' His voice was quite yearning.

'Oh, yes.' Her voice was very low but the thoughtfulness of it was intense and sinister.

'I'm so glad,' said Mr Ellicott. 'Life wouldn't be the same on those long winter evenings without you and Stobo.'

'No, it wouldn't, would it?'

We walked away. Once out of earshot, Angela exploded. 'My mother was right. By God she was. Get your knife and run amok. That's the only answer to it. That mouldy old sod! That's the thanks you get for making a handrag out of yourself. All these years, just rubbing the mist from in front of his life, and this is what you get!'

I guided her into a rising lane that led to the park. There was a bench. I sat down on it and taking hold of her shoulder began to cry tempestuously. She squeezed my hand to her breast with genuine compassion. The grief passed quickly. Then I could feel the black coat of vindictiveness slipping over my heart. 'I've given my life to that sly, muttering old bastard. I've been his mind, his arm, his legs. He baited the trap all right. I nibbled the cheese. What you see on my neck is not a collar, it's the steel, the steel. He's made a gold mine out of me. Do you know that box on the piano? Four hundred pounds in that alone. That's the kind of money I've always wanted to have to spend on you, Angela, to give you all the things I've never been able to give.

'Now there will be a longer wait than ever. There's always a longer wait. He told me himself about the money in that box and whenever he's dangling the key to it on his watch chain I've felt like taking it off him and marching off with my share. That's what I should have done.

'And the way he's looked at you! It's on the mat that he's wanted you, not singing at the piano. He'd have done it too, if I had turned my back long enough and if Dr Poinsette hadn't told him his heart would not stand the strain and shock. He'd have given anything to have his full rights as a lover with you. Him, Ellicott! The pig, the old pig. But let him watch out. Stobo Wilkie isn't going to be a louse any longer.'

22

But he was. Two days later there was a great sensation in Bandy Lane. I got no answer when I arrived at the shop in the morning. I called a policeman and he forced his way in. There was Mr Ellicott on the parlour floor, dead and in what the policeman called a state of disarray. It was a shocking and embarrassing sight. 'You can see what he was up to,' said the policeman callously.

The outbreak of tongues when the news spread was enormous. Mr Ellicott's past was gone through with a fine toothcomb to discover who the woman could be who had called, provoked him to a lethal frenzy and then left, seeing no further possibility of normal relations with the old man. But no one gave a reply that made sense. For myself when I was asked a question I just glazed my eyes and said nothing; letting it be assumed that heartbreak and astonishment had practically finished me off.

The police examined the box on the piano. They asked me if the sum of one hundred and fifty pounds which they found inside was in my view the sum that should have been there. 'Yes,' I said, 'that's the figure Mr Ellicott told me was there: one hundred and fifty.'

A will was found bequeathing the business to me.

Angela left Bandy Lane a week after Mr Ellicott's funeral, saying nothing to me.

I survive. I have made most of the changes in the

shop on which I had set my heart. Mrs Chiddle comes in sometimes and winks when she mentions Angela. Her credit has now developed to a point where she just walks in and takes what she wants. But she is sensible and moderate and I would give even more than that to stop her winking. In the fairest field one must get used to these clownish reservations that will try to cast a shadow over peace and beauty.

I will grow. Over the shabbiness a new lustre will appear; over the wounds a good smooth flesh will form. The gall that has dripped from some of my days will be found to have nourished me, for the will can exercise a weird metabolism even in the most maimed and gruesome life. Colenso Mortlake and my father – who has won a new dignity since I took him out of the porch of The Taj and set him up as my warehouseman – look sidelong at me, laughing with their eyes, saying that I am and always will be a cowardly and unripe dwarf. I laugh back at them, for I feel my limbs grow in this new sunshine. There is no such thing as an unbreakable curse, an unforgettable origin, in the lives of men. No land connects me to the continent of mischance and defeat from which I was begotten.

That is what Wedlake Roper tells me and he is a man who knows. He and I have grown very close over the past year. He was nearly scuttled when the political committee at the Club found he had sold Flaxton Hall and could no longer offer it as a rest home for those suffering from the disease that killed his father. Wedlake made a lot of money out of that and subsequent deals. His wife went to the States in style. There was a rumour that Mr Charles Chiffley, the architect, who went at the same time to inspect samples of the latest American architecture, was partly subsidised by Wedlake, who says that when he finally creates that rest home for the stricken he wants the style of it to be the latest and best and he told Mr Chiffley to keep his eye open over there.

Dr Poinsette, who says he takes a deep interest in Wedlake and me viewed simply as bacilli, spoke up for him in the Club and pointed out to the committee that Wedlake's idea, even if it had not been realised, was a thing of beauty. So Sir Gwydion Pooley launched a fund which will, one day, buy a house similar to Flaxton Hall and which will fulfil a similar function to that conceived by Wedlake.

After that Wedlake went forward as candidate in the Central Ward. He failed, for a prophet, especially if he deals in property and goes about with mortgages and commissions in his hair like Wedlake, has little honour in his own land. Now he has asked me to serve as his agent. I do so with joy and passion, for we are both resolved to wear away the rock of bitter distrust which obstructs the dynamic in this zone.

Sometimes, late in the evening, when Wedlake's face looks lost and in pain, his eyes blanker and damper than a tunnel wall, he says I will one day step into his shoes. We have both come up from nothing. We have as our slogan now: 'Do not coddle the mediocre. Inspire the outstanding.' We do not seem to be making much headway but we think that slogan is a pearl.

And Angela?

Oh, she'll be back.